BLESSINGS AND CURSES

JUDY KELLY

Black Rose Writing | Texas

The final approval for this literary material is granted by the author.

First printing

This is a work of fiction. Names, characters, businesses, places, events and incidents are either the products of the author's imagination or used in a fictitious manner. Any resemblance to actual persons, living or dead, or actual events is purely coincidental.

ISBN: 978-1-61296-989-3
PUBLISHED BY BLACK ROSE WRITING
www.blackrosewriting.com

Printed in the United States of America
Suggested Retail Price (SRP) $18.95

Blessings and Curses is printed in Minion Pro

I would like to thank all the members of my critique group, Rockville Writers', for their encouragement and support.

This book is dedicated to my high school students who felt that since they came from troubled and financially depressed families that they had little chance of making their lives better. I especially recognize Joshua Anton, who had almost given up, but went on to graduate from The University of Virginia's McIntire School of Commerce, one of the best undergraduate business programs in the country and is now founder and CEO of his Company.

BLESSINGS AND CURSES

C<small>HAPTER</small> 1

On the day after Olivia Douglas had completed her requirements at the Virginia Seminary, she made an appointment to see her parish priest, Fr. Wilson. Olivia now sat in the reverend's spacious outer office in St. Luke's Episcopal Church waiting to see him. Even though she knew she had to tell him, the waiting and anticipation made her apprehensive. She had to take her attention off the meeting. She stood and turned to a wall covered with frames and read the certificates, honors and elegantly framed letters of commendation. On the other wall, she read a letter from a parishioner who was obviously elated with the outreach program. When her mind was clearer, she sat down and hummed to the organ music playing softly from the overhead speakers.

The office, with its three stained-glass windows that curved at the ceiling and its English décor — sturdy, high-back, hand-carved birch chairs and furniture, dark oak paneling — gave her a feeling of reverence, and she eased forward on her satin-covered seat, stopped humming, closed her eyes, and prayed that she would not be deterred. She would be strong and tell Fr. Wilson why she wanted to meet with him. Then she sat back in her chair, her body less taut, and feeling happier with herself.

Olivia had asked to see the reverend to tell him that she had decided not to take that final step—her ordination to become a priest. He had gone to great lengths to support and encourage her, she understood that. But she had no choice but to conclude that she will not become a priest. Telling him in person was daunting and she now wished she had just sent him a letter.

Aside from what she wanted to talk about with Fr. Wilson, she worried about telling her parents who adopted her and who would be coming from England to her graduation. She had absolutely no idea what she would tell Fr. Wilson. She never thought she would ever be in a position where she would have to tell anyone. She had always been so careful not to do or say anything that would make her have to acknowledge and explain that "feeling." Even though Fr. Wilson may be able to offer her advice, she couldn't reveal herself, expose this problem, or this curse that had been hanging over her most of her life. So far, she hadn't told a single soul about this "feeling," not even her parents, and certainly not Kara, her sister.

"Can I get you some water or coffee?" the secretary asked.

"No, thank you," Olivia said. She gave the secretary a smile and stepped out into the dimly lit, narrow hallway where she took deep breaths to keep herself relaxed. Olivia worried that she would forget her well planned speech and she would allow Fr. Wilson to council her into changing her mind. She had to hold strong. She knew what she had to do and she couldn't make more of this conference than she had to. All she had to do was just go in to his office and tell him. She wouldn't have to offer an explanation, and even if he asked her, she would just say she had none and leave it at that. She went back into the office and took her seat.

Fr. Wilson opened the door to his office and a man she did not recognize came out. He shook hands with the Reverend and left. Olivia let out a long sigh. "Tell him and get out of there," she silently reminded herself.

"Olivia Douglass. Come in, come in," Fr. Wilson said; a wide smile on his face. He waved her in.

She stood, "Hello Fr. Wilson. Thank you for seeing me," and stepped past him, into the office, which was strikingly different from the outer office. Fr. Wilson's office with a set of stained glass windows across one wall was not only bright and cheery, but also a mass of unorganized books, papers, and magazines. He'd run out of shelves, and several stacks of magazines and books sat on the floor around the periphery of the unusually small office. Fr. Wilson seemed unaware of the mess as he stepped over a stack of magazines and slid into a contemporary leather chair behind his cluttered desk.

Olivia sat in a hand-carved birch wood armchair opposite him. She brushed her beige wool skirt as if cleaning dirt from it, then stretched the material, trying to pull it down to cover her knees. She straightened herself in the chair. She would upset him, and she was now ready for that. During their last meeting, he told her how much he was looking forward to having her at his church and then discontinued his search for an associate priest.

"I'm sure I've said it already, but you're on your way to becoming a fine priest." He moved some papers around on his desk and sat back in his chair.

She tried to keep her perspective by reminding herself about the discussion in the adult Sunday school class she'd led last Sunday. She was sure he heard her comment about the church community. Rumors about that must have gotten to everyone in the church by now and possibly out in the neighborhood.

The memory was certainly clear in her mind. She had expected seven or eight people, ten at the most. Just as she started her talk, the parishioners filed into the room with coffee and donuts in hand until all of the fifty seats were taken. She stopped speaking when she saw people searching for seats and shifting from chair to chair to make room. After everything was settled, she gazed down at her notes to find her place and began again. When she looked up from her notes, she saw four or five people in the front row pointing to their ears.

A man sitting on the back row shrugged his shoulders. "Can you speak up?"

"We can't hear you." One woman yelled out at the same time.

"Yeah, we can't hear a thing with the heater humming," another said.

"I can't turn my hearing aid up any higher," an older man said.

Olivia stuttered out a weak "I'm sorry. Can you hear me now?" as she spoke louder. She tried to remember to speak louder as she continued, but she lowered her voice again and a few parishioners signaled her again. Before she realized what was happening and was able to stop herself, she let slip out, "There's no need to come to church." What she meant to say was, "There is a reason to be part of a church community." She realized her mistake when she heard the moans and groans from the participants. In her nervousness, she tried to figure out a way to correct her error. She sought help from her fiancé, Claude, sitting in the front row, but he shrugged his shoulders. Then he looked at her as if to say, "Don't ask me. I don't know what to do." Still she needed his help. He could have asked her to repeat what she said or explained to everyone what she meant. But not Claude. Claude sat there shaking his head and making faces at her. She should have realized that he wouldn't have supported her. He had already told her he thought she was taking on too much wanting to be a priest, anyway. Then Wesley Johns stood up.

"You started telling us about a need for a church community. Can you tell us more about that?"

"Sure. The meaning and need for a church is not a simple topic. Many authors have written on this subject in much detail. But for now, it is a way for us to understand the death of Jesus. We do this by sharing in his death. Christ loved the church and he gave himself up for her (it). Read Ephesians chapter 5 verse 25."

Wesley had given her a chance to save herself. At the end, several people clapped for her and told her she had done a nice job.

Surely, that mistake was enough for anyone to reassess the situation. She had, and realized that she was just not cut out to be a priest. She'd wanted to offer people direction, discernment, help them see God's purpose, but instead, she'd brought them confusion, frustration, and misunderstanding.

Olivia had to decide whether she should bring it up now or allow Fr. Wilson to bring it up.

"Being a priest. That's what I want to talk about." She had hoped that she wouldn't have to talk about it. She just wanted to tell him and get out of there.

"Is it the procedure? You know you have to do six months of diaconal training before you can be ordained, and if you're planning to start now, which would be good, you can finish the training by July and be ordained in early fall." His was a warm, welcoming smile that should have made her feel comfortable.

Olivia regarded him carefully. His finely chiseled features gave him the appearance of a movie star. She wondered why, with looks like his, he had become a priest. He rocked slightly in his chair, his movements sure and steady. He could have become a movie star, but he became a priest instead. She recognized her own lack of self-assurances and wondered if he'd noticed.

"No, Fr. Wilson, it's not the procedure. It's just that I don't believe that being a priest is what I'm supposed to be. I don't have the character and I'm just not prepared to go any further." She would need to give Fr. Wilson a reason for her decision, and this was where she was stuck. She had to withhold the truth. No one would believe such a thing, absolutely no one.

"I see, you have doubts. Many graduates have doubts." He lowered his voice, and the words seemed to ease out of his mouth, rested in the air. "You needn't worry about that; I'd worry if you didn't have doubts."

"I do have doubts, but not the way we were told in seminary. I have serious doubts about me. Something feels wrong and I can't describe what it is. Maybe I just don't have the right attitude or the right character." She had to skirt the real problem and her nervousness returned. Perspiration rolled down the sides of her head and she hoped her shoulder-length dark hair hid it from his view.

"What do you mean, 'the right attitude'?" His voice was still low, as if he wanted to understand.

"I don't trust that my faith is strong enough, and sometimes I question whether there truly is a God. How can I lead others if I'm unsure about my own faith?" Even though she had to mention her faith, one of the biggest doubts that seminarians had that kept them from going into the priesthood and a doubt that was not very substantial, she was a little less tense.

"Entering the priesthood is a serious step." He glanced at the papers on his desk in front of him. "And from what I have here, you seem to have done well enough to go on. You'll do well."

She tried forming the words to tell him the truth. Her heartbeat sped up and her hands shook. She just could not make herself tell Fr. Wilson. She had to keep it to herself. Not even her parents and certainly not her fiancé, Claude, knew anything about this. After all, how would it make her seem? She was always afraid that telling someone, especially her parents who adopted her and loved her, would cause them to see her as some kind of aberrant, someone with bizarre notions, and then they would steer away from her. Fr. Wilson would do the same.

"Fr. Wilson, I've made up my mind about this. I'm sorry if you feel I've wasted your time, or caused you any problems, but after serious consideration and praying about this over the past few months, I see that I shouldn't become a priest." She wanted this to be enough for him. She wanted him to trust her and accept her decision.

"Olivia, what led you here?"

"What do you mean?"

"What led you toward the priesthood? You have to examine that for yourself. Find the truth as to why you entered the seminary, why you took that first step. What were you searching for?"

She reflected for a moment.

"Right after college, I went from job to job for a few months. Each job seemed to lead me closer to the seminary. And then, I woke up one morning and realized that I wanted to be a priest." Inward, she asked the Lord to forgive her for such a bold sin, or at best, a half lie, but she just couldn't tell Fr. Wilson about that curse that surrounded her.

He studied her as if he expected her to change her answer. She remained silent. He spoke.

"So, you do feel called. That's important."

She hadn't thought about it as a calling. She had to escape that feeling. She thought that by immersing herself deeply in religion and being close to God, those feelings would disappear, but they hadn't.

"Olivia, many graduates stop at this point. For one reason or another, they decide not to go any further. Some come and want to talk about it, others write a letter. What you're doing is common. I suspect something else going on, something you're afraid to tell me. I have summaries of your records here, your performance on the final exams, the recommendations from the bishop, the vestry, your course information, and statements from your seminary priests, and they all indicate that you'll do well. What is your true purpose today?"

She was out of words. Was this why she came? Was it faith in herself or faith in God she lacked? Was it the same thing?

"Father, I—"

"If you don't want to continue with the training, I hope you'll continue leading our prayer team. Olivia, you can always remain a deacon if you decide not to go any further. As a deacon, you may want to consider pastoral counseling or something along those lines. Then again, maybe in time, you'll change your mind." He looked up at her as if expecting her to respond.

She looked down in her lap.

"Search for the truth, Olivia. You may be feeling lost, but you were led down this road for a reason. Maybe you were asked to continue and maybe you were called in another direction. Pray and ask for enlightenment and guidance." He paused as if he wanted to say more but had second thoughts.

Olivia thought the meeting was over when he began again.

"Meanwhile, as our prayer team leader, I have an opportunity that I think will help you. I hope you'll accept it." He said, watching her.

She looked at him as if he knew her curse. Is he asking her to get prayer for it? She wanted prayer, badly, but that would mean that she would have to tell someone about the curse. She wished she had someone to pray with. It would help her get rid of it.

"Yes, I have no plans to leave this church."

"Good, then. I received a request from the men's prison in Virginia, a short ways over the Maryland state line. An inmate is asking for someone to pray with him. He's on death row and will be executed in," he moved a few papers about, sought out his hand-written notes, "two weeks."

"Death row? But, Father, I don't know anything about . . . this is . . . I'm not qualified to do anything like that. This is too huge."

"We all are." He peered at the paper again. "All he wants is to have someone pray with you. You're good at prayer, Olivia. Help this man; pray with him."

She had taken a special interest in praying and healing prayer and had taken on the position as prayer team leader several months ago at St. Luke's Church. She had also taken training in prayer and healing outside of her coursework in seminary and had asked permission from her advisor to attend several training workshops while she was in seminary. Olivia figured that Fr. Wilson knew about her interest and had a list of those courses and seminars she'd taken among his many papers.

"Isn't it dangerous? What did he do?"

"I don't know, and of course, you know you don't need to know what he did. God knows, and that's all that matters. If it helps you at all, I've done this in the past, and I'm certain you'll be okay. He just has two weeks. This should take a day or two, three at most. You go there, and we'll get someone to drive you the first day, meet him, find out what he wants so you can direct your prayers, and pray with him."

"You make it sound so simple."

"It's not as simple as it sounds, but it's not difficult, either."

"Will I have to go inside the prison?" She heard her own voice filled with irritation and complaint; she feared closed-in places.

"Olivia, you'll be okay."

"I . . . don't . . . think . . ." She began to panic, again. It took all she was able to muster up to keep herself under control.

"Even inmates have a right to prayer, Olivia. Surely you don't believe otherwise."

"No, it's not that. Will I have a partner to help with what to do and say?"

"Your Partner will already be there, ready and waiting on you. He's all you need. The only person who is trained is Eva and she's on vacation. You won't need another person to tell you what to do. Open your heart and God will provide the words. He knows everything about this man. Just open your heart."

Olivia was quiet for a moment, taking in the prodigious request.

"Be here at noon tomorrow. I'll get Will to drive you. He has always driven me. Visiting hours begin at 2:00. It's about a two-hour driving time. You'll be fine," he said as he stood, letting her know the meeting was over.

She stood, but she was no longer ready to leave.

"Keep me posted. Call my secretary when you go, and let her know what you're doing, if you have to. I'll get the messages. I'll always make myself available for you in the unlikely event you need anything. Meanwhile, this will give you a chance to do more in the line of counseling. This may help you find yourself, and find direction."

* * *

On the drive back, Olivia gave thought to her new assignment. Going to a prison made her anxious. Praying with this inmate may be a chance for her to find herself. But, as far back as she remembered, she would break out into a sweat when she was in small places or felt locked in. Whenever she rode in a car, she had to have at least one window down, the same way she always had to have a window open in her room. She was uncomfortable in elevators, but it was easier for her if one side was glass. She stayed away from turtleneck sweaters because she felt too enclosed. Just the thought of entering a prison filled her with dread.

Nevertheless, she was relieved. She had told Fr. Wilson her decision to go no further. Now, she worried about how to tell her parents, who were still unaware, and who had already arrived from England to attend her graduation from seminary. They would be disappointed. When her father called to give Olivia their flight and hour of arrival, he also told her that he had told everyone at the University of London, his church, and his club about his daughter headed for the priesthood. She was all set to tell him that she had changed her mind until she heard the boast in his voice.

CHAPTER 2

The weather was above the freezing mark. A light snow fell, and then disappeared into tiny round puddles when the flakes hit the ground. Will drove on the highway for a while, then, when he crossed the line into Virginia, took what he called the back roads. Olivia sat in the back seat of the town car, window let down a little, and Fr. Wilson's notes about the inmate in her hand. She peered out the window glad that she'd remembered to bring an umbrella even though she had hoped she wouldn't need it. They came to a small town and drove down its main street. Three old cars and a rusty-looking pick-up truck were parked on the lot in front of the shopping center. A Laundromat, and a pharmacy, seemed closed. A string of Christmas lights flickered on and off over half of a sign announcing The Wine and Beer Shop. Some of the lights had fallen and rested on the "S" of Sam's Sandwich Shop, next door. Half lit up, the large picture of a foot-long meatball sandwich seemed like half a foot.

There was a familiarity about this small town that brought to her mind the bakery she loved in Cotswold, England with its long blue windows and door. They had the best biscuits she had ever tasted and she would get them early in the morning when the biscuits were just coming out of the oven. Thinking about them now made her mouth water. Cotswold had a certain loneliness about it, the same way she felt about this town as they drove through.

At the gas station, a man wearing a blue baseball hat pulled down to his eyes, and a sweatshirt with faded letters pumped gas in his white pick-up truck. A woman in a short skirt, black high-heeled boots, and a short black leather jacket pushed a baby carriage on a jagged sidewalk alongside the gas station. The baby, a blanket pulled around him, batted his hands at the snowflakes as they fell. The woman turned around several times for something behind her, as she walked fast on the rough sidewalk. Olivia wondered if she was running away from someone, maybe an abusive husband and she was tempted to offer her a ride. But the woman turned the corner and disappeared down a side street. The woman, underdressed for the weather, gave Olivia the idea of starting a coat drive for the poor, especially for homeless women. The weather this time of year was sometimes unforgiving. She would have to talk to Fr. Wilson about it.

About five miles later, and after she'd said her prayers, she looked up and saw that they were driving through another small town. At its edge, by the post office, Will made a right turn, and drove a mile before he pulled up just outside the prison. The snow had picked up, and was sticking to the ground. The large flakes seemed to surround the compound with its purity, edging out the grittiness that hung over the prison. Will put the car in park; turned his head slightly and Olivia knew they had arrived.

"This is it, huh?"

"Yes, ma'am, it is."

Olivia opened the door and got out. Will let down his window.

"Aren't you coming in?" She knew he wouldn't.

"No, ma'am. I'm just the driver. I'll be back in an hour."

Olivia turned toward the huge dreadful-looking mass of gray. A Bastille, a place of confinement stood before her, the only home the man she was to visit, had seen in a long time, and the home in which he would take his last breath. Standing in front of what appeared to be the front, she searched for the name on the building, or some entrance sign. She saw nothing on the side where she stood. Beyond the barbed wire fence and the many locked gates, sat a huge concrete box that though miles from anywhere, was otherwise free of trees, bushes or flowering vegetation. Still, there seemed to be no way to enter. Just about the time she thought she would have to stand outside in the snow for an hour waiting for Will to return, people walking across the parking lot, some with umbrellas, moved toward her and formed a line just outside what she discovered was the entrance. In about five minutes, two guards came and opened the gates for the visitors.

The line of about twenty men, women, and children moved slowly through metal detectors. She heard two visitors answer questions posed to them in Spanish. When Olivia reached the metal detectors, she gave the guard holding a clipboard, her name, and reason for coming. The tall guard, who resembled Lawrence Fishburne, looked at her, then wrote something on the clipboard. He nodded at her and asked her to step to the side. The efficiency and expediency made her nervous, and she wanted to turn back. At that moment, a guard who was two feet shorter than the others and who obviously lifted weights, appeared. Olivia tucked away her nervousness, straightened her spine, and followed the guard a few feet down the hallway. He asked her to wait at a doorway. Overhead on the loud speaker, a tap, tap, tapping sound grew louder. Someone with a southern accent called out the names of those prisoners who had visitors to come to the visiting area. The finality and the intensity of the clanking and banging of the gates locking and unlocking caused a sick feeling to run through her. Her body gave off a ferocious urge to leave, run away; escape the place. Her mind fought against it, wanting her to stay. She doubled over feeling sharp pains in her stomach, and then heaving spasms took over her body. Her mind on her stomach, she reached out to grab onto whatever was there to steady herself.

Just as they got to the doorway, the guard turned around, and saw her. He took hold of her just before she fell to the floor.

"It'll be okay, ma'am," said the guard. "It takes a while," he said with an accent she couldn't distinguish.

Olivia tried to respond, but the pain was so sharp she was unable to speak.

The guard pressed a button on his walkie-talkie and called for the captain of the guards. The captain arrived and the two men helped Olivia to his office, near the visitor's room. The captain offered her a chair.

"It takes a while to get used to all this," said the captain, handing her a paper cup of water.

Olivia sipped the water.

"Hello Mr. or is it, Captain Johns?" Olivia recognized him. He was an usher at her church and the man who asked questions during her discussion last Sunday. She was surprised to see him.

"Call me Wesley. Here, I'm Captain Johns, Wesley Johns on Sunday." He gave her a shy smile. "I thought you might be the one to come."

"I'm sorry, but I don't like closed in places or feeling locked in. I'm not sure I'll do any good."

"You'll be okay in a few minutes. You're here to see . . ."

She handed him the paper that Fr. Wilson had given her, the one with the prisoner's information.

"Yes, ma'am. I know." Captain Johns asked one of the guards to bring the inmate to a visiting room.

She smiled and nodded as if she understood, but she was confused. He sounded like he was expecting her.

In a few minutes, she followed the guard to a small room with a door on either end. The guard pulled out a chair for her to sit. Shortly, two other guards, one on either side, escorted a rotund, bald man with a dark mustache into the room. Tattoos covered his exposed arms, his neck, and around his eyes.

He reminded Olivia of an angry bull—nostrils flaring, deep guttural grunts, and digging in. He was clad in an orange jumpsuit, his hands, and feet shackled, as he shuffled one foot then the other through the now narrow doorway. Were it not for the fact that both guards were taller, Olivia would have thought he'd arrived alone. When the guards sat him down, all Olivia saw was a massive body of orange that spread from one end of the wooden table to the other. She felt like an insignificant little speck. Olivia tried not to reveal how frightened she was of the enormity of this man and the viciousness of his appearance. His face was devoid of any emotion, nothing that told her he understood, and nothing that indicated that he wanted her to pray for him. She had never been this close to a criminal and had no idea what to expect, but this man was so violent-looking that she wanted to ask the guards to remain with them.

One guard did something with the chains around his waist and hands, and then chained and bound his hands to a metal anchor directly in front of him on the table. The table, she noticed when she sat down, was also bolted to the concrete floor. The guards then nodded to her and stood just outside the room.

"What is this? Who the hell are you?" His voice shot out like an explosion that echoed throughout the prison.

"You asked to pray with someone. I'm here to pray with you. You asked for someone to pray with you, remember?" She said, in a shaky voice.

His cheeks were so full and round that his eyes were two slits carved in a pumpkin.

"Hell no! I wanna man, not some bitch." He leaned forward jerking his hands. "What the hell do you think this is?" He turned his head as much as possible and called the guards back. "Guard, guard, get me the hell out a here. What the fuck do you think this is? You think this is funny? Goddammed bitch can't help me. I wanna man. Who the hell do you think you are, bitch? I know what you're thinking. You can't fool me. You think because they say I'm supposed to be a child snatcher, which I ain't mind you, I never took nobody's child, but you believe it and you wanna give me some kind of pep talk. Well, I don't need no pep talk. Shit, you ain't even dressed goddammed proper."

Olivia flinched. She tried hard not to cower. She looked down at her gray tweed skirt and tugged on the pockets of the jacket. His attack on her made her feel diminutive, especially since his presence and thunderous voice seemed to spill out into the halls and beyond. She had an urge to get out of the room, but she was rooted in her chair. Her hands in her lap, she silently summoned all her strength to remain calm, and composed. And before she knew, thoughts about that curse, that evilness that surrounded her flipped through her mind, like pages in a book.

The two guards entered the room. "What's the problem?" one asked.

"He's not ready to pray. He's changed his mind," she began. She knew her voice was not steady, but she tried not to give away her fear.

Several times, the inmate fiercely jerked the chains giving off a strange rattling sound, and pulled at the anchor on the table as if trying to unshackle himself.

"I asked for a goddammed man. I don't want no woman. How can a woman help me? Get me the hell back to my fuckin' cell."

The guard called Captain Johns who appeared within seconds.

"What's the problem?" Captain Johns asked the inmate, as he entered the room.

"I all ready told the guards. I don't wanna talk to no bitch. I wanna man. I thought I was getting' a man. What the fuck is going on here."

"She is who you get," began Captain Johns sitting on the edge of the table facing him, "take it, or leave it. There is no one else. If you want to pray, then you'd better tell this nice lady who came all the way here to see you how sorry you are, and how sorry you are about your language, and ask her nice-like to come back tomorrow." He turned to Olivia, "I'm sorry about this, ma'am."

The inmate and Captain Johns, still sitting on the table, stared at each other.

"Take him back to his cell," said Captain Johns, without letting up his stare. "We'll try this again tomorrow."

One guard undid the inmate's chains from the table, and the two of them stood him up. Then, a guard fettered his wrists to the shackles around his waist. Olivia saw that it restricted his hand movements. As they took him out, an image of a little girl sitting on the floor in a corner of an old house, hands over her eyes, flashed through her mind. She was curious and wanted to understand this image. Did this little girl require help? He mentioned that he was a child snatcher. Perhaps the little girl was the one who needed prayer. But, Olivia worried that a little girl was alone and hidden away somewhere.

She stood to leave. Captain Johns escorted her out of the room.

* * *

"How'd it go, ma'am?" Will asked once she was settled in the car.

"He wasn't asking to have a woman pray with him. He wanted a man."

"Oh, I see. One of those."

"I guess I won't be seeing him anymore."

"Oh, so you prayed with him?"

"No, they took him back to his cell." Tears formed in her eyes and she almost broke down, but instead, she turned toward the window and held strong.

"Oh, don't worry about that. They always say things like that. I guess they have to find a way to feel in control of something, prison life being what it is. Don't you worry; Johns will take care of it. I'm sure he told you to come back." He paused for a moment. "I remember once, when an inmate did that to the rector. After that, Fr. Wilson said that an inmate wanted a woman to pray with him; and then there was the time when an inmate who was found guilty of murdering his wife, just took a knife and slashed her up when she failed to get him his dinner when he wanted it, said he had nothing to pray about. Imagine that?" he said, laughing at the absurdity.

When Fr. Wilson asked her to pray with this inmate, she had no idea that she would have to fight with him to get him to pray. She'd heard that all inmates find God in prison. She had to figure out what this man wanted. She had to get past the huge mass of orange and chains with tattoos and bring him to God. Fr. Wilson said it would possibly take two, three days at most and counting today, she had one, two days to pray for this man.

He had accused her of believing he was a child abductor; the crime he was afraid to admit. The image of that little girl must have been part of his crime. Maybe he wanted forgiveness for what he might have done to that little girl. She hadn't built up any expectations because she had never been in a men's prison before, but this man was a challenge. She was humiliated by his licentious behavior. Yet, at the same time, she had a strong desire to go back at least one more day.

When she first recognized this curse or feeling, she was almost eleven, she thought that she was destined for a life of cruelty, one where she would hurt or torture other people. She learned to keep herself from feeling, as much as possible, so that the curse would be contained and no one would ever see what she held hidden. She was afraid of what would happen if it poured out of her in the midst of her smile or her laughter or her sobs. She held it in; no one would ever know about her feelings. She found it hard to believe that she would hurt anyone, though she did have what she considered dreadful thoughts from time to time.

She tested herself to see if it was in her to kill anything. When she was twelve years old, she picked up her cat, Purdy to kill it. Each time she tried to imagine herself taking her cat's life, the image ended with Olivia playing with Purdy. She loved her cat. Instead of trying to find ways to kill him, she hugged him, kissed him, and kept him close to her. If she couldn't bring herself to killing an animal as helpless as a cat, then how could she harm a person?

When she reached high school, she was desperate to find an explanation for this curse. One afternoon, during lunch in her school lunchroom, her friend, Charlotte, sat down beside her and told her that since she was different from her family that she must be adopted. But Charlotte had no proof of any difference. Olivia's feelings weren't from her adoption.

In one of her classes during her first year in college, Professor Moore showed the students a documentary about a woman who felt like there was something or someone following her. The woman said that many times she would get off the bus and after a half block of walking, she'd turn around, and see a small round shadow ducking behind a building or suddenly turn into a driveway. This woman, too, wasn't able to explain her feelings, but it turned out that she had had a twin that died two days after she was born.

Then, Mark who was in one of her classes, told her at a party one night, that he had lost a twin at birth. He said, "When I was growing up I felt lost, something was missing in my life. I had this hatred inside me and hated everyone who had a good life. I wanted to understand what was wrong with me, but I was afraid to try to understand. I thought I had had a horrible experience, and I was responsible for it."

"My mother told me that I had a twin sister who died at birth. All these years and she never told me. All these years I felt an emptiness in my soul. I saw I had my arms, legs, but I was different, something was missing. For many years, I felt alone because there was no one for me to talk to, no one would understand my missing part. I was a very angry kid because I never understood why I was spared and my twin sister was taken."

Even though their situations seemed different, she, too, felt lost as if she had an emptiness. Mark's feelings were closest to her feelings of loneliness and fear. Mark also said that he no longer questioned things.

This feeling had been inside her, rolling around, making her feel it, and forcing her to recognize it. She hadn't quite felt the strength, the power of the curse until she had entered seminary. After three years in seminary, she realized that the curse—the feeling that drew her to seminary— also made her believe that she didn't belong in the church. She never could describe the feeling. But she believed it was not because she held the wrong attitude, or her belief in God wasn't strong enough, or that her trust in God wasn't deep enough, but it was that she had committed a very wrongful act.

Even though she had just passed her general ordination exams, she decided against her six months of diaconal training and then ordination. After all, who would allow her to be a priest with a curse surrounding her? And even more so now because the power of that curse was greater after her visit with Leon. She saw around him an image of a little girl.

23

Chapter 3

Olivia tapped on the window of *Not the Last Read*, the bookstore the family who adopted her had recently bought a few blocks from their home church just off the main street in downtown Rockville, Maryland. Through the glass window case, she saw her father bent over a box of books and when she tapped on the window again, he stood up, turned and saw her. She smiled as she pushed in the glass door and hurried to give him a hug, the first person she'd learned to trust.

"I knew you'd be here in this store," she said as he stood up.

Her father reached out to her, arms wide to take in the entirety of his daughter.

"Olivia, Sweetheart. Boy, it's good to see you."

They pulled back.

"How was your flight? Did Mom keep you awake like she did during the last visit?" She chuckled.

"Let me look at you. My daughter, a priest." With a loving grin, he gave a sigh, shook his head. "Your mother wasn't as nervous this time. She's getting used to flying over water, I guess." He stepped away but held her hand.

She eyed her father. She'd missed him over these past three years while she was in the Virginia seminary. She was not able to go home as often as she had wanted. Not blessed with intelligence for remembering history, she always had history to learn, and understand. She often found herself at the library. She loved to curl up and study in that worn brown leather chair that she regularly used, the one that reminded her of her father and the times he used to read to her.

She regarded him now, watching for the man whom she knew to be her father; the tall, thin man with a smile that lit up his face, who always had answers, and who doled out serious but tender discipline. The man standing before her appeared tired, worn, almost hammered down from exhaustion and time. He had a slight paunch and filled up his clothes. His full head of hair he was always so proud of had thinned, and his eyes were without that happy gleam. He seemed lost and reminded Olivia of a game show where the contestants opted for a door and when they opened it, found nothing there. It frightened her momentarily as she realized time had crept up and taken hold of her father. She regretted not going home as often as she should have and a feeling of "loss" quickly washed over her.

She turned away and took in the store. "So, this is the new store."

"Yes, and I'm happy that you found it okay." He stood with his arms out. "This is it. Moving up in this world. Your mother and I are now the proud owners of not one, but two bookstores."

She moved toward bookcases where books were already on the shelves and ran her fingers across the spines of several of the books.

She recalled the bookstore they owned in England; she knew that one well. When she'd turned sixteen, she worked side by side with her mother and sister, Kara, three days weekly. Knowing her parents' penchant for familiarity, they would try to make this store very much like the one they owned in England, with its dark wooden shelves and floors, and high ceiling. She'd loved the warmth and coziness of their bookstore in England, the protectiveness of it. For a moment, she remembered how she used to sit for hours at that store, reading whatever she could get her hands on, taking in the aromas. She closed her eyes, inhaled the scents of mahogany, oil and old leather. When she opened her eyes, she forgot for a moment that she was not in England. When she saw the signs on the table, she realized her parents were planning to section this store so that it housed fiction, poetry, political essays, history, and religion. Opposite the books stood a small bar that she knew her parents would use for coffee, tea, juice, pastry, and cookies. Over near the door, by the counter, they would probably display the bookmarks from paper to metal, reading lamps, bookstands, and other things an avid reader should use. In England, Olivia called these things the "extras." She always tried to sell the "extras" whenever she sold anyone a book. Their bookstore in England smelled of Kenyan Tea, and fresh baked cookies just out of the oven and she searched for those aromas now.

She turned toward the large brown box of books, flaps on the outside, and took out a book with a tattered leather cover, and the gold words, across the spine, *Wuthering Heights*, so worn that they were barely visible. "Some of these are vintage, Dad. People still buy these?"

"Book lovers do."

"Why are you and mom opening this store? Aren't you both returning to England after my graduation?"

"We are. I'm going to retire in a few years, and when I do we'll want to move back here. It'll help to have the bookstore going. We want to get it open before we go back. I said to your mother 'I know two beautiful ladies who would run this store for us.'"

"Oh, you did, huh? And what did mom say?"

"Let's just say that the two ladies I had in mind would want more than a minimum wage salary."

"Dad, you know I'll check on it as often as I can."

He kissed her on the top of her head.

Her father was so happy to see her. How would she tell him? In the car on the way to the store, she'd tried to think of a way to tell her father. She had to be honest with him. But she was more afraid of the disappointment her mother would feel than her father. Now, his elation gave her second thoughts.

"Everything okay, sweetheart?"

"Everything's fine. Why?"

"You seem rather unsettled. The graduation is set in two weeks, isn't it?"

"That's a definite."

She wanted to look down at herself, but dared not. She couldn't allow her countenance to give herself away before she was ready to tell them. When she decided to go into the priesthood, they were happy for her, especially her father. Even though she had worked, doing whatever she found at the time, they always sent her money and kept up with her classes. Now, she had to find the right words that expressed what she felt, and she needed to find a way to tell them that wouldn't be so disappointing to them.

"What's the matter? You and Claude still together, aren't you?"

"Claude. Yes. Nothing's changed about that."

"If everything is okay, then why the uneasiness?"

She smiled at him. Even though he had changed, he still knew her, loved her the same way he had before she'd gone into seminary. The bond they had was still there and she felt it with his question.

He took two books out of another box and placed them side by side on an empty shelf.

She, following him, reached into the box and took out several books.

"What's the system?"

"These are all poetry."

Her father, the man she knew, was edging his way back.

"I'm so happy you and mom have come to see me graduate. I'm so sorry I missed coming home so many times. I wanted to come home more often, but I had so much to catch up on, so much about church history that I lacked and had to understand."

"You don't have to explain, Livvy. Your mother and I understood. Remember, we went to college too. I teach Literature and Religious Studies; you know how much history's in those subjects. I had a hard time learning it, too."

"You sure? You and mom are not upset?"

"Absolutely not. But don't misunderstand. We both missed you. After you left, we had to learn to steep our own tea, find good pastry, and find our own way to and from places."

They laughed.

"Sometimes I felt I was overdoing everything. You know, being a know-it-all."

"Sweetheart, it comes with the territory. In fact, your mother and I were happy that you showed us how to make tea and all the things you did. You were never overdoing it."

She gazed down at her shoes, around the room again and back at him, gave him a slight smile. "What if I decided not to become a priest?" She reached in the box for more books, afraid to face him.

He held a space of silence.

He knew she had a worry on her and wanted to tell him. She knew that was the reason why he mentioned her nervousness. She had always found it hard to keep things from her father. She suspected that he also knew about those feelings inside her, though he had never said anything.

"Dad, I know you were hoping that I would be a priest, but I've changed my mind."

He turned to her. "I see."

They continued taking books from the box and placing them on the shelves in silence until they each filled one shelf. She thought he would allow her to leave it like that, but he spoke.

"Are you going to tell me why?"

"Being a priest doesn't feel right to me. I can't explain it, but I just don't think I'm a priest."

He picked up another book and placed it on the shelf.

"Are you angry? Disappointed in me?"

"Angry? Disappointed in you? Are you kidding? Sweetheart, we've been nothing but proud of you? If you've changed your mind, I accept that." He reached out to hug her. "I love you no matter what. You'd make a great priest, but this is something you have to be happy about. It has to feel right to you. And if it doesn't feel right to you, then do what feels right."

"I knew you'd understand." She kissed her father on the cheek. "Thank you."

"I guess we'd better go home and tell your mother. She's home fixing you a special meal. She ran me out of the house earlier. But, you go on ahead; I'll be along. I have to close up here."

She wanted to ask him to tell mother, but she couldn't do that to him. She knew her mother wouldn't take it as easily and be as understanding as he was. "I have to tell mom, but I want to do it my way, if you don't mind."

"Do what you think is best."

He had aged, but he was still her father.

She remembered that after they'd adopted her and moved to England, she was afraid. He thought she was afraid of being so far away and that the darkness frightened her. Every night, after they knelt together and he said the prayers, he stayed with her until she went to sleep.

Some nights, even when it was cold, he found blankets and would take her and her sister, Kara, outside. They would lie down on their blankets or on chilly nights, wrap up in them, and gaze up at the stars. Olivia would try to follow one as they moved across the black sky growing larger or smaller.

During those nights, as they looked up into the darkness of the still night, he taught her how to count. "Hold up your fingers," he'd say and he put up her hands, fingers splayed. He pointed to each finger, "One, two, . . ., ten. You count."

She wiggled each finger, "One, two, three . . ., ten."

"That's right. You have ten fingers," he'd say.

"Ten fingers," she'd repeat.

Some nights, he'd pick out a star and give it a name. He'd tell Olivia and Kara to pick out a star and give it a name, too.

"Pick your favorite one." He'd say to her. And each time she'd pick a different star.

"I don't have a favorite. They keep moving."

One night they tried to race to see who would be the first to count all the stars. He began and pointed his finger toward the dark starlit sky and counted, "One, two, three . . ., ten." When he stopped, he said, "Your turn." Then she and Kara tried to count them at the same time, and the more they counted the louder they got and the more mixed up and confused they became; and being caught up in the warmth and love, they just laughed.

"I counted a hundred," Kara said.

"How could you count that fast? I'm on fifteen," Olivia said.

"Kara are you cheating?" her father asked.

She and Kara laughed because they weren't able to keep up with the stars as they slid across the night sky.

"Do you know about the Milky Way?" he asked them one night.

"I like it," Olivia said.

"We learned about it in school," Kara said.

"No, that was Baby Ruth," Olivia said.

"He's not talking about a candy bar, Livvy. He's talking about the stars," Kara said, laughing her head off. Olivia and her father couldn't stop laughing, either.

Then they would be quiet for a moment as they'd tell their star a secret. Sometimes they would make up stories about their stars. One night in the summer when the noises of crickets and cicadas filled the air, Kara made up a funny one about a cricket living on a star, and it hopping around trying to avoid the gases and craters, she said. During the winter, the blackness of the sky seemed so beautiful, a color that Olivia had never seen in paints or crayons. On those winter nights, Olivia noticed how quiet the sky was and no matter how cold it was, she just wanted to stay there all night soaking up the quiet and watching the stars. She hated it when her father would say, "It's time to go in. It's late and you girls have to get up for school in the morning." She and Kara would reluctantly go back to their rooms.

Her father made her feel safe and she began to open her heart to him, to trust him. She needed to rely on that trust now. She knew he was not happy about her decision not to tell her mother right away. She knew that after all the money and encouragement he'd invested in her that he was not happy with her decision not to be a priest. Why would he be happy? But she trusted him to wait for her to tell her mother when she was ready.

CHAPTER 4

Olivia took hold of the door latch. As she opened the door, a musty, odor much like an old moldy basement escaped and attacked her nostrils. She recalled that her parents had the house closed up after the renters left almost four months ago. She inhaled the stuffiness as she stepped into the dark hallway and made her way to the living room. The plastic covers dutifully protected the furniture and lamps from the dust that had gathered.

The last time she remembered being in the house, boxes and suitcases were packed and stacked throughout the living and dining rooms. The many boxes made it difficult for her to now see the room, feel it, and recall its odors, its cracks, and sounds. Even though she had spent the past three years in the U.S., her home during that time was a dormitory room in the Virginia Theological Seminary. She hadn't been back to this house until now. The humming sound from the refrigerator broke into her thoughts and she turned toward the kitchen.

"Mom, Mom? Are you here?" she inquired as she found her way to the kitchen.

The kitchen was empty, but the aromas from the dinner permeated the room. She spied coffee already brewed, poured herself a cup, and sat down at the kitchen table. She couldn't help but notice the kitchen; she smiled. How amazing, in just a few hours her mother had brought the kitchen to life, given the kitchen that homey feel and even cooked her favorite meal. Her mother had a way of welcoming people and Olivia loved the special touches that she prepared for her family.

The backdoor flew open and hit up against the kitchen wall. Olivia jumped, stood up. "Mom? Is that you?"

Her mother peeped around the large brown paper bag she carried, "Livvy? My Livvy. You're here." She rushed past Olivia and put the large heavy-looking bag on the counter.

"What did you buy?"

"Oh, you know how I am. I just went to pick up some garlic for the green beans and realized we needed so many other things as well." She stood with her hands on her hips. "Let me just look at you. I miss seeing you."

"Mom, I haven't changed that much."

"Oh, honey, you know, every time you or Kara leave, I don't know. I just worry." She wiped at the corner of her eye.

"Mom, you don't have to worry so much."

"Honey, now you're going to make me all gushy and you know I hate that so, tell me all about the seminary." She reached over and gave Olivia a long tight hug.

They pulled back.

"And, your sister was able to come, after all. She flew in with us. She'll be in in a minute, she had to take a call from her boss. She's still in the car." She turned the heat up under the pots on the stove and turned the oven on to warm up the chicken. "Tell me about you."

"Me? I'm happy to see all of you."

Olivia beheld her mother's face, when she turned toward her, saw the love that she hadn't seen in most of the time she was gone, and wanted to cry. She hadn't realized how much she had missed her family. Her mother always bubbled over with her excitement with anything Olivia told her. Whether it was anything tiny or large, she always made a huge deal out of everything. Olivia always held back from telling her things, before she knew it, her mother would be off telling one of her friends. How would she take the news now? The wrinkle lines on her mother's face moved in various directions as she talked and Olivia noticed that her mother's dark brown hair was shorter than she'd ever seen it. Her mother's hair was thinning in the front, revealing part of her white coated-looking scalp that reminded Olivia of a snow-capped mountain. "Can I help with dinner?"

"You may not. I want to know all about the seminary, and about your vows, and about what we should do to get ready for your graduation." She took her by the hand. "Sit yourself down and tell me all about everything."

She paused for a moment, held onto Olivia's hands.

"Livvy, I know you don't like talking about yourself. But just this once, tell me about yourself and the seminary, would you?" Then, she took the groceries out of the bag and began putting them away.

Olivia wanted to hold back and not say too much.

"What's to tell? There was lots of studying to do, lots of praying and practice sermons, and you know, things like that." She got up to help put the groceries away.

"Livvy, honey, in one of your emails, you kinda indicated that Claude wasn't happy about you becoming a priest. Did I misread that?"

Olivia wanted to tell her mother right then. At that very moment, the words almost slipped through her lips, but she stopped herself, held her lips tight, and prevented the words from spilling out. "Mom, you might have misunderstood," she said instead.

"Well good, then. Your father and I were worried there for a while."

"Yoo-hoo! Any of my girls home?" her father called out while walking through the living room on his way to the kitchen.

"We're here in the kitchen," her mom yelled back.

Olivia stood back a second to observe her father as he entered the kitchen. She remembered how he was during the few times she went to visit him at the university. Dr. Vincent Douglass, a stern, no-nonsense professor, his nose propping his glasses as he surveyed the classroom, daring his students to show up unprepared. He walked to his wife, and gave her a kiss on the lips, then to Olivia and kissed her on the forehead.

"Can we eat? I'm starving?" He turned toward the chicken and raised his hand as if he wanted to take a pinch.

"Vinny, don't." Her mother swiped his hand away.

"Elizabeth, honey, I'm hungry." Her mother wouldn't let anyone call her Liz, or Lizzy or Betty, or Libby or any nickname. It was always Elizabeth. She was pretty firm about that.

"Vinny, we'll eat in a few minutes." She pushed herself between the stove and her husband, protecting her precious chicken.

"See how she treats me? She'll let her poor hardworking husband starve when all I want is a taste."

"Vinny, I love you, honey, but you are not getting any of this chicken until it's time."

Olivia laughed. "You two."

He leaned down and gave her a kiss on the forehead. Olivia watched as her mother closed her eyes to receive the kiss. Suddenly she opened her eyes and grabbed both his arms. She laughed. "I thought you were trying to sneak a pinch of the chicken."

He laughed. "Don't trust me, huh?"

Standing between the chicken and her husband, her mother turned to the stove and dished out the green beans and put them into a bowl she had waiting on the counter. Then she put the chicken on a platter and the boiled, buttered potatoes in a bowl.

At that moment, Kara, carrying a brown paper bag in one hand, and phone in the other, came in through the back door. When she closed her phone, she regarded it for a short while before dropping it in her handbag. She set the paper bag on the table. The frown she had on her face just before she gave another glance at her cell phone, turned into a smile when she saw Olivia.

"Livvy. Nice to see you, kiddo." She gave Olivia an air kiss on both cheeks.

Olivia gave Kara a quick hug, then, took a step back, "Good to see you too. Busy as ever, it seems." She felt a bit tense, on edge, waiting for the other shoe to fall as she had when she and Kara usually got together.

"Yes, and speaking of that, that was my boss on the phone. He has an assignment for me and I have to get back right away." She took out her phone again, and walked to another room.

"Let's everybody sit down at the table, shall we?" her mother said. She handed Olivia the dish of green beans and her husband the platter of chicken and directed them to the dining room where she had the table set. Olivia stood in the doorway realizing that she hadn't noticed the table was already set. She admired her mother who always knew how to prepare for her family and kept things together.

"Livvy, you haven't talked about your visit with that inmate on death row. How'd it go?" her mother asked, as she carried the bowl of boiled potatoes to the table and then sat down. After she and her parents were seated, Olivia gave thanks for the meal and their safe arrival.

"I have to say that I was a bit frightened when we found out that you weren't able to meet us at the airport because you had to go to that prison."

"I thought we decided not to bring that up," her father said, a surprised look on his face.

"I just wanted Livvy to know we love her and want her to be safe. That's all," her mother said.

"I suppose it went okay, as well as a visit of that nature could go." She was thankful her mother brought this up, even though discussing what happened in that prison made her a little uncomfortable. It was better than the other topic of her not wanting to become a priest. But, she had to tell them before they finished dinner.

"I don't know why Fr. Wilson would send you there. Isn't it dangerous?" her mother asked.

"The man is heavily chained and guarded," Olivia said. She realized she was defending Fr. Wilson and surprised at herself for accepting this.

"What kind of life is that? But if you break the law —,"

"Elizabeth, Fr. Wilson wouldn't send her somewhere he knew was dangerous. Besides, Wesley Johns works there," her father said. "You remember him, don't you? He's the captain there. In charge of the guards, I believe."

"Yes dear. Oh, and speaking of him, Mr. Johns' call was forwarded here, and since you hadn't arrived yet, I asked to take a message."

"What did Mr. Johns say?" Olivia asked. She tried to remember whether Wesley somehow knew she hadn't planned to be ordained. If he had spoken to Fr. Wilson, Fr. Wilson might have told him. But he wouldn't do that. That wouldn't be ethical. She had to learn to trust people more. Fr. Wilson would have no reason to tell Wesley Johns. Trust. She needed to trust people.

"He called to remind you that you had to be there by 2:00 p.m. tomorrow," her mother said.

"That man doesn't want to pray and he certainly doesn't want me there. "

"What happened?" her father asked.

Kara came to the dinner table, slammed herself down in a chair, and let out a long, loud sigh. The minute she saw Kara enter, Olivia decided not to tell them.

"Glad you could make it, Sweetheart," her father said, as he passed her the platter of baked chicken.

"We were talking about Olivia's inmate," her mother said.

"OOOOOh, scary," Kara said as she held both hands up and shook them.

"Kara! Try to be nice," her mother said.

"What did he do?" Kara asked. She got up, went to the kitchen, and brought back a bottle of wine that she had taken out of the paper bag, and a wine glass.

"I don't know. It was not for me to ask," Olivia said. She now wished her mother hadn't brought up her involvement with the prisoner. Kara had a way of making her feel debased through her pointed teasing. Olivia always kept how she felt about Kara's antics to herself.

"Well, he is on death row, so he must have taken a life," her father said.

"Death row. You have to kill someone or maybe even many people to get on death row, don't you?" her mother asked.

"I don't know," Olivia said.

"I wonder how many people he killed," Kara said. She took a sip of wine.

"It has to be at least one, and that one has to be such a heinous act that it's unforgivable to the court," her father said. He said it with confidence, and gave a slight nod.

"If I were you, Livvy, I would like to know how many people he killed and how he murdered them. Aren't you even curious about that at all?" Kara asked. She said it like Olivia was either crazy or stupid for not wanting to know more about his gruesome acts.

"I don't need to know that to pray with him," Olivia said.

"That's right, the priest thing, huh? Well, maybe I'm just being the reporter, now."

Olivia studied Kara for a moment. The question of how many people this man had killed or how he did it never occurred to her. Either this wasn't important to her, or she wasn't afraid. Wouldn't that sinfulness that surrounded her confer on her the desire to find out? Yet she had no interest in knowing. Maybe she was running from it; and she wasn't willing to stir up anything in her. Or, maybe it was the priest in her—the thing she was denying.

"What about his family. Does he have any family?" her mother asked.

"If he had a good family, he wouldn't be where he is," her father said.

36

"I suppose that's right, Vinny," her mother said.

"A good family is not what keeps people out of jail. A family who shows love and is attentive to each other will keep people out of jail," Kara said. "But I guess some of us wouldn't know about that." She took another long sip of wine, emptied the glass, and poured herself more.

"It helps to have a family who is supportive. You're right," said Olivia. She winced when she supported her sister. She was still trying to win favors with her sister when lately all her sister did was put her down.

"Oh, but I am," Kara said, taking another large gulp of wine.

"Can I get anyone more of anything?" her father asked. He jumped up from the table carrying the almost empty bowl of green beans.

Her mother refilled everyone's water glass, even Kara's glass, a subtle hint that Kara seemed to ignore.

Kara let out a loud portentous laugh. "I am pure evil."

"Here we go, more green beans," said her father bringing back the bowl.

"In all the commotion, I forgot to add the garlic I just bought," her mother said, on the verge of tears.

"They are scrumptious just the way they are," Olivia said, giving herself another helping, and realizing her mother was upset over Kara's comments. Her mother had always wanted her two daughters to get along.

"Livvy, you should pray with that man, find out who he is, who he killed and bring us back the news," Kara said.

She spoke in such a ghoulish voice that it sent chills all through Olivia.

"Maybe you're right, Kara. Maybe I should pray with him." Olivia figured her parents understood Kara's comment about the need for love and attention and were no doubt hurt by it, as she suspected they were with many of Kara's comments, particularly, her comments about the family.

An irritation rose within Olivia. There was a time, albeit short, when she and Kara were inseparable. Even though they were the same age and started out in the same grade, Olivia was put back in a lower grade after the school year progressed. Yet she and Kara ignored the fact that they were in different grades and remained friends. They used to wear each other's clothes and pretended that they were twins. The year Olivia was in the fourth grade and Kara in the fifth, just after the school year started, they told everyone they were twins and that they each knew what the other felt or thought.

* * *

One day after club meeting, standing in the hallway just outside the classroom, Kara had asked a boy if he had seen her twin sister. Just as Olivia walked up and heard everything, the boy told Kara, that Olivia wasn't her twin sister and that twins had to look alike, or at least look related to one another. A crowd of students gathered around them, so he continued. He said that Olivia was taller and thinner than Kara, her hair wasn't the same color or the same type. Kara had short blonde hair, while Olivia had thick dark curly locks and there was nothing similar about them. He said that her father must have made a baby with someone else and was trying to fool every one. The crowd of students laughed and that angered Kara. She just hauled off and socked him in the mouth. Blood spurted out like a broken faucet she hit him so hard. Some of his blood splattered on the face of the boy's friend. Olivia pulled her away, but Kara turned around and gave him another jab in the mouth, saying that he had insulted two of her family members, her twin sister, and her father. The principal, who came running out of her office to the group, gave Kara two days in detention after she'd seen the bloody nose. Olivia refused to go to her classes. She stayed with Kara in detention until Kara's time was up.

Later during that year, they began drifting apart. First, Kara, then Olivia wouldn't show up when they were to meet between classes, or during lunch and sometimes for the club meetings after school. Olivia couldn't remember who started it first. More likely, it just happened. When she first noticed it, she thought she'd made unpleasant comments that offended Kara and Kara turned on her, or Olivia behaved in a way that pushed her away. She also considered that the separation was related in some way to those feelings that filled her and surrounded her. Olivia often wondered if Kara or her mother or father saw that sinfulness in her. They must have felt this "thing" coming from her.

"Livvy? Livvy are you going back tomorrow?" her mother asked.

"Oh, sorry. Mom, it's what I have to do, what I promised to do."

"While you are praying with a mass murderer, I will be traveling back to

England. I have to go back. As you know, my husband is divorcing me and my boss has another assignment for me. He said if I mess this up, you know, like I did the last one when I failed to check all my facts, he would fire me on the spot this time." Kara turned up her glass of wine, poured herself more.

Olivia hated how Kara would make a careless comment like that and just leave it hanging. She observed her father and saw the anger mounting in him. Whenever her father held his head down and kept silent, he was unhappy. Olivia always hated to see that. She glanced at her mother and saw she was near tears. She hated how Kara's barbs affected her parents. And now, she would add to their hurt feelings by withholding the fact that she wasn't going further. This thought left her feeling sad, yet she knew she'd have to hold strong.

"You mean you have to leave now? What about graduation?" her mother asked, voice sounding hesitant as if she was confused as to whether or not she had asked the right question.

Kara turned to Olivia. "Sorry kiddo. Can't wait. I have to leave right away. I'm trying to get a flight back tonight or early tomorrow."

"Kara, can you come back after you do your story?" her father asked.

"Dad, you're on semester break. I don't have that kind of luxury." She took another long sip of wine, examined the bottle, as if she hoped more wine would find its way from a nearby vineyard, and pour itself in the bottle.

"Don't you think you've had enough wine, Kara? At the rate you're going, you'll have a very unpleasant plane ride tomorrow," her mother said.

"Well, Mom, I'll tell you what. Why don't I just finish this?" She poured what was left in the bottle into her glass and tipped it up. "Now, see? All gone. I'll just go upstairs after dinner and sleep it off and be as fresh as a daisy in the morning for the plane ride."

"Are you sure you have to go? We could use help in our bookstore here," her father said.

Kara was silent.

"Tomorrow, I'll go back to the prison and pray with a man who would rather have a man," Olivia said to cover the uneasiness that rested in the air.

"I think that's a good idea," Kara said. "Isn't that part of your new priest job, now? Praying with people? Get the facts, the nitty-gritty, dig into their personal lives to find out why they need prayer. Most convicts don't confess even until the day they die. What will you do if he's the one who's different and confesses? Scary, huh?"

Olivia had to admit that parts of that conversation bothered her. Whatever it was that bothered Kara had gotten worse over the years. Olivia wished there was a way for her to help her sister, but she was afraid anything she tried would run Kara away or Kara would fight against it.

She wasn't sure she was capable of praying with a prisoner. Praying for him would be different from praying for someone to recover from an operation, or cancer, or even praying that someone put aside hurt feelings. His transgressions were much more serious than that. Her hesitation was not whether he deserved praying over. Her hesitation was that he needed to ask for forgiveness and with the curse hanging over her, she wasn't qualified enough to ask for mercy for him. His wrong doings were of such magnitude that someone better than she should guide him. But he would have to accept her. Her church had no one else to send.

Chapter 5

The next day before she left for the prison, Olivia drove to the church to speak with Fr. Wilson about the coat drive. She found him in the outer office, his collar on and without a jacket, talking to the secretary. Fr. Wilson glanced up when Olivia walked in.

"Olivia. How is everything going?"

Even though she expected it, the question still took her by surprise and she was anxious as to how she should answer it. When someone asks "How is everything going?" it usually means that they know things aren't going well and they want you to talk about it. Then she heard Fr. Wilson ask again, "Is everything okay, Olivia?"

"Well, it could have been better." She thought leaving it ambiguous was the better thing to do.

"Don't worry. I'm sure whatever you do is right. It's tough that first day. I don't care what they've done, they always have to test you. Stick with it a day or two longer. He'll open up and things will go smoothly. At least, that's been my experience."

Time. She just had to give it more time. But more importantly, she also had to have patience.

"Thanks. That's good to hear." She paused a second, and tried to phrase her next question just right. Fr. Wilson wasn't someone who liked to be told that things needed to be done, so she started it easy. "I thought we might have a coat drive to collect new or gently used winter coats for homeless men and women. Is that a project we can start?"

"That's a great idea. We can get that in the bulletin right now," he nodded to the secretary. "And if you go downstairs to the Art and Design

Room," he did air quotes, "you'll find what you need to make a few flyers to hang around the building."

"Okay, then. I'll get started."

Fr. Wilson smiled at her and nodded as if to say, "I knew you'd do a good job." Or, at least that's how she took it. She turned to go to the art room.

Before she left the church, Olivia went to the nave to pray.

* * *

The snow from the day before had disappeared but iciness filled the air and clouds dotted the gray sky. When she reached the parking lot, she recollected the protocol from the day before and waited until she saw others heading toward the gate before she got out of her car to wait in line.

At 2:00, when two posted guards opened the gates, another guard rushed out of the building and asked everyone to step back and keep outside the gates. At the same time, the guard's walkie-talkie squawked and he walked away to answer it. The visitors, seemingly worried that they may not get a chance to see their friends or loved ones, asked in an out of tune chorus, why the guards wouldn't allow them their visit.

One woman yelled to the guard, "What's happening? My grandchild came here to see her father and she has to get back to school. How long is this going to take?"

The grandchild, who appeared to be in her early teens, put her hand on her hip, turned herself toward her grandmother and said, "What you tell them that for?"

One guard said again, "We're having a little trouble and we're requiring all visitors to remain outside the compound for now."

Someone behind Olivia tried to make a joke and said, "Maybe it's a prison uprising. They don't like the food so they want to break out and go to McDonald's."

But, no one laughed. Instead, the comment seemed to bring about an unusual and portentous silence among the visitors. In a few minutes, the other guard returned, and spoke to the two guards posted at the gate. They opened the gates and the visitors filed in, passed through the detectors, and disappeared into the visitor's room. Several guards were standing outside the visitor's room, waving the visitors in.

Olivia felt a disturbance in the air, an anxiousness that she hadn't felt the last time, and she thought about the prison break comment that the visitor had made earlier. More guards were patrolling the halls, and she passed two guards on the way to her visitor's room, just down the hallway. The prison seemed noisy, though no one spoke, and busy with movement. She had that familiar urge to escape from closed-in places. Before she had a chance to think more about her discomfort, Wesley met her and walked with her the few steps to the same visitor's room from the day before. She looked over at him walking beside her; his aura of calmness and serenity helped her relax.

When they were inside the room, Wesley turned to her. "Olivia, I want to talk to you before they bring him in. You're not having trouble getting him to open up. What he's doing is rather typical behavior. Convicts don't trust people and he, well, he just doesn't trust you right now. But if you keep at it, he'll come around." He smiled at her and waited for her to speak— an act, a way of listening, that he had to do as the captain of the guards, she supposed.

Olivia suspected that he spent a lot of time in the gym with his model-like body and, on him, his guard's uniform took the shape of an expensive Armani. He was an usher in her church and she noticed how every Sunday he wore a suit that fit him like a key fits its lock. When he had to pass the collection plate to each row, she liked the way he took charge over the plate, not letting it go too far and demanding it back when it reached the end of the row. She saw a man with conviction, a man who knew what he wanted and how to go about getting it, a proud man. But there was a feeling deep inside him, soft and tender, a heartfelt caring about him and she felt it in the way he dealt with her. He was much taller than she was, and had deeply set grey eyes that seemed to give away his feelings.

She wanted to offer an excuse—her inexperience with prisoners, her inability to be confident and that Leon led the conversation—but she thought better of it and remained quiet.

"Not trying to make excuses for him, but I'd like you to know that he's afraid to open up. In a little over a week, he'll leave this world. He wants to straighten it out with 'up there.'" He pointed to the ceiling.

Olivia gazed up at the ceiling.

"So, you shouldn't feel bad or that it's something that you're doing or not doing. It's him. We can argue the fact that he should have done what's right and shouldn't be here in the first place, but he's here."

"What are you saying, Captain Johns?"

"Wesley, remember?

"Yes, Wesley, I remember, sorry." She smiled.

"He wants you to stick with him. Give him a chance to open up a little."

"This should be my last day. Fr. Wilson said that this should take two or three days."

His face dropped a little. "Well, I'll leave it to you. Just wanted you to know. They're bringing him in now." He turned to leave the room.

As the guards brought the prisoner into the room, he was not as tall as he had seemed the day before. In fact, she even thought she was taller than he. Somehow, that seemed to bring her a bit of comfort. The guards seated and chained him, and the inmate was ready for his afternoon's dance around the real reason why he wanted prayer.

He seemed to keep his eyes on her, what she could see of his eyes, and she knew she had to appear confident, as if she had done this a million times before. She sat with her chair a little away from the table, in the event she would have to get up quickly, though she didn't know why she thought that. She placed her hands in her lap, plastered a smile on her face, and opened her mouth to speak.

"So, you came back, anyway, huh?" snorted out the inmate.

Olivia took a minute, not letting him see that he caught her off guard. "Let's start again. I'm Olivia Douglass. I'm here because you wanted someone to pray with you and I'm agreeing to do that." She had a notion to tell him that she wanted to pray with him, but maybe it would be best to save that for later.

He was quiet, and she thought that maybe he was not going to cooperate when suddenly he broke out in a loud belly chortle. The two guards at the door both turned around. One nodded to the other, probably indicating that everything was all right. To her, there was nothing funny and maybe there was nothing funny to him either. He just had to be the one in the power seat.

"Look, mister, sir. Sir, look, I came here because you asked for someone to pray with you. I want to do that. If you want to pray, then we can do that. If not, then tell me so." She waited a second then turned to get up out of the chair.

"Sir? Did you just call me sir?"

"I don't know what to call you. Why not tell me your name?" still turned sideways.

"No one has ever called me 'sir' or 'mister.' It's always been 'hey you' or some other names that the captain asked me not to use with you."

She turned around in her chair. "I don't want to offend you."

"You didn't. Olivia, huh? That's a nice name. Has that movie star appeal, or sounds like somebody important. What do you do?"

"I pray with people. That's what I do. What is your name?"

"You have a job like that? How much do they pay you?"

"Okay, let's pray now." She placed her folded hands on the wooden table and leaned forward, remembering that he was chained to the table.

"How can you do that? You don't know anything about me."

She wanted to tell him that dealing with him, she was the one who needed prayer, but she kept that to herself. She brought her hands back to her lap and gazed at her watch.

"Leon. My name is Leon."

"That's a nice name, too. Is it your last name or first?" She finally felt like she was getting somewhere with him, pulling a car out of mud inch by inch.

"Leon Sunstrik Wilkerson is my full name. And lady, I don't get to tell that to many people."

"Thank you for telling me, Leon. May I call you Leon?"

"Whooooaa. 'May I'? You one of those proper ladies, huh? Sure, call me Leon."

"Okay." She found humor in his comment, but she dared not smile. "Leon, can you tell me a little bit about yourself, what you want to pray about?"

He broke out into another loud guffaw. "Lady, where do you think you are? Why do you think I need prayer?"

One step onward, two steps back, a monopoly game.

"I don't know. Men and women die in prison, and they don't always ask someone to pray with them, but you did. Knowing why you want prayer may help me form the prayer, that's all." She had no idea if that was true, and knew he had no idea. She needed to encourage him in some way, convince him he needed to pray.

"You wouldn't be trying to find out what I've done, would you? Trying to get me to confess to something I didn't do and I know nothing about. You know the police lied on me. They made up stories about me. They said I killed someone, but I never killed no one, not one single person."

"Leon, I wasn't sent here for any of that. I came because you asked, remember?"

Captain Johns opened the door and stuck his head in at the same time a loud, piercing intermittent blast like that of a foghorn went off. The noise was so loud and intrusive that Olivia frowning, covered her ears. She saw guards run by the door.

"Ms. Douglass, visiting hours are over. The guards have to take him back now." Wesley yelled over the loud noise.

"Naw, we're just getting started, aren't we, Sugar?"

"Hey, watch it. I thought we talked about what to say to her and what not to say," Captain Johns said. "Get him out of here."

She heard the urgency in his voice and just knew something was wrong.

"Come back tomorrow. Please," Leon said. "Come back tomorrow."

"I can come back one more time." As she stood to go, she had a strong desire to get out of there immediately. The blasting of the horn and the exigency she heard in Wesley John's voice created an anxiousness in the air and in her; and she knew that there was a reason they had to leave and that there was trouble with the inmates.

"I'll see you tomorrow," said Leon. "Okay, then, okay." He smiled an uncanny smile at Olivia.

Olivia left the room. Even though she needed to leave, she stopped for a moment. Through the window, she watched the guards unshackle Leon to take him back to his cell. He used the word "please" when he asked her to return. She was beginning to break through. Maybe tomorrow they would pray. She thought about her conversation with Wesley. He was right, Leon was afraid.

He reminded her of the time in England when she watched her father and his friend try to help a wild horse that got his leg caught between two boulders while fighting another horse. The three of them were out riding. They decided to cut across a meadow and came across a pack of wild horses, where two of the horses were in a terrible fight. One stallion had backed up into the boulders and had gotten his right rear leg caught between them. The screaming was excruciating as he tried to extricate his leg and at the same time, fight back. Olivia couldn't watch the beating that the horse was taking, unable to defend himself.

Her heart went out to this most magnificent beast, the most beautiful shade of ecru she'd ever seen. Without presence of mind, she urged her horse toward the pack yelling and screaming hoping to frighten the other wild horses away. But, all they did was turn around and stare at her. Her father and his friend galloped on horseback to the pack also yelling and screaming. They flung their arms and her father waved his hat, and the pack of wild horses took off running.

Her father got down off his steed to try to help the stallion. Olivia ran over to help free him. She saw the deep wide-open gash that exposed the veins, cartilage, muscle and whatever else was inside a horse's leg. The stallion continued screaming and jerking around, making the wound worse and Olivia knew that in order to free the horse, she had to calm him down. In as soothing a voice as she was able to muster, she spoke to the horse then sang a hymn to him so that her father could take his leg out. Her father and his friend were able to move back one of the rocks. Once the horse was free, they needed to take him home to fix his leg, Olivia begged. Her father tried to put a rope on him, but when she saw the fear and horror in the stallion's eyes, she asked her father to let him go. He would cause more damage to himself as they tried to get him home. Many days after that incident, Olivia rode out in that direction searching for the stallion, hoping that he was still alive and maybe even healed.

Wesley rushed her to the front and out the prison where the other visitors were racing to their cars. She could still hear the earsplitting siren of the horn and like the others, wanted to get out of the environs before anything serious happened.

* * *

On the drive home, she thought about Leon and how he knew he needed prayer, how he wanted someone to pray with him. Maybe prison life had restored his faith, and he understood the power of prayer. She couldn't remember exactly when she began praying by herself. It just seemed to happen when she was ten and she was upset about her classmates calling her dumb. After she told her mother, they sat together on the couch, both in tears. Her mother wrapped her strong arms, around her so tightly that she felt the warmth and love exuding from her mother's body and surrounding her, like a cocoon. She buried her face in her mother's long hair and the scent of apricot permeated her nose. Olivia closed her eyes and repeatedly wished that the moment would never end. After a while, she asked God to make that moment and moments where her mother held her and comforted her, happen again, and again.

CHAPTER 6

Olivia unlocked the door to her new townhouse, the one she'd lived in since she left the seminary, and headed down the main hallway to the kitchen. The blinking red light on her cordless phone caught her attention before she reached the kitchen. The first message was from Claude reminding her, as he did about everything, of the dinner party that he was having for Margaret, his new partner in his dentistry office, and her husband, Casey. She winced and groaned when she heard the message and drew it out longer when she took a glimpse at the clock and saw that she had thirty minutes to get to his house. She had hoped for a few minutes to herself to relax, and pray. She was tired, and just wanted to order take out and eat at home. But telling him that was out of the question. She hadn't told him about her assignment from Fr. Wilson and doubted that she would. He would try to talk her out of it and then it would turn into something with a different purpose— she'd want to continue because he would want her not to. The second message was from Fr. Wilson saying that he had six people who wanted intercessory prayer training, and had scheduled her to do the training.

She gave herself a "high five" and a "well, okay" head tilt to Fr. Wilson's message, pleased that he had chosen her. She was anxious to do the training and she was good at it, even if she did have to give herself the credit. She called Fr. Wilson back and left a message thanking him for asking her help with the prayer group, and asking how they would go about selecting the books and tapes for the training. She also told him that she had placed four flyers advertising the coat drive throughout the building. Then she danced her way up the stairs to change. Five minutes later, she was downstairs feeling like a new person and ready to go.

Soon, she stood at Claude's door. When he opened the door and saw her standing there, appearing as what she hoped was fresh and newly revived, he let out a smile so enormous that his entire body beamed, like a spotlight. Sometimes she thought he loved her, like at this moment, and other times, she questioned his feelings. She wished she had a way to capture this smile, keep it with her, to remind her of how he felt or could feel about her. When he smiled at her the way he did at this moment, he almost made her feel valued.

She stepped into the living room where two people were already seated on his new mocha color microfiber couch, a bottle of red wine on the glass top coffee table in front of them and wine in their glasses. Claude looked at his watch as he began to introduce Olivia. Tardiness was an annoyance to him. When she glanced at her watch, she saw she was a little late. The loving smile had now disappeared and a flash of anger crossed his face. She tried to ignore that. She learned that sometimes when she ignored him, he wouldn't yell at her and storm out of the room, or make remarks that made her feel little. Often, she controlled him, but sometimes she was frightened of the other side of him, when he would just let go of his self-control, and anger poured out of him.

"Hi. I'm Casey Moore." The man stood, pointed to the woman, "and this is my wife Margaret." He extended his hand.

"Nice to meet you both," Olivia said. She extended her hand.

Claude handed her a glass of red wine and pointed her toward one of the large matching armchairs across from the couch. He sat in the other chair opposite her and took a sip from the wine he'd poured for himself.

"Are you getting settled in your condo okay?" Claude asked his guests.

"Trying to get used to things, our new jobs and the condo," Margaret said. "This town is quite different from the small town and the large home we had."

"Where are you from?" Olivia asked.

"We just moved here from Colorado. Casey has a new job in the Department of Transportation, Federal Government. He was unemployed for a while then he landed this job in the Federal Building downtown, so here we are." She raised both hands, a magician making a rabbit appear.

"You'll love the area. Most people do," Olivia said. "Isn't that right,

Claude?"

"Yes." He took a sip of wine.

"We hope so. We're starting over, after fifteen years of marriage, we're starting over," Margaret said. She watched Casey as she said it. She tried hard to blink away the tears that were forming.

"We've been having a hard time, since I was laid off. Of course, Margaret was working as a dentist, but in the small town where we lived her job wasn't paying the bills." Casey paused for a moment and there was a hint of sadness in his voice. "But we're here now and we want to put things back together again." He smiled at Margaret and took her hand as if to assure her. She returned his smile.

Olivia saw that they hadn't worked out their problems and were hoping that a move would make everything work out for them. She had a desire to give them words of encouragement, words that expressed hope for their effort. Claude's lack of trust in her vocation, weighed on her and she had trouble praying for them. Besides, even if she thought of a prayer or Bible verse appropriate to offer them, Claude would just use his favorite degradation for her saying, she was "being a priest." She shouldn't let that bother her; she was being a priest. But he had a way of saying it that made "being a priest" seem despicable, something vile.

"This is a good place," Claude said. He turned toward Olivia, but quickly turned away.

"Claude, what made you decide to take on a partner in your dental practice?" Casey asked.

"I've been in solo practice since Al, my old partner, died eight years ago and left everything to me. He was older and well established, had no family. I never bothered about another partner; he had just enough of a patient list. Almost all of the patients wanted to continue on, even encouraged their friends, and family members to come and see me. I never thought about adding another dentist until I met Margaret at a weekend dental conference. We got to talking and she asked if I'd be willing to take her on. You gotta know that this is new and different for me. Eight years is a long time. I've been able to spread out, take up the entire office. And, my patients know me and how I operate. They don't like a lot of change. I want you to join me, but you have to know that the practice will have to stay the same."

"Thank you. I'll remember that."

Olivia couldn't remember the conference or Claude telling her about the dental conference or this woman. He must have told her, otherwise they wouldn't be here sitting in his living room now. Somewhere along the way, she'd stopped listening to him.

The hunger pangs in Olivia's stomach ready to begin a symphony called her attention to the fact that she wasn't taking in any of the aromas that signaled food was in the oven. Claude knew when you invited someone to your home at the dinner hour you actually served dinner. She stealthily grabbed hold of her stomach to soften the array of sounds that would soon burst forth. She turned toward the kitchen. He, no doubt, had everything covered in foil as he usually did.

"I know how you wo . . .," he glimpsed at Olivia, then cut his eyes down, "how you would like to make some changes, change things around to suit you. You need to know my patients will get upset if you tried to do that without my knowledge." He gave Olivia a smile, a proud peacock.

"How will that work out? Will you have to get your own patients?" Olivia asked, trying to divert her attention away from the food and Claude's last comment.

"Well, no; not at first. She'd handle the emergencies, and do cleanings, and when I'm not there, things like that, and eventually she'd get her own patients." Claude made a face at her as if to ask why she would ask such a question. He slid to the edge of his seat. "Can you get those appetizers in the kitchen for me?"

Olivia got up and went to the kitchen. There was a crystal plate covered with foil. She pulled the foil back and exposed the three-section platter of shrimp salad, stuffed mushrooms with artichoke, and spinach dip. She'd never known him to put things together this well. Maybe there was hope for him after all. Next to the platter was a dish filled with an assortment of crackers. Olivia took a sneak peek in the oven and saw several covered dishes. This was his way of keeping the dinner warm. She turned her head in the direction of the living room not believing that Claude had done this. Maybe things were picking up with him. She grabbed up both platters, brought them to the living room, and placed them on the coffee table.

"What do you do?" Margaret asked when Olivia sat down.

"She's a priest," Claude said. "Or she'll be one soon. She graduates in a little over a week."

She should have told him she had changed her mind, but since he believed she wasn't cut out for the priesthood, anyway, what was the point? Telling him would just feed his ego. She hated that this lie or this change in her life she was keeping silent about was now getting out of her control. She had hoped to keep this to herself for a while longer, until the graduation and break it to everyone at that time. She just couldn't correct it now. Her father had kept quiet about it and if she told anyone else, her mother would be next. So, she refused to correct Claude.

"Oh, really?" Casey asked. "My grandfather was a Methodist pastor. What denomination?"

"We're Episcopalian. She's learned that she has a long way to go to be a priest. Don't you, Livvy?" He turned to her and smiled as if she agreed with his assessment.

Olivia wrinkled her face, gave him a "why would I agree with you" look.

Casey and Margaret didn't seem to know how to respond. They both gave off a nervous laugh and a helpless appearance. Casey helped himself to a double portion of the appetizers.

Though Olivia was disappointed in Claude, she was not surprised.

"I understand that it's a long tough road into the priesthood," Casey said.

"Well, that it is. Are you two very religious people?" Claude looked from Casey to Margaret as he asked the question.

Olivia wondered why he would even ask. He was not very religious himself.

Casey turned to Margaret before he spoke. "Well, I don't guess you'd call us religious, but we do try to attend church somewhat regularly."

"I can't remember why we don't go more often," Margaret said.

"Religion, it's a mystery, an enigma that I can't feel or touch. I like dentistry because I can see the problem, feel the tooth, almost feel when someone is in pain. But religion—it's just a mystery I can't define," Claude said.

"I like dentistry for that same reason. I started out wanting to be a surgeon, but there are too many guesses about that. I wanted a surer thing,"

Margaret said.

"Exactly. We seem to think alike about this," Claude said.

"I guess you're pretty excited about Olivia going into the priesthood." Casey asked.

"That's a vocation that she wants to do, don't you?" He smiled at her. "Frankly, she could do other things with her life. She's a beautiful woman, smart, clever, independent. A little too independent, but a good man, like myself, can keep that under control. She has other choices like a nurse, or a food critic, mother, oh, she'd make a good mother, and even a nutritionist." He cast his eyes toward Olivia. "We may not have to worry about her becoming a priest, anyway. She has a habit of starting things and not completing them, don't you, Livvy?" He laughed as if he thought everyone present would see that was funny.

And there it was. Everything that she believed was still true about him, those things that he refused to admit to himself or to her, openly confessed. She realized how these few simple remarks, that he so casually, but proudly released, gave her permission to recognize her true feelings for him. He had promised her that he wouldn't be like his father who abused and abased women. Claude told Olivia that he hated the way his father treated his mother and that he detested the expression on his mother's face after his father tore his mother apart. Claude even further confided in her that he thought his father sexually abused his mother, but his mother never let on. He even told her how he not only hated his father, but he hated his mother for not standing up to him and every time she cowered to him, he lost more respect for her.

Three months ago, just before he had asked her to marry him, Claude had asked Olivia to help him be a better man. At first, he had slipped up too many times. The task seemed too daunting and Olivia believed he'd never change. His yelling, storming off out of anger, calling her names, and putting her down far outweighed the minimal love and attention he showed her. Then, he made a change. He seemed to try harder to keep his notions about women under control and until now, he had been careful about what he said, and she thought he had begun to see women differently. On one occasion, he had asked her advice about a female patient who seemed uncomfortable when he let the chair back. Claude told Olivia that the female patient also had nosebleeds. Then there was the time when a female patient was sensitive about her partial that she was having made. Claude asked Olivia's advice about what to say to her and patiently listened while she gave it. She was so happy that their relationship was changing and she thought he cared and that his love for her made him want to be a better man. She thought that he had begun to see her as his equal.

She tried to recall what it was that drew her to Claude. She was just dating, nothing serious, no special person. It was just after Christmas break during her first year in the seminary and after a short visit to England to see her parents, she'd returned to the states a few days early. A girl friend, Ann, asked her to go to a dinner party with her that her brother and his wife were having. Ann's brother and his wife had invited a man for Ann to meet. Ann was a little anxious about going alone. Maybe she'd end up stuck with someone who possibly wouldn't interest her; so, she asked Olivia to come along. Ann had cleared it with her brother and sister-in-law.

It was obvious that Claude was more attracted to Olivia than Ann and Ann saw that. Later, Claude called Olivia, and they began seeing each other. Olivia was worried that she was turning twenty-five and Claude was her only prospect. Ann confessed to Olivia that she was happy that she and Claude had started seeing each other.

Ann found someone else and later she invited Olivia to her wedding. During the wedding, Olivia thought how nice Ann's husband was, kind and thoughtful. She had wished Claude was more kind and thoughtful like Ann's new husband. When Claude had asked Olivia to marry him, Olivia hadn't given it much thought, she just said yes. In the back of her mind, she had wished that Claude was a better person.

During her later teen years, when she began dating, she had read a book about relationships. The author said that children change into teens and teens change into adults. But adults don't change unless they want to and even then, they have to work at it. Olivia saw now, that no matter how hard Claude tried, he would be the same unchanged Claude. She had stayed with him because she thought he would. She hadn't liked the man she saw inside him and she hadn't liked herself when she was in his presence. Before, she had given him a pass, ignored everything he had said and done, and all the while hoping he would become that better person. But lately, she'd had trouble accepting Claude's yelling at her, or the way he made her feel small and empty, and like everything she did and said was wrong.

CHAPTER 7

Olivia wasn't able to sleep at all. The conversation from her fiancé the night before took up permanent residence in her mind, refreshing itself throughout the night grating on her, irritating her, the way a swarm of flies hovered over food at a picnic. For reasons not quite understandable to her, she suspected that Leon had something to do with why she couldn't shake Claude's comments about her. She questioned whether one day Claude would hate her or any woman so much that he would turn into a Leon and take a life.

She rose up out of bed when she heard the paper thump up against her front door, put on her robe, and went to retrieve it. When she opened the door, she found Kara huddled under the mailbox, her suitcase next to her.

"What on earth are you doing out here?"

Kara squinted up at her. "Bout time you came to your door. What does a person have to do to get in?" slurring over each word.

"Did you ring the bell?"

"I don't know. Is there a bell?"

Olivia helped Kara stand. She put Kara's arm around her shoulders and took her inside. When Kara was safely seated on the couch, Olivia went back to get Kara's suitcase and the paper.

"Did you miss your plane?" Olivia asked while closing the door.

"Plane? What plane?"

"Your plane back to England. Your job, remember? The one you have to rush back to?"

"Oh, yeah. That job," she giggled.

"Kara, what's wrong? I thought it was very important that you go back."

"You diiid? Well, sit down and I'll tell you aaaalllllllll about it. You do want to hear all about it, don't you?" She laughed.

"Yes, why wouldn't I? I'll make us coffee." She walked to the kitchen to put on a pot of coffee, but from the liquor on her breath, Kara needed to sleep it off. When she returned, Kara was standing, trying to find her way to the kitchen. Olivia helped her back to the couch.

"Hah! Wha waz I saying? Oh yeah, never mind, oh yeah. B'cause you always want to hide the truth, that's why?" She fell back on the couch.

"Hide the truth? What truth are you talking about?"

"Okay, you asked for it. Here goes. You ready?" She clapped her hands and laughed. "The truth is I lost my job." She gave off a loud vigorous laugh.

Olivia couldn't understand the reason for her laughter. "Is this a joke? I thought you said the truth?"

"See, there you go."

"Kara—"

"Okay. Okay. I'm serious now. I lost my job. I started working part-time, but lost that job about a month ago. And, I had no money to pay the rent on my apartment. And I bet you can guess what happened." She sang out as she laughed and pointed to Olivia. "You got it. I lost it. My husband or ex-husband wants a divorce, and I used all the money I had for an attorney. We don't have much, but he wants it all." She gave a sly look to Olivia. "But don't you worry, my angel sister. I'll have another job soon and I'll be back on top."

"A month? What have you been doing all this time?"

"You know. Staying with friends."

"What friends, Kara?"

"Oh, now you don't think I have any friends?"

"Kara, I don't mean—"

"Oh, yes you do. You think I don't have what it takes, don't you? You wonder how I got to be a journalist in the first place, don't you?"

"Kara, I never—"

"Oh, don't give me that high and mighty act. I know you, mom, and dad have been placating me for years. You're the special one, you're the good little girl, and you're the one that everybody loves."

"Kara, how can you say that? All these years I felt mom and dad pushing you, favoring you. You ended up a journalist, while I ended . . . .."

The drunken appearance and wrinkled smelly clothing were evidence that Kara had been and maybe still was homeless. In fact, if Kara hadn't been so drunk, she, no doubt, would have cried. Olivia wanted to cry. This was the sister she'd grown up with, and whose playfulness, and adventuresome spirit endeared her to everyone. She had done so well, on top, one of the best journalists in the country in just a few years. She took many tough assignments and went into areas so dangerous that even her editor feared for her life, her mother used to say. As she examined her sister now, Olivia couldn't believe that what she just heard her sister say about how their parents treated them was enough to bring about what she saw before her now. There were other reasons, other matters much bigger than these worrying Kara.

"You'll have to stay here, then. You know you always have a home with me. Why don't you get some rest?"

Upstairs in the guest bedroom, Olivia watched her sister unpack. Kara pulled out a pair of pajamas, and in a few minutes, slumped down on the bed under the blanket. Olivia stepped out the room and closed the door behind her.

* * *

Olivia thought she knew when Kara separated herself from her. She couldn't admit to herself that it happened, but in her heart, she knew. It was in the spring of her sixth-grade year, and the leaves began to appear on the trees, the flowers in her garden began to bloom, and the earth seemed to change its colors from gray and black to the hues of green, yellow and blue— welcoming sights after the long hard winter they'd had that year. Olivia was happier than she ever remembered. She had learned to read, caught up with her classmates, and knew how to solve all sorts of math equations and science problems. At the end of that year, she had looked back over all her school years and was proud over the progress she had made. She felt good about herself, so good in fact that when she cast her eyes down at the floor, she was sure that she was standing on a cloud.

When her sixth-grade science teacher told her class that they would have an important science test, Olivia went home to study. She became a master of studying. At her desk in her room, she laid out her class notes and made herself a study schedule. Over the week she read over her notes, reviewed every experiment they did in class, and reviewed each chapter and the charts the teacher handed out. She even went over everything a second time and third time. Then she declared herself ready for the test.

Waiting to get her test paper returned was pure torture. She had fixed in her mind that all her answers were wrong and that she had failed the test. On the day her paper was returned to her, she felt like she had been given a crown of brilliance, whatever that was. Anyone seeing her would have sworn that she was of intellectual royalty the way she held her head up. The "A" that she had received and every question answered correctly, sent her into another world. She wasn't the dumb girl that Jean and Robert, the two top students in the class, said she was. They could no longer make fun of her. In fact, she was so proud of herself that she wanted to do some kind of Mensa royal dance right there in the classroom, but couldn't. She just didn't know one. As soon as the bell rang, she darted out the door to go show her paper to Kara.

Olivia raced to the eighth-grade hallway and waited for Kara. As the eighth graders came to their lockers, Olivia realized that she had blocked Clayton Harrison's locker and with the other students crowding the locker area, it was difficult for her to move or make her way out of the crowd. She was so excited she didn't think about what it would be like on the eighth-grade hall.

"I gotta get to my locker," Clayton said to her, in her face.

"Sorry," Olivia said, crunching her face back at him.

She tried to move away, but a group of students had assembled in a circle on the corner where she stood and even though she asked them to let her out, they ignored her. She asked them to let her out a second time, but the locker area was so noisy, and Olivia figured it was impossible for them to hear her over the noise. Then, Clayton yelled at her to get away from his locker.

"You retard, what're you doing in the eighth-grade hallway anyway? You lose your way or something?"

At this point, silence fell over the hallway and everyone turned around to see why Clayton was so angry.

"Maybe they should give you retards a map or give you guides. Or better still, put you people somewhere else."

The students laughed at her and she heard some of them call her "retard" also. When she saw the students staring at her, she had wished the floor would open up and she just slip through. Concentrating on getting out of there, she made herself walk away. She cast her eyes beyond the students to see how to get out of the crowd, and down at the end of the hallway, saw Kara walking away in the opposite direction. Olivia just knew Kara saw and heard everything and decided to save herself embarrassment by going the other way. The proof was that after that incident, Kara seemed to have lost interest in doing things with her.

Now, Kara needed Olivia. Olivia had to help Kara. Kara was the only sister she knew. Olivia was almost afraid to leave the house with Kara in it. Only drunks and alcoholics have the smell of liquor on them that early in the morning. She took all her money with her, the little that she had. She had very few things of value in the townhouse, nothing that couldn't be replaced if Kara decided to pawn anything.

* * *

When she arrived at the bookstore, her mother was busy dusting off the books and shelves. Olivia noticed that many of the shelves were full and empty boxes were stacked near the door. Since she'd decided that she wasn't going into the priesthood, she should let her parents know that she would be able to manage the bookstore for them when they went back to England.

"Hello, sweetheart," her mother said.

"You're starting early. I thought I'd beat you two here, and have everything ready before either of you got here," disappointment in her voice.

"No such luck. Your father insisted that we get up early and finish putting the books up. He just left to go get us more coffee. I can call him if you'd like." She leaned over and kissed Olivia on the cheek.

"No mom, that's okay. I'll get something a little later." She stared at her mother, not sure whether to jump right in or hold back. "You could have told me about Kara." She sounded accusing, but she didn't intend to accuse her mother or jump right in.

"Kara? Where is she? I got up this morning and she was gone."

"She's staying with me."

"Well, that's a relief." Her mother went back to dusting and rearranging

60

the books on the shelves. "There's nothing to talk about."

"Mom, Kara is out of a job and she drinks too much."

"I'm sure that's just a little setback. She'll get back on her feet soon."

"You can't believe that."

"I do. I've tried to help her, but you know how she is. It's hard to help someone with a smart mouth like she has."

"Mom, you can't ignore this. She's in trouble and I don't know how to help her. I don't know what she wants, but you do."

"I'm not ignoring anything. We told her we needed her help here in the store."

"Maybe she feels you're ignoring her. I can't help but I believe that her smart mouth means that she's asking for help. You don't think she's pleading for your help?"

"But she says ugly things about me. You've heard her. It gets worse every time I see her. I just can't stand it; and she just doesn't listen to your father. She doesn't listen to anyone." Tears formed in her eyes.

"She's saying what's on her mind, what she feels," Olivia said, nodding to her mother.

"You two are different. She says it and you hold everything in."

"Yes, we are different in that way."

"What are you holding in?" her mother asked.

"Not me, Mom, we talking about Kara. Maybe we are ignoring her hoping she'll change. She's not going to change, unless we help her. I want to help her, but I need you and Dad. Do you know anyone? Maybe you and dad can make some calls and find her another job as a journalist. Isn't there someone, some good-hearted parishioner who has contacts? Some journalist contacts?"

"We are helping her. She lost her job and we want her to work here in the store. Manage it after we leave to go back to England."

"But she wants to be a journalist. She's hoping for a job as a journalist," Olivia said.

"She may not be a journalist again."

"Why not?"

"Because she went out on dangerous missions," her mother said.

"Yes, I know that."

"Livvy, she wanted to do that."

"What are you saying? I thought she took those chances to become the best?"

Her mother studied her face a moment as if she was weighing the purpose of telling Olivia a secret. "Livvy, those chances were unnecessary. Kara wanted those assignments and took those risks on her own. Her boss asked her not to. After her boss called, your father dropped everything, got on the first available flight, and brought our daughter back home."

"So, you think . . ., what are you saying?"

Her mother kept quiet.

"Mom, wait, no. You think she's trying to hurt herself? Take her own life? Mom, Kara's not like that," she said vigorously shaking her head.

"I used to believe that. On her last job, her editor told her not to go. He fired her, took away her authority and tried to take away her insurance. I don't know if the camera people she found knew she no longer worked for that paper. I don't know how they got paid. She was out of control and had been for a while."

"Okay, so we'll get her help. A counselor. I can call Fr. Wilson, he'll know someone. Let's get her an appointment."

"We've tried that. Your father and I set up an appointment with someone in England. She met us there. Just before the therapist called us all into his office, Kara got up to go to the ladies' room. We waited and waited, but she never came back. We've tried talking to her. Your father and I want to know what's wrong. She won't let anyone help her."

"If you ask me, she believes the idea of me becoming a priest is distasteful."

"She does seem to have something against you being a priest. That's why we thought you were better able to help her."

"She and Claude. Maybe they're right I . . ."

"It is Claude, isn't it? He doesn't want you to be a priest, does he?"

"No, he doesn't." She said, softly. "Mom, I—"

"I'm a good mother. I know I am. Kara's a good daughter. She's an excellent journalist and maybe one day she'll be back on top." She took Olivia's hands, held them tight. "But you," she began.

"Mom, what's the matter?" She directed her mother to a wooden chair and found a second chair for herself.

"Tell me, Mom, please. Whatever it is, tell me."

"It's just none of your concern. I'll be okay."

"Mom, something is bothering you. Can you tell me?"

"It's nothing, and it certainly doesn't apply here."

"It must, or you wouldn't be worrying about it now."

"Livvy, no, I—"

"Mom, just let it out. I'll bet it's been worrying you for a long time."

Her mother appeared surprised, but gave in. "After your father and I were married for almost a year, your father came to me and said he wanted to be an Episcopal priest. I was afraid I would let him down. I just wasn't cut out to be a priest's wife. I wasn't as religious as he was at the time, and I just wasn't sure I could do it. After talking about it for several weeks, I told him. I've been sorry about that decision since then. I just don't want the same thing to happen to you."

"You've never mentioned that before."

"I know. I'm not particularly proud of what I asked of him. He lost some part of himself that day, some of the happiness disappeared. He gained it back first with Kara and, after you became our daughter. When you left to come back here to the states, that sadness returned and Kara got worse. I know we've done everything to help Kara. But I just can't stand it if I'm the cause of everyone's unhappiness."

Olivia reached over and gave her mother a long, tight hug. "You're not the cause of anyone's unhappiness. We all have choices. We can make decisions for ourselves."

"You're such a good girl, Livvy, such a good girl." Then she pulled away from Olivia.

"Do you believe that?"

"Yes. I do believe that you're not the cause of anyone's unhappiness. And I'll try to help Kara."

Just then, the front door scraped open and her father appeared carrying a paper tray with two paper cups of coffee and two pastries. Her mother got up and headed toward the bathroom.

"Livvy? Should I go get another coffee? I can go back for another coffee. Here, take mine. I don't need it anyway." He held out his coffee to her.

Olivia walked toward her father, kissed him on the cheek. He gave her a big smile.

"I can say all that again, if you like." He chuckled and placed his coffee and the coffee tray on the counter.

"I'm not staying. I came to help get these books on the shelves, but I see you and mom have most of them up, already."

"There's always work to do. We've ordered a big coffee machine, new racks, and furniture. You'll have an opportunity to help," he said.

"I'm on my way back to the prison."

"Oh, you decided to continue? Good for you. Did you ever find out his full name?"

"Yes Dad. I did. Leon Sunstrik Wilkerson."

He stared at her before he spoke. "I see."

They held there for a minute. Olivia thought he had more to say, maybe another question to ask, but he stared at her, lips pressed together.

"Hope you have a good session this time, Sweetheart." He kissed her on the forehead.

On her way out, a book on top of a box caught Olivia's eye. It was a book of essays and articles by Kara Douglass. Olivia picked it up off the box.

"Is this Kara's book?"

"Yes," her mother said, walking back from the bathroom, a tissue in her hand. Kara wrote the book when she was starting up her career. It sold pretty well, too."

"I forgot that Kara wrote this book. Why isn't this up front or out where everyone can see it?" Olivia looked from her mother to her father.

"Ask your mother about that," her father said. "I don't remember why it isn't out?"

"Vinny, what are you saying?" her mother asked.

"I'm just saying that you made the decision and I agreed. That's all."

"But we agreed."

"I know. That's what I said."

"Vinny, a long time ago we made these decisions—"

"Elizabeth, all I'm saying is that she should ask you. Now why don't you tell her?"

"What's going on?" Olivia asked.

"Nothing Livvy. It's just that when you girls were young, your father, and I decided, you know . . . when you became ours." Her mother turned to her father for help. Her father nodded his head encouraging her on. "You were so . . .. you just needed to learn so much to catch up."

She loved it when her mother said things like "when you became ours" instead of "when we adopted you." It gave her such a warm feeling and made her feel loved. She couldn't let that distract her now. "What do you mean?"

"We had to do so much, tutors and everything to help you get caught up. You and Kara were becoming such good sisters that we thought you would recognize, what I mean to say is, we thought you would start to turn away from each other."

"Mom, could it be that the attention you gave me made Kara feel left out? Or maybe she felt like she had to hold back because of me?"

"Olivia, how can you say that? You needed so much, much more than what she needed. We don't think that she felt left out."

"Before me, Kara got all the attention and she did so well in school. But then you adopted me and things must have changed for her; she received less attention."

"Kara understood that your needs were greater. I know she did."

Olivia was mixed up about what to think or say and frustration began to build inside her. Olivia faulted herself for not understanding that her position in her family upset Kara's place. To keep from saying or doing anything she would later regret, she turned to leave, grabbed the book off the box, and let the door slam behind her.

She remembered Kara as being strong. Kara would hardly let the fact that she required more bother her in any way. Kara had always been her own person, done her best job for everything she did. Olivia gained from her strength and learned to be strong through her sister.

In the car on her way to the prison, she put all that behind her and got herself ready for another round, this time with Leon.

CHAPTER 8

As soon as Olivia passed through the detectors, she saw Wesley standing in the hallway tall and confident-looking. He was talking to another guard who nodded back several times in response. Olivia was disappointed that Wesley was tied up with the guard. Just as she began to think that she would have to walk to the visitor's room alone, the guard hurried off and Wesley turned to her.

"Hello," he said.

"Hello, Wesley, I hope you're not busy."

"I have time to walk you to the visitor's room."

They walked the few steps to the same room, the room Wesley must have reserved for her visits. From the opposite direction, the same two guards brought Leon through the door and chained him to the table. Wesley pulled out a chair for Olivia before he left.

"Well, well, well, so you came back, huh? I'll bet you just couldn't wait to see me."

"I came back because you asked me to." She paused expecting him to respond. Then she asked, "Are you ready to pray now?"

"Do you," he cleared his throat, "have family, Olivia Douglass?"

"More questions? Leon. I see you don't want to pray. Maybe you don't believe in prayer." She thought this would challenge him enough and he'd want to pray, and by this time she was out of things to say to convince him to pray.

"I bet you have an older brother who told you all about life, huh?"

"No, What about you? Did you have a brother?"

"No brother?" He asked.

She waited to respond. She had a desire to let him talk. His future was short and she saw he wanted to talk about his family, if he ever had one.

"No brother, Leon. Did you and your children do many things together? When I was little, my father used to take my sister and me outside at night and we would stare up at the stars."

"That was nice. You had a good father?"

"Yes, I do."

"Me and my kids, we had a garden."

"Oh, that's nice. You grew vegetables?"

"Yes." He stared down at the table.

"Are you a mother, Olivia?" He asked, looking up at her.

"I'm not a mother. I hope to be one someday," Olivia said.

"I know you have a mother and a father. Tell me about your mother. Is she still living?" Leon asked.

She'd learned in her psychology class in undergraduate school, that often when clients wanted to disclose information about themselves, they would ask a question about the therapist, wanting them to give up some of their personal life before giving up information about themselves. It was a sign of trust. However, the question about her mother gave her pause and she couldn't understand why it bothered her. "She's an optimist. Everything is good to her and she loves books. She and my father own two bookstores."

"Everything is good to her. That means that she's had a few downs in her life?"

"She lost her sister to cancer almost two years ago."

Leon's face dropped, as if he was disappointed in the way her mother had lost her sister.

"What's the matter?" Olivia asked.

"Nothing. Your mother likes books, what else does she like?"

These questions made Olivia uncomfortable, and for a moment, she saw Leon breaking into her house to take her mother's life. Then she remembered that he was in a maximum-security prison and would be removed from this earth soon. This man wouldn't be able to harm her so she answered.

"Every week, she helps the secretary at her church by answering the phone, sending out notices, arranging meetings, and things like that."

Leon stared at her. Maybe she had taken him by surprise.

"You should be a mother."

"Maybe one day—"

"I mean you'll be a good one."

"What about your family? Tell me about you," she said, sticking her neck out.

"You know. You remind me of somebody."

"Who?"

"I don't know. I'll chew on it a while and let you know."

She thought she saw a smile appear on his pudgy face, but she couldn't tell.

"Tell me about your mother," Olivia said.

"You want to know about my mother?"

"Sure."

"I don't think you're ready for what I have to tell."

"You don't have to. It's up to you. It would be okay if you want to tell me something about your mother; but only if you would like."

He paused for a moment and she saw the anger twisting and fuming inside him and contorting his face. She was ready to let him know that he could remain quiet for as long as he needed to, when he spoke.

"My mother was nothing but a whore. She made me do things. I don't want to talk about it. I would never do anything to any of my kids that she had me do. Never. Do you hear me? Never. Never, never, never." Leon leaned toward her as much as possible for him, face red, nostrils flaring shouting louder and louder with each "never."

The guards entered the room. One guard used his walkie-talkie and summoned Wesley. Within seconds, Wesley rushed into the room.

"I told you to speak to her nicely. No shouting."

Leon rolled his eyes and sat back in his chair.

"Take him back to his cell," Wesley said.

The two guards undid the chains to take him back to his cell.

Olivia hated to hear him speak like that where he allowed his anger to get the best of him. She was familiar with his ways. He did that on purpose. Wesley had told her that these prisoners don't like to give away information about themselves. Maybe Leon thought she would find out too much about him.

Leon glanced at her with what seemed like tenderness, a gentleness even, as if he wanted to tell her how sorry he was that he let himself get out of control. But she figured she had misunderstood his appearance. Leon would not accept responsibility.

"Come back tomorrow."

"Tomorrow . . .." She began. She was dumbfounded as to why he would want her to return.

"Please. Please. Come back tomorrow. I won't get upset."

When Leon turned toward the guard, Olivia noticed a scar or maybe a birthmark on his right cheek, along his jawbone. A scar, a birthmark. It was in the shape of the country, Italy. It was rather small and she hadn't noticed it at first. Yet there was a familiarity about it. She passed it off understanding that she recognized Italy, and that it was just a strange looking scar. He must have been in a fight and the scar was his trophy.

She stood up and watched the guards take Leon away. As much as he was able to, Leon turned around twice as he walked away and then stopped to study her. At that moment, she saw a tiny movement that she'd seen a moment ago in this strange and hardened man. He almost seemed soft, warm and he dropped his head slightly as if a word or statement she made or he made had embarrassed him. He bent down as far as he was able, swiped his cheek with his shoulder, turned, and walked out. For a quick second, the image of the little girl cowering in the corner, hands over her eyes, flashed through her mind again. She needed to find a way to ask him about the little girl. It was not her job to dig out information about why he was in prison, but she worried that a little girl may still be held captive somewhere and hoped to be rescued.

Olivia and Wesley walked in silence. When they reached the entrance, he stopped and turned to her. She felt his hand brush against hers and it made her smile.

"I joined your prayer group."

"Wesley. I'm so happy to hear that. You'll make a good prayer person. I'm just curious, how did you hear about it? Fr. Wilson just asked me."

"It was in the notice that we got. I called and signed up. Fr. Wilson said that there were five others in the group and he expected several more to sign up."

She wanted to chuckle, but tried to hold it in. Fr. Wilson had organized the prayer group, sent out a notice, and selected her to do the training all before he'd asked her. He knew her too well.

"Wesley, it's nice to hear that you're interested in a prayer group."

"I've been giving thought to taking the training. I've always been interested in intercessory prayer, but never had the time until now."

She was surprised when she saw his uneasiness. He shifted from one leg to the other.

"The training will require many sessions, some of them could get long, but I'll try to keep them short as much as possible."

"Not too short, I hope. I'll need long sessions."

"Then, after the training, the second part is praying. People will want you to pray with them and lay hands on them and that will require much of your time."

"I'm willing to give of my time."

He said it with such tenderness that it made her feel all mushy inside and her heart beat in a strange and thunderous rhythm. She wanted to touch his face and struggled to keep her hands by her side. He turned away.

"I would like us to get started soon," Olivia managed to say.

When he turned toward her, his stare was so intense, like a magnet, and she had a hard time making herself turn away.

"So, do I," Wesley said.

* * *

She sped to the nearest library, the one she found off Main Street. Inside, she headed toward the reference section and for a map of Italy. The scar or birthmark or whatever it was she saw on Leon's side chin was in the shape of Italy. She knew the boot shape of Italy; after all, she had studied it in school. What was this anxiety? Why would she have to research that? She closed the reference book, calmed down, and reasoned that if she knew about the shape of Italy, then she shouldn't be so compelled to get information about it. There was just something about the shape of this scar.

It was at that moment that Kara's idea to find out more about why Leon was in prison came to her. She went to one of the computers that she saw along the wall, powered it up, and found the website for Leon's correctional facility. She typed in his name and his record appeared on the screen. She saw his picture along with his height, weight, race, and birth date, July 6, 1955 and under "Identifying Marks," she saw "birthmark in the shape of Italy along the lower right cheekbone." His aliases were Leo, Wilkes, and Lonny. She scrolled down and saw that Leon was charged with twelve counts of murder and his sentence, death.

Olivia searched in the newspaper archives for more information about Leon. With twelve counts of murder, there must have been a news article about his capture. After a few minutes of nonproductive attempts, she found an article on the front page of the Carrville Post, a Virginia newspaper.

Leon had abducted and killed twelve girls in the state of Virginia. The police dug up twelve bodies of young girls that he and his son, Tony, had buried around the farm he rented. According to the coroner, ten of the remains were of girls thirteen and up, and two of the remains were under thirteen. The coroner estimated at the time of the discovery, that some of the remains had been in the ground for several years. Leon and his son, Tony Sunstrik Wilkerson, were captured at their home on a rundown farm five miles outside of Carrville near Dawn's Creek. Leon called the girls whom he abducted his wives, though he had no marriage licenses to prove it. When the officers raided his home, they found ten children and two girls whom he later said were his wives and children, all shackled together to beds, posts, and furniture. The officers also said they were malnourished, and dehydrated. It was believed that Leon had taken the lives of more young girls and began abducting in another state, but so far, no one had come forward to give the police any information about that. Leon was discovered when the state police went to his farm to deliver an eviction notice. The property owner stated that he was eight months behind on his rent, very uncooperative and had done nothing to keep his property in good condition.

When Olivia finished reading his record, she put her hand over her mouth and tried hard not to throw up. How could anyone do this sort of thing to another human being? She closed down the computer and sat there a while, her hand still over her mouth, and trying to absorb what she had just read. She'd watched many police shows on TV where she saw child abductors and killers, but to meet one face to face was beyond anything comprehensible. She was almost sorry that she found out what he had done. She hoped that this new information wouldn't affect her ability to or her want to pray with him.

She tried to feel afraid, tried to tell herself that she should never go back to the prison again. However, she wasn't afraid, nor did she feel hatred toward him. Maybe some part of her did have what Claude referred to as "priestly feelings." Finally, she realized that the feelings that haunted her, that curse was the thing that kept her from feeling afraid of this man.

CHAPTER 9

At the prison the next day, a guard told Olivia that he had orders to take her directly to Wesley's office where she was to wait for Wesley's return. Olivia began to worry about why she had to wait. She had hoped that the wait was due to Wesley trying to figure out how to ask her out. She had to smile to herself. She hadn't realized that she wanted Wesley to ask her out. She tried to imagine a conversation that the two of them would have, but she got stuck on the, "Where would you like to eat" part. Since she had been going out with Claude, she hadn't kept up with the good dining places. Claude liked to eat out at two places and she wouldn't suggest either of them. She hated them both.

Within minutes, the door opened and Wesley stepped inside, a wide smile on his face the moment he saw her.

"Hello, Olivia."

The way he said her name so soft and warm made her lose all her thoughts, forget about anything she had to say. He made her feel as if she was an angel with large, fluffy wings, and who gently slipped in and out of places as she helped people. He made her feel like someone who made things happen.

"Hello, Wesley."

"I asked to have you brought to my office when I found out this morning that Leon wouldn't be here during the time you regularly see him. I'm sorry, Olivia. When you were here yesterday, he hadn't received permission. When I arrived this morning, I found out that his request had gone through and he starts his visits today."

"That's okay."

"Let me walk you out."

"I have time to wait—"

"No, no. He's at the hospital."

Olivia gazed at him for more information.

"His son, who was also in this prison, is very sick and Leon went to visit him."

"Oh, I see. I'll just wait."

"It's not as simple as that. You see. Tony, Leon's son, contracted HIV/AIDS some time ago and he's not expected to live out the week. Leon was granted visitation rights and I imagine he'll stay for as long as he can."

"Where is he?"

"What?"

"Where is he? I should go pray with him."

"Olivia, you can't be there with both of them. You can't do that."

"If his son needs to pray, then I should go pray with him. I have the time and it wouldn't hurt to pray before the priest gives him his last rites."

"Olivia—"

She saw the look on his face. He wanted to do whatever she wanted. It was not her intention to take advantage of him. "You can fix it, Wesley. I know you can."

"Let me see when Leon is scheduled to return. If this happens, I'll have to drive you. You understand that, right?"

"I know you can do it."

"Wait here." He pointed to a chair in his office.

She couldn't understand her want to see Tony. She had never met him, never even knew he existed until this moment. She had no idea why she was so driven, why seeing someone she'd never seen before was so important to her. But for some reason it was. She had no idea what to expect or what she would see. She just knew that at this moment, a strong feeling consumed her and she was determined to get to the hospital. She felt compelled to follow that urge and see where it would lead. The main question she was anxious to answer was: Was this Tony's need or her need? She only hoped that her visit to Tony would do him some good and help settle the unrest inside her.

Chapter 10

The temperature dropped, the weatherman predicted snow again; the kind that stuck to the ground. By the time they left, a light snow had begun to fall. Olivia left the "how" up to Wesley, and he managed to get permission for her to see Tony. In the car on the way, Wesley told her that Tony had been taken by ambulance to the AIDS ward of the nearby county hospital when he had taken a turn for the worse. The doctor thought Leon had contracted AIDS during the early years of his prison term. Wesley also told her that prisoners were brought to that hospital when they were seriously hurt or ill, so usually, the hospital was heavily guarded. He warned her that she should expect to go through the detectors, the same way she did when she came to the prison.

"Are you sure you want to do this? We can turn back now. It's not too late," he said.

A strange rippling feeling like a hot wave washed through her at that moment. "Yes, yes. I'm sure. I'm fine. I have to do this." She was certain that her uneasiness came through her voice. She was antsy, and shifted her weight from one side of her seat to the other, the way she felt when standing in a line that moved too slow and she was in a hurry.

Wesley gave her a sideways glance that held a questioning look.

"I'm sure," she said. She had a strong desire to see Tony. For some reason, she needed to know more about Tony's childhood. Maybe he knew something about that little girl. Surely that would help her know more about why Leon wanted to pray but was afraid. She also knew that her desire to see and talk to Tony exceeded what Fr. Wilson had sent her to do. She was taking a chance and hoped that she would not be put in a position where she had to explain her actions. The rippling feeling turned into a sour feeling in her stomach that rose up in the back of her throat. She was compelled to see this man who helped his father abduct little girls. She had to admit that this was a "priestly" act as Claude would have said. She was beginning to get caught up with them, like a fly caught in a spider web, and she was unsettled about what it was about them that worried her so much—this father and son.

At the hospital, Wesley directed her to the waiting area. Olivia thought it best not to ask questions so she took a seat while he went into a small office. When Wesley came out, he walked her down the hall in the direction of Tony's room. They had to pass through metal detectors again. After they checked in at the guard's station, a guard took Olivia to Tony's room. Wesley waited for her just outside his room.

The room smelled like rotten meat and blood mixed with alcohol, along with other odors she couldn't distinguish. As she walked to Tony's bed, she tried to keep herself from throwing up the smell was so rancid. She had begun to think that seeing Tony was a bad idea until he managed to turn his head in her direction.

"Hi, you come to see me?" he whispered, his face straining as he tried to smile.

"Hello, Tony. You don't know me. My name is Olivia Douglass." Olivia moved closer to his bed.

"You're Olivia. There's a chair, if you like." He tried to point to a chair. It took all his strength, so she grabbed the chair.

"How do you know me?" She began to shake, wondering if she would say the right things, or say the right prayers for him. She had never done anything like this before and said a silent prayer, asking for help.

Everything she saw, thought about touching was vile to her, almost as if she touched anything, and she would contract AIDS. She remembered from a class she had taken during her second year in seminary that this reaction would happen when visiting those in a hospital. She tried to recall the technique that was presented. The nurses, counselors, and hospice workers demonstrated what to do to get over fetid odor in a hospital room. She held her breath for a few minutes, then let the air out slowly. If she relaxed, she'd get used to the smell faster.

"My father said that you were praying with him. Did you come to pray with me?"

"Yes, if you would like." She looked at his gaunt face and down at the outline of his emaciated body under the sheet.

"Yes, I would, but I don't think God wants to hear from me. I did some bad things, Olivia. Some very bad things. I'm so sorry. I'm so sorry. I didn't mean to. I didn't want to." Tears swelled and ran down Tony's cheeks. Olivia heard the sincerity in his voice.

"Let's pray." She knelt beside his bed. "Heavenly Father, I raise up Tony to you, now. Thank you, Father, for your love of Tony and the many blessings you've given him, even those blessing that he wasn't able to accept . . .." As she prayed, she barely heard herself over his ragged breathing, his sobbing and repeating how sorry he was. When she finished she asked him to say the Lord's Prayer with her.

"I don't know it. I'm sorry. I don't know it," he sobbed.

Tony cried hard for his weakened state, sobbing and trying to catch his breath. Olivia worried about him getting emotional in his fragile state.

"That's okay. It's okay, Tony." She began, "Our Father . . ."

When she'd finished she attempted to get up, but he took her hand.

She cringed at his touch at first, and tried not to show it. Then she gave in and relaxed.

"Don't go yet. Can you stay with me a little longer?"

"Sure." She wasn't sure she should stay much longer. He was the color of ash, strands of short gray hair gathered in thin patches on the top of his head and his eyes sank back into his face.

"Olivia, you know something," he began with labored breath, "I never went to school. If I had another chance to live my life again, I want two things—go to school, and play baseball. My father, he didn't allow us school. When I was a kid, I used to sneak away sometimes in the day and evening. I hid outside the school, but got as close as I could and listened to kids talk about school. Some hated it, the homework. I just wanted to go so bad." He stopped to catch his breath. "One day I saw some boys coming out the school. They had some balls, a bat and that thing you put on your hand and catch with."

"A mitt?" Olivia asked.

"Yeah. A mitt. Then I heard them talk about baseball and I followed them to a field. Saw them hit a ball and run. It looked like so much fun. I wanted to play, but I knew I couldn't. One night I sneaked away to that field. I acted like I was on one of them teams. I hit a ball, ran around the make-believe bases."

"You scored a homerun, huh?"

"Yes, I did. I'll never do any of those things." He began to sob so hard and loud that Olivia found it difficult to keep herself from crying. Her heart went out to this gray-haired man who had his entire life stolen from him by his father. She saw that even though he participated, Tony was also a victim just like the girls he helped abduct.

"I'll never learn to play baseball or go to school or live another kind of life." He coughed and cleared his throat.

"What kind of life did you want?"

"Don't tell my father, I always wanted to get away. I had a sister once, she got away. At night, I used to try to talk to her wherever she was and hoped she was happy and living a good life. She wanted to go to school." He coughed again.

"A sister?" On one hand, she wanted to know more and on the other, she was afraid to push him in his fragile state.

"Olivia, I don't want to die. I don't want to die."

"I know you don't. But you'll be okay, Tony."

"Will God ever forgive me? Will he know I wanted to stop doing those things?"

The revolting sound as if someone was violently scraping his throat with a metal object as he coughed and gagged sent chills throughout Olivia. The nurse came in and asked her to leave. She peered down at him coughing, trying to talk. He reminded her of the time she had tried so hard to keep her hydrangea bush alive.

When she lived in England, their neighbor had a hydrangea bush and when Olivia saw the beautiful blooms, she wanted to grow one. Her neighbor gave her a cutting from her bush and Olivia planted it in a sunny spot recommended by her neighbor. She watered it, gave it plant food, talked to it, loved it, and couldn't wait to see it grow. Then one day she came out and there were buds on the bush. She ran to her mother. "Look at my bush. It's alive. It's growing."

"So, it is," her mother said. "I'm so proud of you."

Then, she ran to her neighbor, Mrs. Bixley, and made her come outside,

"See the bush? Isn't it beautiful?"

"You're going to have a beautiful bush. Just keep up with what you're doing."

"Mrs. Bixley is right. One day you'll have a hydrangea bush as pretty as hers," her mother said.

Olivia ran off to tell everyone on her street about her bush. However, the bush never grew beyond the buds and soon the bush began to wilt. Olivia continued to water it, maybe even over watered it, and feed it, but it wilted away to nothing. In tears, she dug it up and threw it away. She realized that the bush required more than watering and a fanciful love. It also needed a better place to grow and a caring kind of love.

Before she left the room, she turned around to Tony. He had stopped coughing and his face held a gentle, peaceful smile.

"Tony, God knows you and what's in your heart." She said and left the room.

Wesley stood when he saw her coming out of the room. He put his arm around her shoulders and pulled her close to him when he saw she was crying. She tried to stop herself from crying. She couldn't breakdown in front of him and the hospital staff. They walked out, his arm still around her.

* * *

In the car, he started the engine and drove a little before he pulled into the parking lot of a nearby park. The parking lot was empty and the light snow had not yet accumulated. Wesley pulled into the first space and parked.

"Why are we stopping here?"

"Olivia, are you okay?" Wesley asked. He reached out his hand, and took it back.

"I'll be fine. I've never done anything like this before." She wanted to cry for Tony, but held her tears.

"I've never seen anyone go this far for an inmate, especially, someone they don't know. Usually they don't see the value," Wesley continued.

"I know I'm a little unnerved right now, but I'm so thankful that you made this possible and stayed with me."

"What made you want to do this?"

She tried not to let out her emotions. "He doesn't want to die. He just did whatever his father told him to do. He talked about another life. I believe he held onto the thought that one day he would get away from his father and have another life, a better life. But that never happened."

"You're a brave woman, Olivia, kind and considerate. What you just did was difficult for anyone to do, yet you were courageous enough to do it; head on, you did it. I admire you for that." He reached over and put his hand over hers.

She was a little uncomfortable, not knowing his motive. "Thank you. You're no longer upset with me for making you bring me here?" She had to lighten the mood.

He gazed into her eyes for what seemed like an eternity. She was embarrassed at first, and blushed, cut her eyes downward. He moved his head toward her, just a little. He put his hand under her chin and tilted her chin upward, just slightly. She was almost paralyzed by his touch. She thought he was going to kiss her but instead he said, "I was never upset about that." His voice was barely above a whisper.

She smiled a nervous smile at him. Then, he let go of her hand and started the car. She gave him a sideways glance, and wondered if he'd planned to kiss her, but stopped himself. For a moment, she wished he'd just taken her in his arms, protected her from the twists and turns that her life was now taking.

Wesley was so gracious, not like Claude who often acted as though women were nothing. Wesley was a pure gentle man—kind, understanding. Nothing she did was wrong in his eyes. In the past, she'd dated men more like Claude. Wesley made her feel dainty, feminine, like the women she read about in her romance novels when she was a teenager. In those novels, the men always opened doors for the lady, pulled out her chair, carried the heavy bags so she wouldn't dare sprain a muscle, protected her from danger. The men in those novels made the women feel like queens that sat on their high thrones. Wesley made her feel like a queen. He respected her and now, she saw that she had to have more respect for herself. But, just because Wesley appreciated and had high regard for her didn't mean that he had romantic feelings for her. Maybe he just valued all women, an honor Claude found impossible to do.

On the drive back, after Wesley took her to her car, her mind went to Tony. He never got the chance to do the little things that so many took for granted. A dreaded trip to the grocery store, or the cleaners, a walk in the park, blowing out candles on a birthday cake, raking leaves for an elderly neighbor or friend were things denied to him and he grew up without experiencing any of these. According to the article she read, they lived in an out-of-the-way farmhouse and he and his father chained Leon's wives, and other children to beds, posts and whatever they could. Jail, though a different confinement, may have been a welcoming change for him, but one that he was not even prepared to handle.

She imagined Tony hiding in the bushes wanting to learn how to play baseball, watching others freely play, knowing that he couldn't. She thought about the sister and wondered what happened to her, and whether she cared about Tony, the brother who never forgot her, wanted to do what she did. Olivia tried to imagine the run-down farm where they lived with bare floors, broken windows that let in the cold or the rain, and that was sparsely furnished. She imagined Tony sleeping on the bare floor beside his father's bed, huddled under a blanket against the cold. She saw him help his father take another girl and tried to see him consoling her after taking her to the farmhouse. She saw the terror on the faces of the girls, scared to death knowing that there was no way out for them. She imagined Tony helping the others chained or tied wanting to let them loose, but afraid of what would happen to him. She saw him wanting to help all the girls escape, and realizing he had no place else to go. She felt sorry for Tony and wished that his life had turned out differently, that he had had the simple things that meant so much to him.

CHAPTER 11

Olivia's visit with Tony had drained her of energy and she felt an emptiness that chilled her. She entered her church through her door. She'd come through the side door so often she was beginning to think of it as her door. She slipped into the pew, knelt down on the kneeler and prayed. She said a prayer of thanksgiving for all her blessings, then read psalm 51. She read a prayer for Tony and his illness. She ended with the prayer she loved to say, *The Lord's Prayer.*

Afterward, she stopped by the office to get the key to the storage room where they were keeping the coats for homeless men and women.

"Olivia, your coat drive is catching on," the secretary said.

"We got a few?"

"Go see for yourself. You're going to be surprised."

She ran down the hall to the storage room to see the coats. When she opened the door, she was lost for words, so amazed at the number of coats. There were so many that they had run out of space on the racks. Someone had started stacking the coats on the floor. She pulled back some and saw that they were men's, women's, children's coats in different sizes, different colors, and different styles. There were so many that the small stack had turned into a large pile that was so high that the coats had begun to fall over. "Thank You, Lord," Looking up, Olivia prayed out loud. Now, she just had to arrange to deliver the coats to the two places in the area that cared for homeless men and women. She closed the door and headed back to the office, a wide smile on her face.

Just as she got to the office door, a woman dashed out and almost slammed into her, leaving her off balance. Olivia grabbed onto the wall to stop herself from falling. She got control of herself, turned to speak to the woman when she saw the lady running out the front door.

"Oh, no! Oh no!"

Olivia heard someone scream from inside the office. She went in to see.

"The money bag. It's gone. The money" stammered, Delia, the treasurer while pointing to an empty spot on the edge of her desk that sat across the room from the secretary.

"What happened?" Olivia asked.

"Someone took the money bag off my desk. The children's donation to the cancer center. I just went to get my coat. I'm responsible for that money."

"I know what happened." Olivia, Delia following behind, ran out of the church and onto the street to see if she could find the woman who'd almost knocked her down. She spotted a woman standing at the bus stop across the street from the church and holding her coat closed. When the woman saw Olivia and Delia watching her, she turned her back and then walked in the opposite direction, away from the bus stop.

"That's the woman who almost knocked me down running out of the office a few minutes ago."

"That's Mrs. Cox. Are you sure it was her?"

"Let's go talk to her," Olivia said.

Olivia and Delia caught up to Mrs. Cox.

"Hello, Mrs. Cox. I'm Olivia Douglass," she yelled out from behind Mrs. Cox.

Mrs. Cox wouldn't turn around. She walked faster.

"Mrs. Cox," Olivia shouted again.

When Mrs. Cox still hadn't turned around, but tried to walk even faster, Olivia ran around her and stood in front of her. "Stop, Mrs. Cox." She held out her hand, asking her not to take another step. Mrs. Cox stopped walking.

"Mrs. Cox, by mistake, you picked up the money bag that was on the desk."

"I don't have anything. What are you talking about? What money bag?"

"The one that you may have under your coat. Can you unwrap your coat so that we can see what's under it?"

"No. Why should I do that? I just told you I don't have a money bag."

"I hate to ask you this, but could you just open your coat or take your hand out of your coat so we can see that we're wrong?"

"I'm telling you now, that you're wrong. I don't have to open my coat, or take my hand out."

It dawned on Olivia that Mrs. Cox could have a weapon of some sort under her coat that she was prepared to use. But, Olivia needed to get the money back for the church, and she had to take a chance.

"Mrs. Cox, the money that you have is the donation from the children. They baked cookies, had several car washes, and did many things to earn the money that is in that bag. They did it to give the money they earned to the families who have children with cancer. They've been collecting that money for over a month. Won't you please give it back?"

Mrs. Cox made a jerking movement with her hand under her coat. "What about my child? What happens to my child? We can get money to help other people's children, children we don't know, never even seen before. Well, who helps my child? Who, Olivia, who?" The woman tried to ease past her.

Olivia noticed the bus was two blocks away.

"Tell me about your child. I wasn't aware that you were having a problem." She tried to stall her to keep her from jumping on the bus. She noticed three other people at the stop which she hoped, complicated the woman's plans.

Mrs. Cox seemed confused, like a person out of options and mixed up about what to do next. Her eyes filled with tears. "My husband took my two daughters."

"You mean your husband has run off with your daughters?"

"Yes, the court told him to. They said I wasn't taking good care of them. How can they say that about me? I'm their mother. I do the best I can."

"What did the court say, Mrs. Cox?"

"They said I wasn't a fit mother. My ex-husband makes more money than I do and he says he can take better care of them. I can't live without my girls."

"Mrs. Cox, please give me that money bag. You can't fix your children by doing this. I need you to see that."

"Seven thousand dollars. That's what's in this bag. I can provide better for my girls with this money. I have to have this money. I have to have it to get my girls back. Don't you see that I need this money?"

The bus was now a block away and the three people waiting stepped closer to the bus sign. One lady turned around toward Olivia and Mrs. Cox.

Mrs. Cox turned around and saw the bus approach. She tried to move toward the bus stop, but Olivia stepped in front of her, again.

"I can't let you get on the bus. Please give me the bag and come back to the church with me. I want to try and get you help. Would you let me do that, please?

Mrs. Cox tried to get around Olivia on the other side, but Olivia blocked that as well.

"Let me go. I have to get my daughters back; I just have to."

"If the court has granted your husband custody, then this money won't help. It will get you in trouble. Right now, you mistakenly took the wrong bag. But if you get on that bus, then this turns into a crime. If that happens, Mrs. Cox, you may never get your daughters back. Please, give me the bag, come back to the church with me, and let's try to get you the help you need. Please, Mrs. Cox, please."

The bus pulled up to the stop, opened its doors and one by one, the three people started up the steps. Mrs. Cox pushed Olivia out of the way and ran to the bus.

With her foot on the first step, she turned around to Olivia.

She turned toward the inside of the bus.

Mrs. Cox got off the bus, opened her coat, took out the moneybag, and handed it to Olivia. Olivia handed it to Delia who had been standing near the bus stop. Delia opened the bag and counted the money.

"Thank you, Mrs. Cox," Delia said, and took off for the bank.

Olivia took Mrs. Cox by the arm and they walked back to the church. Before she left the church, Olivia had appointments set up with an attorney, a health specialist, and Fr. Wilson for Mrs. Cox.

"No one has ever done anything like this for me until now," she said. Her cheeks gave off a twitch as if she wanted to cry. Instead, she held it.

"Help is here for you, Mrs. Cox. You just have to let us know you need us." When she felt Mrs. Cox would be okay, Olivia left the office.

Olivia remembered how earlier she felt drained of everything. Helping Mrs. Cox revived her, filled her with a special energy. Before she left the church, she arranged to have the coats taken to the shelters.

CHAPTER 12

In the bookstore, Olivia worked quickly to finish before her parents returned. Growing up in England, she had taken pleasure in doing things for her parents. Many times, she would wait for them to leave the house or the bookstore, and then clean the house or do some work in the store so they would return to a nice surprise. She learned to watch their faces for happiness, and when she saw how pleased they were, she would plan for the next time. Her parents teased that that was Olivia's way of softening them up to ask for a favor. However, Olivia never asked for anything.

Today she was busy wiping down the tables and chairs, adding a vase with flowers to every table along with a small rack for books—things that she'd found in the dollar store earlier. If she had time, she would bundle the books that a few customers from their church had ordered off their website, and then take them to the post office. As she worked, she felt like a young girl again, the girl who used to surprise her parents with niceties.

The bell over the door tinkled and she noticed that her parents had put a bell over the door. It reminded her of the aroma of the tea and butter cookies that she always took in whenever she entered the bookstore in England, but were missing in this store. Olivia looked up and saw Kara.

"So, this is where you are. Mom and Dad here?"

"They went out for dinner."

"Another one of your surprises?"

"Yes. What's wrong with that?" Olivia handed Kara a vase. "Would you like to help?"

Kara took the vase and stuck a yellow and red plastic flower in its opening.

"What's wrong? You seem nervous," said Olivia.

Kara placed the vase with the two flowers in the center of the table that was next to her. "Do you," Kara began, "never mind. I just need to talk to mom and dad." She gave the vase a pat and headed for the door.

"Kara, can I help?"

"No sense bothering you. I'll just come back."

A few minutes after Kara left, the bell over the door tinkled again and in walked her mother and Kara.

"Look who we found outside," said her mother as she entered the bookstore.

"Mom, you back all ready?"

"Yes, but your dad went to pick up some sandwiches or something. Livvy, what are you doing?"

"Oh, just a little surprise." Olivia stood in front of the table she was working on to cover up.

"We'll leave you to it. Come on Kara, you can help me with these internet orders."

"Oh, so now I've been reduced to a clerk, huh?"

"Honey, no. I need help. Your father always does it, but he went to get your dinner. The least you can do is help."

"Kara, how can you say that? We all take the orders off the internet. Why not help her?"

"Oh, miss priest over there who doesn't have to do this. She can go back to priesting, or whatever you do, talk to prisoners. Now, that's an important job."

"Kara, stop it," her mother said. Come, help me take these orders off the internet."

The bell over the door sounded again and her father entered carrying a large brown bag in one hand and something furry and brown under his arm. The aromas wafting from the bag, alerted Olivia to delicious food. He came in and sat the bag on the table.

"Anybody hungry? Since I knew you two were here, I thought I'd go back to the restaurant and bring you something to eat." He began taking small packages and containers out of the bag and Olivia, so drawn by the aroma, went to help him.

"See what I found outside?" He reached under his arm and pulled out a furry brown teddy bear with one eye missing and a hole in its chest. Some of the filling had already fallen out.

"Vinny, where did you find that?"

"Just outside. By the door." He turned to Kara first, then Olivia. "I remember that one of you had a brown teddy bear that seemed very much like this one."

"I did," said Kara. "You found this just outside the door? It wasn't there when we came in, Mom, was it?"

"I don't think so. Vinny, let me see that." She took the teddy bear from him and held it up. "Kara, I remember you loved that bear so much."

"She used to pretend that it was a puppet. I remember she tried to make us think that the bear was doing the talking when we all saw her mouth working," Olivia said.

"I know, but I fooled you a few times. Remember when he said he was thirsty and wanted a drink of water? Each of you brought him a glass of water. He said he'd drink it later."

"Kara, I remember you couldn't go to sleep without it. What was the name you gave it?"

Her father said just as he laughed.

"Yes, it was something funny. I remember that too," her mother said. "But, what was it?"

Kara burst out into laughter. "I remember. It was Sleepy something. No, I think the name had a bunch of "Bs" in it, like Benny Bean Baby Bear or Barking Bear, or something."

"Kara, Barking Bear?" her father asked.

"I was young then. I thought bears barked."

"I thought it was Curly Whirly Twirly Bear. You remember, Kara, when you and Livvy came home from school and the twins next door were using the bear for a baseball?" her mother asked.

"I remember that. Kara, you left the bear outside, remember? You said you wanted it to have fresh air. The twins, who lived next door to us, had found it and was batting it back and forth. I remember seeing Curly Whirly Twirly flying and whirling and twirling through the air while they ran around those sandbags they said were the bases," Olivia said.

"Curly Twirly Whirly or Betty Beenie Bear, either one, I don't see how I named the poor bear any of that," Kara said.

"It was rather funny to see a bear flying from first to second base, arms out, twirling, whirling. . ." Olivia tried hard to contain her laughter.

"They said they weren't going to give it back. When we saw them batting poor Curly Whirly, we went out to get it back and they made us chase after it," Kara said.

"They started throwing it back and forth to each other," Olivia said. "But when one of them dropped it, that's when I had to step between Kara and Danny."

"When Danny saw the look on my face, he and Denny took off running," Olivia said.

"Kara put the bear in the bear hospital," her mother said, "to get him fixed up."

"I remember those huge bandages that covered almost his entire body," her father said.

"But whose bear was it?" her father asked turning from Kara to Olivia. "I remember you both had it, right?"

"Dad's right. It was Kara's but she gave it to me," Olivia said.

"That's right," her mother said. "Kara gave it to Olivia after we moved."

"You're right. I did. I remember now. I gave the bear to you, Olivia. I thought you were afraid and I wanted the bear to keep you safe."

"Right," Olivia nodded. "But I gave it back to you because you couldn't sleep without it."

"What should we do with it?" Kara asked.

"It's broken, with a missing eye and hole in its chest. Kara, take it to the bear hospital," her father said.

"Let's try and fix her and take it to a homeless shelter," her mother said.

"I brought my girls food. Eat this dinner before it gets cold." Her father opened the bag. Olivia and Kara helped take the rest of the food out of the bag and set a place for each of them. Her mother made coffee using their new coffee maker. Her father had brought dessert and he and his wife sat down to eat the triple chocolate cake while Kara and Olivia dove into their salad, spaghetti with mushroom sauce and warm garlic bread.

CHAPTER 13

A week had passed since Olivia had begun her visits with Leon. To her surprise, knowing that Leon had one more week made her sad more than anything else. She had always believed that everyone had good inside them, and given the chance, they would show it. She'd arrived to church earlier than usual on this Sunday, and on her way to the church office she almost bumped into Fr. Wilson as he was coming out of his office.

"Olivia, I'm sorry. I wasn't thinking." He said as he stopped himself from colliding with Olivia.

"Fr. Wilson, are you okay?"

"Yes, I'm fine. My mind is elsewhere is all. I have to try to find someone at the last minute. I hate that. Wallace Conway, you know him, right? The Lay Eucharistic Minister? He was offered the job he's always wanted and flew out last night for an interview early tomorrow. I can't locate the Verger. We need someone to read and assist."

"Do you want me to serve, then?"

"That would be a big help." He gave out a long sigh. "You're a God send, Olivia. Truly you're sent by God."

Olivia recalled a sermon that Fr. Wilson gave just before she went into the seminary and she heard again, from one of the priests at the seminary. There are no coincidences. Everything is the work of God and his plan for us.

Olivia went to the sacristy to get an Alb and cincture. Then she made her way to the Narthex, or the entryway into the sanctuary where everyone participating in the service assembled beforehand. The members of the choir appeared one by one or two by three. The two teenage girls with the lit tapers appeared; behind them, the crucifer carried a large and heavy-looking brass

Cross. He was tall and the verger, who had been walking through the building trying to find a substitute reader, pulled the crucifer to the side and asked him to practice holding the processional cross. After two or three times of demonstrating how to hold the cross high enough, the verger asked him to let it down a little. The crucifer rested the base of the Cross on the floor in front of him. When the verger saw Olivia in her Alb, he smiled and whispered a "thank you" to her. The assistant priest, Fr. Burgess, stood off to the side talking to one of the choir members—the tenor—who would sing the solo. Olivia noticed Fr. Burgess rocking from heel to toe. Priests may appear confident, but even they can be nervous at times. As the Narthex filled up, the noise, even though in whispered tones, became disturbing so the verger asked the ushers to direct people into the sanctuary through another door. He closed the main door.

Olivia was so excited that she had to get ready for the service. It gave her a sense of belongingness and made her feel like she belonged to a special community. Even though she'd made her decision, she already missed this part. Fr. Wilson had just told her that she was sent by God. He was trying to get her to recognize how much she would miss this. When Fr. Wilson began the prayer before the service, she smiled not at him as much as about him. When he had finished, the organist began the first hymn, the verger opened the doors to the sanctuary, and the processional began.

The crucifer, with the processional cross and a taper on either side of him, led the way down the center aisle. The congregation members stood as the crucifer, carrying the cross, passed them. Behind them, the choir, an acolyte with the flag, an acolyte carrying the Gospel Book, then side by side Olivia and the verger, Fr. Burgess, and finally Fr. Wilson, the Rector.

At the conclusion of the hymn, when everyone was in place, Fr. Burgess gave the opening sentences. Olivia glanced out at the congregation and saw Wesley ushering people to their pews. She saw him extend his arm to help the elderly Mrs. Moore, and a tinge of jealousy rippled through her as she recalled how he had made her feel when he had put his arm around her when they left the hospital the day before. She watched them as he slowly led Mrs. Moore down the center aisle to her preferred pew and then walked back to the back of the church. When she thought about it, Wesley had ushered almost every Sunday. Somehow, he'd managed to get on every usher team.

Just after the prayers, Olivia eased herself to the lectern to read from the Old Testament. She began with a reading from Deuteronomy, chapter 30. "See, I have set before you today life and prosperity, death and adversity. If you obey the commandments of the Lord, your God . . . I call heaven and earth to witness against you today that I have set before you, Life and death, blessings and curses. Choose life . . .."

Later in the service, at the time for communion, the ushers directed the parishioners toward the altar and to the railing where they knelt down to accept. Olivia, with the wine chalice, followed Fr. Wilson who offered the bread. After everyone had been served, the ushers came up to the railing. Wesley knelt down in front of her to receive. When she offered the cup to him, he placed his hand over hers and took a sip. His touch sent a surge of warmth through her, the same feeling she had in the car after they left the hospital. After he had taken a sip, he fixed his eyes on hers, sending her heart into twirls and flips. She grasped the chalice tighter, so as not to spill any of the wine that was still in the chalice. She gazed down and saw his hand on hers, his grip tighter. Then, he eased his hand away, stood up, turned, and went back to the usher's station.

After the service, during coffee hour, Olivia, already changed out of her Alb, went to the Community Room to greet the parishioners and meet newcomers. Across the room, she saw her parents talking to a group of people. She turned and over near the door, saw Wesley with a small group of men. Just as he looked up and saw her, a couple wanted to engage her.

Even though her mind was on Wesley, she tried to hold a conversation with the two people who wanted to know more about the prayer group that Fr. Wilson wanted her to lead. The woman said that Wesley suggested that they join. She wished she knew how to read the signs that men gave off. Was Wesley interested in her? From his touch earlier that morning, he had stirred up feelings inside her. Was there a book somewhere? The "hand holding" in the car and earlier with the chalice, confused her. The last thing she wanted to do was to mistake his intentions. Either he wanted to learn to pray or he wanted an opportunity to see her. Why couldn't this "man-woman" thing be simpler, a lot simpler?

Olivia brought her attention back to the couple who wanted to join the prayer group. She told them about the training and suggested that they attend the sessions. After they left, she turned to find Wesley, but he was gone. She looked around the room for Claude but he wasn't there. Funny, she hadn't thought about him during the service or noticed his absence until now.

"Can I offer you a cup of coffee?" Wesley asked standing behind her.

Her face must have produced an appearance that said she was glad to know he hadn't left. She felt the warmth on her cheeks when she turned to him.

He handed her a cup of coffee, steam emanating, and the aroma wafting to her nostrils.

"Thank you. I could use it."

"Can I just tell you how much I enjoy your reading? I get so much meaning out of the passages that you read."

"Wesley, that's my intent."

"They must teach you how to do that in seminary, don't they?"

"You have to read the Bible with your heart. When you do that, you get the meaning and you'll see things that you missed during your first reading."

Olivia was struck by his professional manner of the conversation. But, she was ready for it. If she could just figure him out.

"I haven't been doing that. Maybe we need a class or workshop for us lay people on how to read The Bible."

"That's not a bad idea." She paused. "I understand you're recruiting people for the prayer group."

"I thought people would want to know about it. Hope I haven't done anything wrong."

"No. You haven't. A prayer group would help us connect to each other."

"I'm hoping it will. A few people wanted to know what we'll be doing, Wesley said."

"How many people have you spoken to so far?"

"About ten."

"Will everyone join?"

"About eight of them. But don't worry. I have a few more people to ask," Wesley said.

"Can you send me the names of the people who wanted to know more?"

"Sure. I'm just asking people. Everything else, I have to leave to you," Wesley said.

"It seems as though the ushers were shorthanded today. Some of the ushers were out this morning. I'll bet."

"We handled it," Wesley said.

"Were you a substitute?"

"I was here, so I offered. We have to jump in where we're needed."

Wesley is the calm and relief that the sun brings as it settles over an area that was just struck by a severe storm. He was covering for Claude. Claude no doubt did the same thing he pulled a month ago. He just didn't bother to show up or let anyone know he'd be out. This time, Wesley was kind enough to take his place. Yet at this moment, when she glanced at him, she thought she saw something else in his face, pain, a need, a man hurting; feelings she'd not seen before.

* * *

That afternoon, when Claude opened the door to his townhouse and saw Olivia standing there, he gave her a Cheshire cat grin, stealth around the edges, and opened the door wider. He was in his sweats, hair mussed.

"I'm glad you're here. You're just in time for coffee." He took her arm, pulled her inside, and closed the door.

"You missed church this morning. You're just getting up?"

"What are you questioning me for? A person deserves to sleep in once in a while."

He walked back to the kitchen to make coffee; she thought she heard him mumbling or talking to himself. She followed him. She took off her coat, placed it on the back of a chair, and sat down on one of the stools behind the long counter that separated the kitchen from the dining room. He stood in the middle of the kitchen, scratched his head, and looked around the room as if he couldn't remember where he kept his coffee.

She had come there to tell Claude that she needed space; she needed to take a step back from their relationship. Before she found the right words, he started in about his work and how the new female dentist, Margaret, was making a mess of his office. He complained that he couldn't find his equipment when he needed it. Olivia sat on the stool listening to his grumblings and discontent, one after the other each one debasing Margaret.

94

She held her tongue. Responding would just encourage him. She wasn't surprised by his put-downs and disparaging comments and Olivia questioned why he would even take on a female partner in the first place, given his views about women. Olivia watched him, his face contorting as he told her about how Margaret left her space messy and others had to clean up for her at the end of the day, and how she wanted to talk about Casey all the time. Annoyed, Olivia tried to find an opportunity to cut in to tell him that they needed to separate. The disgust in his voice, his attention to himself, and his needs were glaring examples of his inability to become that better person.

Olivia thought about how Wesley would respond. Wesley took the time to recruit people for her prayer group. Claude complained about his partner intruding in his space. Claude cared little, if he cared at all, about Margaret and the transition to her new life in this town. He knew she was in a difficult situation when he took her on. From the bits and pieces that Olivia was now hearing, he wasn't cutting her any slack at all, and nor did he care to. After Olivia had had enough of his ranting, she cut him off mid-sentence.

"Claude, you left the ushers shorthanded. Wesley had—"

"Oh, that Wesley, huh?"

"What do you mean?"

"I see how he looks at you. Eyeing you up and down. I know what he wants." He stood over her as she sat on the stool, his arms on the counter, enclosing her.

He was too close to her. She tried to stand, but there wasn't enough room. He leaned in further. Now, his face seemed less than an inch away and she broke out in a sweat. She saw the bristles of hair on his face and chin and he had that morning bed odor. Her heart sped up and she had trouble breathing. She tried to push him away. Before she realized it, Claude had pulled her up off the stool and had her up against the wall, his arms on the wall on both sides of her. Beads of perspiration formed on her forehead and her palms were sweaty. Her heart pounded so hard that it felt as if it would explode.

Again, she tried to move one arm out of the way, and tried to go under it. He tightened his arm preventing her from moving it. "Claude, what are you saying? How could you believe that?" She tried moving his arm again and he tightened his hold on the wall. With her fist, she beat him on his arm and chest, but he was too close, she couldn't get the momentum she needed and her punches were weak.

"You think I don't know it, don't see him watching you?" He took hold of her chin, turned her head, kissed her hard on the lips.

When he stopped, "He doesn't see you're mine."

"Claude, what are you doing?" she said, trying to turn her head. She tried to push him away again, get under his arm, and get free.

"I just wanna kiss my girl. I can kiss my girl, can't I?" As he slid his hand under her skirt and touched her, he kissed her neck.

"Wesley may want you, but you're my girl," he said as he worked his fingers on her.

She flinched. And in trying to pull herself away from his hand, she pushed herself harder into the wall. "Claude, please don't, you're hurting me. Stop." She pushed him again, but she couldn't budge him.

He kissed her again, and again, hard on the lips, around her ears, her neck, all the while pressing himself closer to her, gyrating. With one hand, he unbuttoned her blouse, slid his hand inside. He grabbed hold of the center of her bra, kissed his way down from her neck to her breasts. Then he hiked up her skirt, bunched it up close to her waist.

"Claude, what are you doing? Stop, stop. Get away from me!" Olivia screamed out, as she frantically beat him in the face and arms with her fists. "You said you wanted to be a different man from your father. You're not different; you're just like your father; you're just like your father."

Claude stepped back, put his hands over his eyes, dropped down on the nearby stool, and began crying. "I'm not like him; I'm not like him. Don't say that, please don't say that."

Olivia straightened her clothes, brushed a hand over her hair, got her coat off the chair, and started for the door.

Claude stood up, "I'm sorry, Livvy, I'm so sorry."

Olivia had nothing to say.

"I just thought, well, we're getting married. It's not wrong if we're getting married. Don't go, Livvy, don't go. We're getting married."

"I have to."

"I thought you had something to tell me."

"I do, I mean I did. But I don't need to say anything, now."

Quickly, she continued down the hall to the front door. With her hand on the knob, she turned to him. "You know, you have never told me that you love me. Do you love me, Claude?"

"Don't be upset with me. I know you are, but don't be, please."

Olivia opened the door, stepped outside.

He looked at her.

"Good-bye." Olivia made her way to her car.

She was glad to be out of his townhouse. Until now, Olivia hadn't noticed Claude's jealousy over Wesley because Claude's ego wouldn't allow him to recognize that Wesley was a threat to him. His aggressiveness frightened her more than he ever had. He was more forceful, almost frantic as if he needed to overpower the thought of her and Wesley. He had tried to have sex before marriage several times but she never had to fight her way out like she did this day. He usually stopped when she asked, even though one other time she did have to ask him several times. Olivia always thought that the reason he stopped had to do with that "priestly thing," as he called it and she never wanted to disturb that idea.

She realized that in the past, she wasn't afraid that he would harm her if she refused to go along with it, she was afraid that if she did refuse, he would leave her. She was always relieved that she had found a way to escape that experience. Her fear of Claude's rejection, was stronger than her fear of his aggressiveness. Earlier, she had almost acted out of habit— the fact that she wouldn't be able to face herself if she was rejected, the failure of a person wanting her, loving her. She now realized that she was no longer afraid of being rejected by him. Listening to him talk about Margaret also made her see that he would never change. She saw that now and knew that she would never give him another chance. She was through. She hadn't realized it until she got outside, but the way she kept her head and fought back was due to Wesley. She held her thoughts on him.

On the way out of Claude's house, she had asked him if he loved her. She realized now that she never loved Claude.

* * *

97

That night Olivia wanted to put all thoughts of Claude out of her mind and after an hour of worrisome sleep, she drifted off.

It was dark in the dense woods. The green trees were so tall and full and they formed a canopy over her, hiding her and closing out the sky. She was lost. She tried to remember what happened, how she became lost. She peered behind her to find a path, a road, anything that would take her back to her house, but the path had disappeared. She took a few steps, saw an opening and ran toward it, hoping it would take her out of the darkness. But that path disappeared. She walked on through the woods anyway, certain that she would find the right way, that she would find her way out of the woods. She saw a path, and ran until she fell over a boulder that suddenly moved onto the path and blocked her way. She tried to stand, but she was in pain. She wasn't able to move her leg. A man came to help her, but he couldn't help her stand. She saw that he was too young. He wasn't strong enough either and he ran to get an older man who had a mark that was the shape of Italy on the side of his face. The older man gently picked her up. She thought the man would be mad, but he wasn't; he seemed so happy to see her. He kissed her on the forehead and held her close to him as he carried her back to a house.

Olivia woke up, clothes wet from perspiration. After a warm shower, she was able to sleep.

CHAPTER 14

The gray blanket that covered the sky gave way, dumping thousands and thousands of large, wet flakes on to the earth, covering the parking lot and creating a barrier between the prison and the rest of the town. Amid the heavy snowfall, Olivia made her way to the prison to see Leon. His scheduled execution was Friday, five days.

When she arrived, Wesley met her near the entrance, and as they walked toward his office, he said, "Tony passed away over the weekend. Leon was at his side. Of course, the state buried him."

"Maybe now he'll be at peace," she said.

"I understand. I hated to see him suffer so," Wesley said.

"He was used to suffering."

Wesley nodded.

"I'll bet Tony never told his father that he wanted a different life."

"No, Wesley, he didn't. Nor did he tell his father that he wanted to play baseball, or that he wanted to go to school to learn to read and write."

He gave a slight grunt.

"I suspect that up until the moment he left this world he was still afraid of his father or maybe he thought it just wouldn't matter."

"You're right," he said.

"Wesley, Many people, in fact too many, leave this world filled with hate, anger and bitterness. Now I know what people mean when they say make things right before you die, or get your affairs in order."

"I used to think it meant to get a will or sell your house, name your heirs, things like that. But I see what you mean."

"But I believe Tony will receive the love he'd always wanted and would even learn to play baseball and go to school."

"Fr. Wilson left a message saying that our first training session has been cancelled," Wesley said, voice slightly monotone and his face void of expression.

"The weather is expected to pick up," she said, trying to be more cheerful.

A guard stuck his head in the door of Wesley's office.

"He's here. I'll walk you down," Wesley said.

Olivia loved the feel of him walking beside her, his sureness, his authority, the eloquence in his movements. It gave her a powerful sense of confidence that seemed to stay with her throughout her visits with Leon. She hoped he felt the same way. Or at the very least he felt her support for him.

When she entered the room, Leon was already behind the table and chained.

"Hello Olivia Douglass."

"Hello Leon."

"You don't look too happy today. Want to talk about it?"

"Now, you want to offer me therapy?"

"Naaaaw. I ain't no therapist. Just see that something may have disturbed you that's all."

What would Leon's defense be today? Every day so far, he's done everything possible to get out of praying. She looked at the man across the table, the one who was out of time and realized that he was afraid to pray, scared out of his mind. He was terrified that he would die and not know what would happen to his soul. He was afraid that he would not be allowed into heaven. Another thought came to her. This was his last week and she was his only visitor and in his eyes the only person who cared enough about him to visit him.

"Your man not treatin' you right?"

"Leon . . . ."

"What do you want from me? If you spend time in jail, you learn how to read people real fast. Your life could depend on it."

She tried to put a smile in her voice. "I appreciate your concern."

"I think if he ain't treatin' you right, you ought to get rid of him. A lady like you, you deserve respect. Treat you like a queen, give you everything you want, show you love. That's what he ought to be doing."

"You think you know me?" was all she wanted to say to Leon. She had to admit that she was completely taken by surprise. She hadn't thought that Leon would say anything like this.

"I heard you went out to pray with my son."

"Yes. You never mentioned him. Why?"

"What are we now? Best friends? Father and daughter?"

"No, it's just that he needed someone to pray with him, just like you do. The difference is, I prayed with him."

"Maybe he just. . . Maybe he only. . .."

"Why don't we pray, now?"

"How do you know what to pray for?"

"Considering that you only have, I mean that in five, well you know. Considering that, I know what we could pray for now." She remembered his birthmark and wanted to get another glance at it.

"Oh, I see. You pray I go to hell, huh?"

"I'm sent here by my church. I wouldn't dare pray for anything like that."

"Okay."

"Okay, what?"

"Pray."

She bowed her head, linked her fingers and began her prayers.

"Lord, I bring before you today, Leon. Leon will leave here soon, Lord, but before he does, he wants to open his heart to You . . .." When she'd finished, she read from her prayer book. "'Jesus said, "I am the light of the world; he that follows me shall not walk in darkness, but shall have the light of life."' Next, she read a general confession from the prayer book. After the "Amen," she looked up at Leon who sat with his head bowed. For a moment, she was surprised to see him so reverent. Then she turned to the Lord's Prayer. She watched him from time to time as she read, and listened for him to join in. She continued alone. She ended the prayers with, "In Jesus's name we pray. Amen."

Leon turned his head up and was quiet for a minute. She saw that tears were forming and he tried so hard to keep them back.

Olivia closed her prayer book.

"You sure it'll take?"

He was determined to hold strong to the very end. Obviously, he wanted to laugh at his clever comment, but she was sure that the expression she gave him stopped him.

"You asked for prayer and we just prayed. God has heard you. I don't know what you mean when you ask if 'it'll take.'" She was offended by his statement and wanted him to know it.

"Remember you asked me about my family?"

"Yes."

"Well I just want you to know that whatever you heard about me, I always loved my children. I admit that I had different wives, but I always loved my children."

"How many children did you have?"

"They say I have seventeen."

"Leon, why do you say 'they say'?"

"About seventeen."

"Did all of your children live with you?"

"Yes; all but one. I never forgot that one. She was special, my special one."

"What happened to that one?"

"My beautiful girl. She left me. Just left me. Of all of my children, I loved her more." He paused for a moment and she waited. "I always wanted to know how she turned out, ya' know?"

"Tell me about her."

"I trusted her. I cried for three days after she left. Couldn't eat, couldn't sleep. Tony brought me around. I know you may think that's strange coming from me. But that's the g —, I mean, that's the truth."

"She's still alive?"

"As far as I know, and I'd like to be sure if she is. Years ago, an inmate told me that he knew her and she's dead."

"Are all of your other children still alive?"

"As far as I know."

"You never heard from your daughter?"

"No. I guess she don't want nothin' more to do with me. Or maybe she is dead."

"Maybe not, maybe one day you'll meet her again."

"Huh, real funny."

"Tony loved you."

She tried her best to ask questions that would get him to open up and talk about what he did to these girls and his children. He needed to say that he was sorry for taking them, doing unspeakable things to them, forcing them to have his children and then abusing them. She thought her questions would lead him to see that. But he had not said in any way how sorry he was. Leon thought he did the right thing.

"Tony was my oldest. He was a good boy. Did he talk about me to you?"

"He just said he loved you." She paused, reflecting on their conversation and not sure what to say to Leon. "He told me he wanted to learn to play baseball and that you taught him." Olivia wasn't sure why she lied. Maybe she couldn't stand the idea that Leon would leave this world not understanding Tony. Maybe she felt she had to get it out for Tony. She hadn't planned to lie. She just did.

"He said that? That I taught him?"

Olivia held herself from answering even though he looked for her to confirm it.

"I remember how he loved it. He wouldn't tell me how he found out about baseball, but I knew he was watching those kids at the school. Sometimes, when we had time we would play. We . . ."

The door to the room flew open and the two guards entered.

"It's his dinner time," one of the guards said.

"Come back tomorrow. Would you?"

"We prayed and that's why I came."

"Come back tomorrow. I just have this week."

"Okay." She sighed. She saw the pleading appearance of his face and remembered that she was all he had.

The guards had Leon up, re-chained, and ushered him out by the arms.

Wesley returned to the room, and stood in the doorway.

"The snow is coming down pretty hard out there. Why don't I follow you home?"

She turned in her chair. "Wesley, that's so kind of you. But, that means you'll have to come back." She stood up to face him.

"Don't worry about me. I just want to see you safe."

She glanced at her watch and was surprised to know that it was later than she thought. The traffic would be a problem.

She saw his need to take care of her. Prison was an unhealthy and dangerous environment and even though she was relaxed with Leon, she couldn't afford to be too confident. As strong as she was, it was nice to have him want to see to it that she be unharmed.

"If you promise to keep us both safe."

"I'm sure I can do that." He gave off a smile that seemed to light up his entire body.

* * *

When Olivia entered the bookstore, the bell over the door tinkled out and Mrs. Andrews, who was a new part-time clerk that her mother mentioned she had hired, was helping a customer. Olivia was amazed at the number of people who came to the bookstore and wondered where these customers came from. She was delighted to know that people still read books.

She remembered that the bookstore was her father's idea. He had to come up with something to keep his wife busy. When Olivia and Kara were in high school, they needed their mother less and less, which left her feeling unwanted, their father told them. He told his daughters that his wife tried to solve her need by pouring herself into his teaching. She asked him about his philosophy of teaching, the assignments that he gave to the students, the students' names and many other things that her husband couldn't and wouldn't tell her. He said that she tried to tell him how to teach his classes and even offered grades for their work. He was in a panic and called his daughters to his office for help.

"She actually wanted me to change the grade on a student's paper," he said, outraged at her interference. He wanted his daughters to help him come up with ways to get her out of his classes.

"She needs a hobby or an activity," Olivia said after she managed to stop laughing. "She tried to give out grades to your students?"

"Olivia, this isn't funny . . ."

"Oh, Dad, yes it is."

"Okay, maybe a little," he began to laugh, a little at first and then a big chortle.

"Dad it's really funny," Kara said, "Can't you just see her now?"

"Okay girls, you're having your fun. I need your help. Let's get back to what she can do. What is that?" Her father asked, voice sounding frantic. "You know she's not the nursing or nurturing kind so don't say anything like helping at a senior center or hospital or with children."

"Yeah, mom likes to talk to people," Kara said.

"And read. What about a bookstore? That man, Mr. Martin, who's planning to close his shoe store, you could take it over, Dad," Olivia said.

"A bookstore? I'm not so sure about that."

"Dad, picture her teaching your class," Kara said.

"You're right. First thing tomorrow, but you girls be on the standby in case that doesn't work."

In a few weeks, he bought the building and their mother spent most of her time turning it into a bookstore and, more importantly, out of her husband's classroom. Olivia and Kara worked in it while they were in high school and college. The store carried modern titles and many of those books were on England's best seller list.

Olivia waited until Mrs. Andrews finished ringing up the customer, who went out the door with several books in her arms.

"Hi. I'm Olivia Douglass. I guess you're the new clerk. Don't know if you know me—"

Nodding, "I know you. They're in the office," Mrs. Andrews said before Olivia finished.

In the back room, her mother was on the computer and her father sat next to her, an open notebook on the desk in front of him. They took orders from their website.

"I don't want to disturb you two. I'll come back another time." She turned around to leave.

"What is it, Sweetheart?"

She heard her father ask.

"I just want to talk. I need to ask something."

"Sure. And if we haven't mentioned it before, thanks for the beautiful vases, flowers, and book racks. That was so nice of you. Where in the world did you find those nice racks?" her mother said.

Her father closed the notebook and stood up. "Just like old times, huh?

Well, I'll leave you two to talk."

"Dad, what's wrong?"

"Nothing."

"Why is it that every time you and mom are alone and I walk in, you have to leave?"

"I hadn't noticed that. I just thought you'd want to talk."

"I do. But with both of you."

"What do you want to talk about?" her mother asked.

"I was thinking about the man in prison. You know, the man I had to pray with?"

"Yes," her father answered.

"We prayed together." She pulled up a wooden chair that was against the wall, and sat down. "I don't know why, but I know it has to do with his son, Tony. Tony got me to wondering about myself. While I was visiting him, he talked about his childhood."

"What was his childhood like?" her mother asked.

"He had a very hard childhood. The thing that I can't get out of my mind is that he remembered some things about his childhood."

"Is that unusual?" her father asked.

"I don't know," Olivia said.

"May not be the best memories," her mother said.

"Mom, the thing is that he remembered."

"What are you saying?" her father asked.

"I don't remember much about my childhood. I just have one or two memories. I mostly remember things when we lived in England, and when I was older, nothing much before we moved to England."

"Well, that's not unusual. Many people don't remember their earlier childhood. You just said so yourself."

"But, Mom, I don't remember anything until I was seven, eight, or nine. I can't figure out how old I was when I have these one or two memories. It bothers me that I don't remember."

"What's the memory that you do have?" her father asked.

"It's about you, Dad. I remember you teaching me how to read. We sat in a big brown leather chair and you read stories to me almost every night."

He turned away.

"What's the matter?" Olivia asked.

"Sweetheart, we never did that."

Olivia felt as if a bullet had pierced through her heart, split it in half, even though she didn't quite know what being shot felt like.

"No," she yelled. "We did. You did. You taught me how to read. We sat in a big brown leather chair, like the one at home. We sat in it together."

"Livvy, we read together, but we either sat on the glider on the back porch or we read in your room. And sometimes we sat at the kitchen table."

"That can't be true. It just can't be. You just don't remember. You just don't remember." Olivia got up, ran through the store, out the front door and found her way to her car. She opened the door and sat inside. She could hardly breathe. She had to understand why this memory was so important to her, or why she wasn't willing to hear the truth.

By this time, the snow was sticking to the streets, and trees. She had to turn on her windshield wipers to see. She started the car and drove the few blocks to the church. The side door was open and she entered the sanctuary, walked down the center aisle, and sat in a pew, about mid-way.

Since she'd starting visiting Leon, her life had become much more complex. She had unexplainable feelings. She had found out that Kara lost her job and was homeless, she came to some realizations about Claude, and Wesley, and she strongly felt her parents holding something from her. She hadn't expected her parents to keep secrets from her, but, they were for some reason, she just knew it.

On Sunday, she would have her graduation ceremony. She had to get her mind on that, leave everything else alone for now. Then she remembered Leon, and realized that Leon would be gone when she graduated. She pulled the kneeler down, folded her hands, and got down to pray. She had a list of things that she needed to have straightened out for her. But before she began her prayers, she felt a presence behind her.

She turned. "How'd you know where to find me?" She asked her father.

"I figured you'd be here. You okay?" he asked, leaning on her pew.

"I don't know." She turned to face him, her back against the pew. "It's just been so much for me lately."

"You and Claude broke up."

"Yes. How'd you know?"

"I knew it was coming. Something you said the other day got me thinking."

"I should call him, shouldn't I?"

"Why would you want to do that?"

"I don't know. I know who he is. I know how he treats people and women mainly. But Dad, there's no one else for me."

"Look Livvy, you're my daughter and I'm not just saying this because of that, but you deserve to be treated much better than the way he treats you. When you brought him to England to meet us, I was ready to put him on a plane and send him back here to the U.S."

"You never told me that."

"No, and I never would have, but now I sense so much going on with you that you need to hear it. You are such a beautiful person, loving, kind, generous and committed to people. He's the very opposite, but the opposite that won't work with you, you know?"

She gazed at her father, love pouring out of her eyes and heart and patted his arm.

"I do need to hear that now. I love you, Dad."

"I love you, too Sweetheart. And there is somebody else. Give it time."

He leaned over and gave her a kiss on her forehead. "Tell me more about the prisoner."

"I'm not quite sure why, but Leon and his son, Tony, bother me. I don't understand why I can't remember things that happened to me before you and mom. I just seem to have that one memory. But Tony, remembered things that happened to him in his early life and it's likely that many other people have early memories. Is there a reason for this? Is there something wrong with me?"

"Your life is far different from Tony's life. Maybe the few memories he told you about were bad memories for him. You had a slew of good memories. You and Kara and your mother we all did so many nice things together. We should all have good things to remember."

"You're right. Maybe I should just leave it alone."

"You could do that. Or you could keep tugging, but if you want." He stood up. "You need to get home. The snow is really coming down out there."

She took her father's hand and they started out of the church. She peered up at him as she got in her car and noticed fear as it surged across his face. She dismissed those thoughts when she saw the snow settling in his hair and shoulders. She almost saw him stick his tongue out to let the flakes melt on it, like he showed her the first winter they were in England. Then she understood that he was worried about her drive home in the snow. She also understood that there was something in her past that they couldn't have her find out. He had just told her to keep trying, that is, if she needed to find out. More importantly, she hadn't asked him to clear up the memory about the reading in the chair, the wrong memory. Instead, she ran away, feeling there was something she feared and couldn't face. Her parents were obviously dodging it, which made her question whether she wanted to know. No doubt, it had to do with that curse that surrounded her and at this point, she needed to get to the bottom of that feeling.

CHAPTER 15

When Olivia walked in her front door, Kara was sitting on the couch in the living room, a whiskey bottle in one hand and a half-empty glass in the other. When she looked up and saw Olivia, she poured more whiskey in her glass. Kara hadn't done much about cleaning herself up. She had on the same faded top and dingy pants and each strand of her hair seemed to have its own idea about the direction it wanted to take. Olivia felt a strange distance with her sister, a dark cloud between them and it was hard for her to understand her sister anymore. Just the other day she seemed almost happy. But now, seeing her unkempt and drinking too much made Olivia cautious about her sister.

"What took you so long? Have a drink." She held up the bottle and tipped her glass to her mouth.

"Mom must have called again. Was she talking about the bookstore or was she trying to get you to take care of yourself?"

Kara rolled her eyes at Olivia.

"Kara, what's bothering you?"

"Having a nice drink. Want some? It's yours. Here, you have a message from Claude." She handed the note to Olivia, but took it back before Olivia had a chance to take it. "Want me to read it?"

"No, Kara. Hand it to me. I can read it."

"No, I'll read it out loud." She tried to giggle.

Olivia wanted to snatch it from her, but changed her mind. Why should she? Besides, Claude doing something nice, writing a note? It just wasn't like him.

"Olivia," Kara began with a dramatic voice, her hand over her heart. "Where have you been, my love? Don't you know that I need you? I wish we were together now. I want to tell you how much I love you. I'll be waiting to hear from you."

For a second, Olivia almost wished that Claude had said that. "Are you going to give me the note?"

Kara laughed. "The great priest is —,"

"Kara stop. Stop it, please." She moved toward Kara.

"Okay, I was just kidding around. He just said he hadn't heard from you and call him. I'm just teasing you. Can't you take teasing?"

"I thought you were going to clean up."

"Why?"

Olivia wanted to ask about the job, but knew that Kara lied again.

"Have a drink." She found another glass and poured Olivia a drink. "I've been reduced to helping out in a bookstore. I don't even have a legitimate title. Wait, is 'helper' legitimate?"

Olivia took a sip and made a scowl. "How can you drink this stuff?"

"You don't think about it."

"You need coffee and something to eat. Have you eaten at all today?" She walked to the kitchen to start the coffee brewing.

Kara followed her. She pulled out a chair and sat at the table. "Don't sound like Mom. I don't need a mother."

"What do you need?"

"I need a friend, Livvy. I need a good friend." Her voice sounded serious and she watched Olivia as if she wanted to ask Olivia to be her friend.

"Kara. You have friends. I'm one of them. Remember how we used to be?"

"How long ago was that?" Kara asked.

"When we were growing up. Do you ever think back about us growing up?"

"You kiddin'? Why are you thinking about that?"

"I went to see Tony, Leon's son. You remember Leon is the man who asked for prayer. Tony talked about his life. He's, I mean he was, a grown man with graying hair and the one life he'd lived was helping his father abduct little girls." Olivia turned on the coffee maker.

"You found out why he was incarcerated."

"Leon's in for twelve counts of murder. He was sentenced to death for abducting young girls. His son, Tony was in the same prison. I wonder if that was planned, somehow. Anyway, Tony spent his life in some run-down farmhouse somewhere and I got the impression that he had to stay inside that farmhouse, that he wasn't allowed to leave. I try to imagine his life and I can't get Tony and his circumstances out of my mind. We are blessed. I know I'm blessed."

"Now you want to run a guilt trip on me."

"No Kara, I was just thinking about Tony."

Olivia poured coffee for Kara. She took a frozen pizza out of the freezer, and stuck it in the oven, then turned on the timer. Olivia took the cup of coffee and started back into the living room. Kara followed and took a seat on the couch. Olivia placed the cup on the table directly in front of Kara. She watched Kara for a reaction, knowing she always had to be ready for a rebuttal. Kara poured herself another drink, instead. Olivia opened the drawer of the end table next to the couch, and pulled out a velvet lined leather box. She took the top off exposing a book titled, *Stumbling Through the Woods*, by Kara Douglass. She took the book out of the box and placed it on the coffee table in front of her sister. She watched as Kara stared at the book as if it were something harmful to the touch, something that was tainted. Sitting next to Kara, Olivia picked up the book, and held it like the Bible, and it contained precious proverbs and moral teachings. She moved it in front of Kara, wanting her to take it. Kara sat back on the couch and turned her head away.

"Take it, Kara."

"No, I can't. Where did you get this?" With the back of her hand, she attempted to wipe the tears from the corners of her eyes.

"Take it, Kara, take it."

"No, I can't. I hid this. Where did you get it? You have no right."

"This is you Kara. This is who you are."

"No. That woman, she never was. That woman was someone I wished I was. But I'm not her. Why can't anyone see that? I'm not her, I never was."

"No, Kara. That's not true. These essays and poems say who you are. They talk about the things that made you, your struggles and loves, just like we all have."

Kara moved away from the book.

"Kara, please take your book. This book is so beautifully written. These words came from your heart and you poured that all out to us on every page. This is the Kara I know. Take your book, please." She held the book closer to Kara.

Kara stood up. She reached down and picked up her glass, and the bottle of liquor and she started up the stairs. "You don't know . . . you just don't know." And she wobbled her way upstairs.

The bell in the oven went off; the pizza was ready. However, Olivia would have to wait.

Chapter 16

Olivia waited for her parents to leave their house for the bookstore so that she could use her key and let herself in the front door. She wanted to be alone in the house to try to remember when she was ever in the house. She must have spent some time there. She must have had a bedroom; maybe just being alone and trying to recall would help bring back some memories that lay deep in her mind.

"Mom? Mom? Dad?" Out of habit she called out to them after she stepped into the foyer.

She took in the entire foyer, searching for any kind of markings on the walls she might recognize, marks on the wooden floor that she might have put there, and that, if she was ever there, happened long ago. She may have been in that foyer earlier in her life, but it was not familiar to her now.

In the living room, the plastic coverings that were over the furniture were removed and left folded on the floor next to the couch. She noticed that her mother had found the opportunity to dust and rearrange the chairs and lamps. She walked to the brown leather chair that sat in the corner facing the hallway and front door. The chair was the one thing she remembered from her childhood. She bent down and ran her hand across the smooth-leather-texture of the arm until she hit the graininess of the chair's wear. Bending further, she ran her hand across the seat, and when she found the same coarse texture, she let out a loud sigh of relief. She recognized the chair, or thought she did.

She eased down in the chair feeling the wholeness of it, stretching out her arms and legs. Laying her head against its back, she closed her eyes and tried to remember when she and her father had sat together and he taught her to read. She knew it had happened the way she thought, she knew it. Her parents for some reason just couldn't remember; that was all there was to it. She closed her eyes and tried to remember.

One day when she'd come home from school, she had told her father that the children made fun of her because she couldn't read as well as they. She stood in the kitchen and announced to her mother and father, through a stream of tears, that she refused to return to school until she learned to read and stomped off to her room. She had carried on as if learning to read would happen when her mother or father handed her a book. But her father knew how she felt and the next day, he went to her in her room with a book, the story of the *Three Little Bears*, and asked if he could read it to her.

After that day, he brought home more books and read her those stories. He also taught her some of the words in the stories and made word cards for her. She had a desire to learn to read so badly, and more importantly, she wanted the kids to stop teasing her so much so, she practiced with those word cards from the minute she arrived home from school until it was bedtime.

On the nights when she tossed and turned unable to sleep after her father had finished reading and gone back to his room, she would get up and read more during the night. Within a few weeks after she'd learned more, she began reading whole pages of the stories to her father, with his help on a few of the words. Whenever he began a new story, Olivia would interrupt him and ask many questions. She found it hard to understand what a runt was, and why someone would want to get rid of an animal because it was born different from the others. Nor could she understand how a twelve-year-old boy survived the wilderness for so long. Her father did his best in answering her. He told her that they were just stories and stories were not always true. She laughed with her father through *The Wizard of Oz*, cried during parts of *Charlotte's Web*, hid her face during the reading of *Hatchet*, and stood with her hands on her hips on *Bridge to Terabithia*. She remembered these things happening, but her memory failed her when it came to where these things happened. When she thought about these times before, she saw herself in the brown leather chair where she sat now. She remembered she referred to it as "the settee." She named it that because she found it in one of the stories that her father used to read to her. She recalled turning the pages, and now looking back, she saw a man's hand, turning the pages with her. It was her father. The only man she had ever known as her father.

When she was older and had learned to read better, her father took her to the library, showed her how to use the internet and when she had to write a paper or an essay, he helped her with those. She remembered all of these things. She remembered begging her mother to take her to the bookstore to buy *Charlotte's Web*.

But, no matter how hard she tried to remember her early life, she still had trouble imagining herself before she was seven or eight years old and she questioned that. Whenever she thought of this, she became more and more frightened of what she was trying to hide, and why she refused to let it surface. She prevented herself from remembering. That evilness, that curse that surrounded her was so horrific that she refused to remember. She had tucked it away so deep inside her that it would never come out. She had to find out and now, she was determined to find out who she was before she was seven or eight years of age. She was stuck and in order to move on she had to find out and figure out how to move on.

Leon with his birthmark in the shape of Italy along his right jaw line flashed through her mind. Before she had a chance to reflect on Leon and his scar, the front door rattled and her mother opened the door and came rushing in. Olivia stood up when she saw her mother, and the vague image of Leon with the birthmark disappeared.

"Oh, Livvy, honey. You scared me."

"I don't want to intrude, Mom."

"Your father asked me about the insurance policy, so I ran home to get it. Is everything okay?"

"I just wanted some space to think. That's all."

"I have to get back. Some kind of rodents made a hole in the side of the store and got inside the crawl space. Your father boarded it up, but we have to call a professional. I have to get back. Is there something that you need?"

"Mom, I'm sure that dad and I sat in this chair, right here," she turned and pointed to the chair, "and read stories. He taught me how to read right here in this very chair."

"Livvy, he taught you how to read, but not in that chair. I don't know what you want us to say."

"Did I read with some other man? My real father, did I read with him?"

JUDY KELLY

She hated to use the words "real father." It was upsetting to her mother and father. At this point, she had no choice.

Her mother gave her a look like a person who had just taken a chance on running to the bathroom nude, and was caught in the hallway. "We talked about this before. You—,"

"I'm sorry, Mom. I really am. . . ."

The phone rang and her mother went to answer it. Olivia heard her whispering something. When her mother returned, she waved the insurance policy at Olivia, and headed toward the front door.

"Honey we'll talk about this later. Your father is waiting for this right now."

"Will you, mom, will you? Something's wrong. You and dad keep putting this off."

Her mother opened the door and started out. She turned around to Olivia. "Why can't you just leave it alone? You're our daughter now. Livvy, you're our beautiful daughter, now." She turned around and left.

After a few minutes, those words sunk in and Olivia grabbed her purse, ran to the door and out on the porch, but her mother was half-way down the street by then.

She went back to the living room to sit in the chair again. "Why can't you leave it alone?" Her mother's words ran through her mind and crowded out anything else. Leave what alone? Why should she leave whatever "it" was alone?

Over the years, her parents talked very little about the fact that she was adopted and she was so happy with them that she had no need to bring it up either. When she got older, she remembered thinking how she hated herself for growing up and becoming a teen where it just wasn't cool to have her mother or father kiss her good-bye or drive her home from school, or even go on a family vacation. She wasn't quite finished with their show of love, and she needed them to continue doing and saying loving things to her, different from what the other teens said they needed from their parents. Now for some reason, her past wanted to find its way out of her deep dark crevices where she must have had everything neatly and securely hidden, and confront her. She never had a reason to want to find out about her real parents, or even broach the subject until now. She just thought they died somehow, or worse, was glad to be rid of her. Her mother's words now made her feel like she would not love her parents anymore. She loved them more than anyone believed possible. But she had to find out about her past, brace herself, and deal with whatever she uncovered. She folded her hands, knelt down in front of the brown leather chair and prayed.

* * *

When Olivia entered the prison, two guards took her directly to the usual meeting room. While she sat waiting on Leon, she watched for Wesley. He wasn't there to accompany her, as was his usual manner. Before she was able to think more about it, she heard the sounds of Leon's feet dragging across the floor and his chains hitting against each other. When she saw him, she almost smiled, but stopped herself. She was happy that he wanted to open up, but he was still a convict and convicts tried to take advantage. She couldn't let him think that she was weak and if he tried, he could take advantage of her. The guards sat him down and chained him to the table as usual.

"You came back to see me, huh?"

He made it sound like she volunteered.

"Yes, you asked remember?"

He gave her a depreciatory look.

He needed to believe that she came back on her own. "I agreed to come back again," she said, giving in to him. This was his last week and maybe a little give here and there wouldn't hurt.

He gave her a quick smile.

"Tell me more about your children, Leon. Can you talk to me about them?"

"You want to know about my kids? Why?"

"I don't know. Maybe it'll help me understand you."

"Nobody understands me. Sometimes I don't understand me." He looked around the room, toward the guards, back at her. "I love my kids, every one of them. I know I favored one over all the others, but I love them all."

She heard something in his voice, a slight stop, a quiver.

"I took them to Disney World every year. My six oldest went to college and are now doctors and lawyers and we had a Christmas tree every year and all the kids hung their ornaments on it."

Olivia scowled.

When he saw her frown, Leon broke out in another one of his loud laughs. "Well, what did you want me to say?"

"I thought you'd tell me a little about your family. I thought you'd tell me something true."

He looked at her, and down at the table. He tried to move closer as if he wanted to share a secret with her.

"We lived on a farm. We worked the farm growing tomatoes, potatoes and a little corn. Then we sold it when we could. Our life was different, not like everyone else, but we got by. The older ones showed the younger ones what to do." Leon sat back and when he spoke again, he seemed to be delving into his past. "They missed out on some things they wanted and sometimes we all had to go to bed hungry. They needed new clothes, but we managed. I had to. I had to keep them with me. They were mine and I had to keep them with me."

"What do you mean?"

"Sometimes, one or two of them would get the idea to leave, and I just had to keep them with me. That's all."

Olivia thought she'd leave that alone. The article that she read in the library said that he chained the children to things in the house and to each other. She sensed he was being very careful about what he said to her.

"What did you and your children do together?"

"We did a lot of gardening. They liked playing in the woods, but I made them promise not to go too far. They liked catching crickets and fireflies. Things like that."

"You know, I read this article once about a woman who had fifteen children. Fifteen children. Can you imagine?" She paused and smiled. "I would have trouble remembering their names." She laughed. "Do you miss them?"

"Yeah, I do."

"Why did they want to leave?"

"Leave? Naw. They weren't gonna leave me."

"I'm sorry, I misunderstood. Did any of them go to school?"

"I did that whatchacallit kind of school." He snapped his fingers, thinking.

"The kind you do at home."

"Home school?"

"Yeah, that. I taught them what they need to know at home."

"You understood your children."

"Pretty much. I had a lot, but it was easy for me to keep up with them. I remember not only their names, but what they were like. I liked to think of them with the names that I gave them, names that meant something to me, to us, more than to outsiders."

"How did you come up with the names?"

"I remember when each of them was born and how I took each one of them in my arms and promised them my love and that I would take care of them. You know, babies are so tiny and beautiful." He gave the last word an extra syllable. "They need their parents to help them grow and understand things, you know?"

"You had a special relationship with each one." Even though she couldn't see how that was possible, she was surprised to hear him say it given his current status. But she was learning Leon and Leon seemed to believe he did everything right.

"They need us to give them food and love and shelter. It would be mean to try and take any of that away from a baby. I liked to watch them grow up and learn to walk and to talk, but I don't like no back talk. Whenever they gave me back talk, they got in real trouble with me. I always told them no back talk. When I tell you to do something, you do it."

"Tell me about the one who left."

"My daughter. She left. That's all for now."

"Tell me about Tony?"

"Tony was a good boy. Remember, he was my first child and he never gave me no back talk. I loved that boy. I was so sorry he caught AIDS. He wasn't able to defend himself and gave in to the ugliness that goes on in here. He just got used too much. I'm sorry about that. Really, I am. He was a good boy."

She wanted to know more, yet was afraid to ask for fear he would shut down.

"The past. All this is in the past. That's all I have now. You know something? I wish I could do my life all over again, no I wish I had a different life."

"I guess we all would like that," Olivia said.

"Yeah, but some of us should have had another life."

"What do you mean? Who are you talking about?" Olivia asked.

"My mother."

"Tell me about her. When I asked before you got angry with me for bringing her up. Maybe now, you can talk about her a little. And if you want to, we can pray about it."

"My mother and I lived in one room. She always had a man in her bed and I slept on the floor in the closet so I wouldn't hear them or see what went on. I don't remember a father, that's why I wanted to be a good father to my children. I heard someone say that a person can only be as good as they know how. I was too young to figure out what a good father or mother was supposed to do. I went to school whenever it was convenient for her. If she was entertaining, then I went. If not, I had to stay home and clean up the mess that she and whoever she brought home made the night before. I never learned to read good and never made it to high school. Schooling wasn't important to her. I was important because I helped her do things. Things I can't talk about."

He paused for a moment; his face held that faraway stare and she knew he was going to a place deep inside him that perhaps even he had never been before.

"When I was ten years old, I was ready to run away. I had had it and at ten. I couldn't take anymore. My mother told me that she was pregnant and that the man who was the father wasn't going to have any more to do with her. The morning she told him she was pregnant, he put his clothes on and left. He never returned. Before that, he was pretty regular, coming round, and I know she thought they would have something other than him just coming over for sex whenever he was able. He was married and when I found out, I didn't see how he would leave his wife. I followed him home one day. I saw him and his wife had a much better life than we had. His wife was also pretty. That's how I knew that when he left, he wasn't coming back, and I never saw him again. She kept hoping even up till the day the baby was born. But I knew. We couldn't go to no hospital, so I had to help her with the baby when he was born."

"You had to help with the delivery of her baby?"

"There just weren't nobody else. She hadn't asked no one in the rooming house to help us. After the baby was born, I had to watch him and take care of him. I was ten. I didn't know what to do. What my mother told me to do was all I knew to do."

"She gave the baby away?"

"No." He gave off a deep sigh and then he paused.

She wanted him to continue talking. He was talking about his past. He continued before she had a chance to ask him to go on.

"It was during his nap one afternoon and she was gone. I had to take care of him again. I went into the bathroom, and when I came out, I found him dead. When she got home, I tried to explain to her what happened. She blamed me for his death. I had to go down the hall to the bathroom. She should have understood that, don't you think?"

"She blamed you? Why would she do that? You were ten."

"Yeah, but she blamed me and for the longest time. Thing is, I can't get that image out of my mind and I still have nightmares about seeing his face under water in the bathroom sink. I still feel the baby's squishy neck and still see the life go out of the baby."

Olivia tried not to seem stunned or shocked, but she was. Before she was able to regain herself, the two guards entered the room. Something rumbled through her head and she wasn't able to hear anything they might have said. They undid his chains. Leon stared at her and she kept his stare. She wanted the truth. Was that what he'd just told her? The guards took him out, as he continued holding her stare. He must have been searching for a reaction to his story or rather nightmare? She tried not to give him what he wanted. Then she reminded herself that he had had a nightmare no doubt due to the huge responsibility that his mother had dumped on him when he was ten.

After Leon left to return to his cell, Wesley appeared. She and Wesley walked toward the entrance.

"Are you all ready for the graduation ceremony?" he asked.

She tried to turn away from him, but she couldn't. She saw gentleness in his eyes, the soft touches of the curves around his mouth, the easy way he had of talking to her. Not the same pain in his face she saw the day before. Not to mention that he just wasn't the prison guard type. She realized that she had made a decision about not becoming a priest and only her father and Fr. Wilson knew about it. She still hadn't told anyone else. Maybe she was holding it open. Maybe deep down inside she wanted to change her mind about that decision.

"Oh, I don't want to pry—"

"You're not prying."

"Oh?"

"I'm getting myself ready. Or at least I will be on Sunday."

"Well, I hope you have a wonderful ceremony as I know you will. I was just wondering; is the public invited?"

"Invitations are given to family members and friends."

"Oh, I see. I only ask because I would like to attend."

"Wesley," She paused for a long moment,

"What is it?"

"I . . . Wesley, I'm sorry. I have to go."

She turned to leave, but he took her by the arm and gently turned her around toward him.

"What is it?" His voice was low, but strong.

She didn't quite know what to do with this man. She really liked him, but was it right for her to saddle him with her problems? He seemed nice enough, and she wanted more from him, but was he only nice because she needed someone to help her with Leon? She continued to study his face for a long moment longer, weighing the benefits of telling or not telling him.

"I don't plan to become a priest." She just blurted it out.

For a moment, he seemed okay with her plan. He made no effort to lecture her. He just kept his eyes on hers.

"I do plan to graduate," she said in a nervous high tone.

"This is what you're supposed to do?" he asked.

"I don't know what I'm supposed to do. I don't feel I do much good here."

"I don't think Leon would agree."

"He has made a change. We did pray together after dancing around it and avoiding it every day," Olivia said.

"What do you plan to do about your gift?" he asked.

She wished she could just reach up and caress his face, give him a passionate kiss. Just when she needed something, he came along and handed it to her.

"I would love for you to attend. You know the seminary in Virginia, right?"

"Yes, I do. I have all the information. I'll be there."

"I'll let my parents know, so they'll watch for you."

She almost let slip out, the words "I love you," and just before they poured out of her throat and tumbled passed her lips, she stopped them and she let out a slight grunt, instead.

As he looked down at her, she saw his eyes glisten and he gave off a long heavy sigh.

When she held out her hand to him to say good-bye, he took it and kissed it.

* * *

When she got in her car, she realized she was breathing hard and took several deep breaths before she started the car. Her gift. Her gift to pray, to love, to do good works, to do God's work. He reminded her of her gift—the reason why Fr. Wilson chose her for the prayer group leader.

The reason why Fr. Wilson asked her to pray with Leon.

The reason she insisted on praying with Tony in the hospital.

Her gift—the gift that helped her see her connection to her God and the thing He had given her. She had to remember that she had to use her gift. It would help her deal with everything she had before her now.

CHAPTER 17

Just before Olivia reached her townhouse, her cell phone rang. A man who identified himself as a bartender at Wonderers' Tavern asked her to pick up her sister, Kara; his tone bland his message short. She barely had time to pull over to take down the address; he hung up before she had a chance to ask anything. Olivia hoped it was good news. She had to believe it was good news. She needed to be optimistic for her sister. She wanted to be happy over the fact that Kara had found a job and was writing a story about alcohol. Or maybe about people in bars. Or any writing assignment. But there was something in the bartender's voice and abrupt manner that made her feel otherwise.

Olivia entered the dimly lit almost empty barroom. When she panned the area, she was drawn to a woman, and a group of men in the back near the kitchen door. There, she noticed Kara balancing herself, arms out, and walking on the edge of one of the long and empty steam tables, as if she were walking a tightrope in a circus. Olivia's heart sank. She would have given anything to know that Kara was working on a story. Kara was dressed in a white, low-cut blouse and a skin-tight blue skirt that stopped mid-way up her thin, but muscular thighs. The skirt was so tight that when Kara turned sharply to go back the opposite direction on the steam table, she couldn't take a wide enough step and almost lost her balance. Arms extended and rocking sideways, she managed to steady herself before she tried to walk again. A man dressed in shorts and a T-shirt, and who was sweaty like he'd just finished taking his run, stood up to help her. He reached out his hand, but she ignored it. "Whoooa," she said now bending over. She eased herself up, and waved her arms. She suddenly stopped to give some kind of speech to the other two men sitting at one of the tables. But Olivia saw it as "drunk talk"– idle prattle from people who drink too much.

Kara's "table trapeze" act reminded Olivia of the year when Kara, her parents and she went to the zoo one fall afternoon when they were still newcomers to England. She and Kara, being the same age, were seven or eight at the time. Olivia had never been to a zoo and couldn't wait to see the animals. Her father had told her not to try to touch any of the animals. After they had just arrived, Kara said she wanted to go see the lions first. She ran off and the other three followed her. Before anyone knew it, Kara had climbed up on the stone wall that separated the lion exhibit from the spectators. "Get down," her mother tried calling to her several times and extended her hand. Still Kara wouldn't get down. She kept saying things like, "Look at me. See what I can do?" Then, when she was about to stand on one foot, her father snatched her off the wall. She fell and scraped her knee. Both her parents were so angry that they left the zoo right then. Still holding on to Kara, her father marched her straight to the car and then drove everyone home.

He was so angry that not one word came out of his mouth the entire way and he never took his eyes from whatever he saw in front of him. Throughout the drive home, her mother continued with questions. "What were you thinking about? You could have been killed. Do you realize you put everybody in jeopardy? Why on earth would you do anything like that? You embarrassed us all, your father, your sister and me. Why Kara? Why would you do anything like that?"

After Olivia got in the backseat, she pulled the armrest down, separating the two of them. The more anger and barrage of questions their mother threw out, the more Olivia recoiled from Kara until she had pressed herself to the door and held onto the door handle for the entire trip home. Kara never said anything to defend herself.

As Olivia thought about that, she also remembered what her mother told her about her sister—that Kara took dangerous assignments. Olivia remembered when Kara took an assignment deep in the jungles of South America where an American student traveling with friends had been kidnapped by what was discovered a gang. The gang members had made the student contact his family for ransom money. Somehow, Kara had found out where the gang was hiding out. She put a camera crew together, and found a group of soldiers from somewhere—Olivia never did understand that. They went into the jungles to get the student. A group of reporters had followed behind at what they thought was a safe distance. Olivia remembered Kara's comments in an interview when the officials rounded up the gang members, even those who tried to escape. She had said that the U.S. Embassy, government, and soldiers were too slow in saving the student.

"No one has the right to capture another person and hold them for ransom. Or hold them against their will. We are human beings to love and cherish. You can't just take people and do what you want with them. You can't just do that," Kara said, facing the camera.

The reporter asked her, "Weren't you afraid?"

Kara's answer surprised Olivia.

"I'm never afraid because God is with me. He protects me."

"Do you honestly believe that?" the reporter asked.

"Look around you. You yourself arrived here safely. How do you think that happened? The student will go home, back to his family where he belongs. How do you think that could happen? Who do you think kept you safe today?" Kara even sounded offended.

Olivia thought about something her mother almost said—Kara went into danger. Now, as she watched her sister on that steamtable she thought about another time she went into danger. It was when a father had taken his daughter and fled to Canada. The court had denied him custody or even the opportunity to see his daughter without supervision because he was accused of sexually abusing her. Kara did her research and found him in a house in Canada where he had his daughter locked in a bedroom. Again, she somehow found a group of what might have been soldiers, talked to the Canadian police, found a camera crew and a group of reporters from somewhere who all followed her to the man's house. The man held them at bay with several blasts from a shotgun that damaged two police cars. The police had refused to rush the house saying that the daughter could get hurt. Kara just walked up to the front door and told the man to let her in and that she was there to tell his side of the story. When she found out the man had his daughter locked up she made the father unlock the door and release his daughter to her. Then Kara and the daughter left while police took the man in custody. Most of the facts about what happened were unclear. Kara refused to give all the details, but she did walk out of that house with the daughter by her side. Olivia wasn't sure which made the better story Kara's over done bravery, or the man taking his daughter out of the country. Certainly, both made front-page news and it must have been a long while before the community would talk about other things.

As Olivia crossed the bar and moved closer to the group, she saw another man in jeans and a jeans jacket who seemed to be trying to get Kara down from the table, by standing beside her and running his hand up the inside of her thighs.

"Come on, let's get out of here," said Jeans.

Kara took his hand away, and jumped down off the steam table. She grabbed Jeans by his belt, pulled him close to her and kissed him. She pushed herself close to him. Then pulled away from him and stumbled over to the other two men, laughing and swaying.

"I need another drink," she said.

Jeans motioned for the bartender to bring Kara another drink. The bartender shook his head. "No," he yelled back, "and don't climb up on that steam table again."

"She's had enough. Don't do that," said the runner seated at the table.

"I just need another drink. That'll make it all right. I swear it will," Kara slurred out. The other men laughed.

The runner at the table took her by the hand and sat her down in one of the chairs at the table. "I'll call a cab for you. You need to go home."

Olivia looked at the bartender who found a cloth and began wiping down the bar.

"I want another drink. If you want to do something for me, get me another drink."

"Come on, lady. Let me put you in a cab. Where's your coat and bag?" the runner continued.

"I'll take her home," Olivia said walking toward the group. "Thanks for helping."

"Oh, my sister, the priest. Everybody, look. My sister. She's a priest." Kara stretched out each syllable. "You know what they can do." She let out a loud laugh. "She can preach the good word," Kara said in a louder voice, hands in the air.

At this moment, Olivia wanted to shake her sister, bring her to her senses. She wanted Kara to be all right, to face whatever was bothering her. She wanted Kara to stop drinking and get a grip on herself, tell someone whatever this thing was that bothered her.

Olivia managed to get Kara into her car and fastened the seat belt across her.

"You're upset with me, I know," Kara said, singing and stretching out her words.

"Silly me. I actually thought you had a job."

Kara laughed and laughed. "You, you," she pointed to Olivia, "you thought I had a job? Doing what?"

"Writing a story about alcohol or alcoholics or something. I mean the bartender asked me to pick you up in a bar. I wasn't thinking you—,"

"What? Would stoop this low? Go on say it. You, the priest, didn't think your sister would stoop this low."

Olivia refused to respond. It would do nothing but encourage the disagreement. She glanced over at her sister and, mercifully, Kara had fallen asleep. A light snoring created a boundary between these two sisters.

When they arrived home, Olivia managed to get Kara to bed. After Kara was changed and all tucked in and she had dozed off to sleep, Olivia sat on the edge of the bed surveying her sister trying to understand what happened to her. Olivia folded her hands and tried to recall her early life, tried to recall the exact point in her life when Kara changed. Her earliest memory of Kara was when they first met in elementary school. Was it second grade, or third grade? Olivia knew she lived in England yet, in the few times she tried to recall her earlier life, she couldn't tell where she was and thinking about her earlier life always left her so confused. She saw the two of them coming home from school, but they parted ways. She saw herself walking through woods. Whenever she tried to recall anything about the woods, she had an unnerving sense of vulnerability that caused her to push those thoughts out of her mind.

Nevertheless, she tried hard to see farther into the woods, but her memory wouldn't allow her. Olivia tried to remember whether she and Kara were friends or just in the same class. When they parted ways in the woods, where did they each go? There were instances Kara's face came to her when she tried to remember anything about a house. Maybe she and Kara played in the woods. Since it was hard for her to recall, she should find someone who asked the right questions to help her remember. A memory therapist, she needed a memory therapist, if there was such a person. Maybe a therapist could help, but more than likely, they never had the close friendship that Olivia thought they had or rather, wanted them to have had.

Until now, she hadn't worried about remembering, but now she would give almost anything to know what kind of life she'd had before she was seven. Whatever happened in those woods, whoever she was then, wouldn't be the same person she is now. For reasons not clear to her, she had blocked it out of her mind. Then there was the strong possibility that what she recalled would be a distortion of reality— a trick of the mind that sometimes fills in the gaps.

Her father had once told her that she was their child now, and showed her some papers he said were adoption papers. He read portions to her, but she was too young to understand what it all meant. Recalling this, she remembered a feeling of relief, of being made new, of being in a new family, a feeling that she would be free. She even felt a little happy. However, at the time, she couldn't put words to what she felt, and very soon after, the four of them moved to England. This part of her life happened so quickly and she was so young that there was no time for her to think, time to decide whether she would like her new parents. No time for her to understand where she was going; or whether or not her new parents would like her.

Olivia only had a few clothes. Since she was close to Kara's size, Kara shared some of her clothes with Olivia. When they arrived in England, she recalled that her mother bought her new things. Olivia loved her blue pleated skirt and white shirt with the round collar. Her mother bought it for her the minute she saw Olivia marveling at the skirt and shirt on the rack in the department store. She was fascinated with her new clothes, shoes, and she had her own room. She made herself part of the family.

Olivia recalled that when she had gone to school, the other children knew more than she did, could do things she couldn't, and she couldn't read. She remembered now, that she was so busy catching up, making herself part of her new family, loving them, accepting them, so that they would love and accept her, that she forgot everything about her past. She wanted it that way. Relief. That's what she felt when she went with the Douglasses. Relief. Freedom. And, later she felt love.

For a while, Kara told everyone that Olivia saved her from hurting herself in the woods, except Olivia never remembered saving Kara from anything. Olivia remembered how happy Kara was when she was accepted to college. Kara wanted to attend The Walter Cronkite School of Journalism at Arizona State University in the U.S. She told everyone that she had been accepted there and she had planned to leave for the United States and spend the next four years of her life becoming a journalist. But she attended another university instead. Olivia wasn't certain what happened. She thought it had to do with the expense of that school. Kara had gotten into a screaming match with their mother and father and in the end, Kara ended up attending the University of London. When Olivia graduated, she also went to the University of London. When they were in college together, and they ran into each other on campus, Kara usually waved and, had a reason to leave. "I'll see you at home," she would always say. She claimed that her classes and assignments kept her so busy that there was no time to even do the few things that they used to do outside of school. Olivia tried not to feel hurt or abandoned; she, too, had to attend more to her studies.

For years Olivia tried to make herself believe that it wasn't possible for Kara to have overheard Troy when he had called her a retard in the spring, just before Kara had graduated and gone on to high school. She saw Kara's back that day, and reasoned that it could have been anyone, but in her heart, she knew it was Kara. At that time, she needed Kara, needed her sister to stand up for her. Kara turned her back on her and Olivia was hurt by it, so she fooled herself into believing that Kara never saw or heard what happened. That day had been wearing on them both since then and had brought them to this point.

CHAPTER 18

Leon leaned on the table as much as he could. "One last time," he said.

Leon's "puppy dog" appearance made Olivia feel sorry for him.

"That's okay. You don't have to say anything."

Olivia took comfort in that. Nothing else came to her mind.

"How's that man of yours treating you? He showing you some respect? Giving you what you need?"

"Leon, I'm fine."

"I thought I told you to get rid of him, anyway. You don't need nobody that mistreats you. You the kind of woman a man needs to do things for. You need a good man to take care of you."

"I appreciate your concern. Thank you. How are you doing?" she said almost in a whisper.

He looked down at the table and then up at her. "Yeah, I'm sad. I'm real sad today. Tomorrow's my last day on this earth. Nothing more for me after tomorrow."

Olivia wished she had more to say to him. This was her last day with Leon. She found it sad that, like Tony, he lived a life that he didn't want to live. It was his choice to follow that lifestyle even after he knew he wanted a different life. At this point, he wasn't in need of advice and she wasn't sure where he'd end up. She could make no promises.

"I guess the only thing I'd be remembered for is what they say I've done."

"I know no one will remember me when I'm gone," she said, trying to brighten his spirits as much as possible.

"You kidding? Even in here, the inmates mention the men whose time is up."

"Any last wishes?"

Leon laughed.

"What's funny?"

"You wouldn't believe my last wish."

"Why? What is it?"

"Never mind. You'd just really believe that I'm some kind of freak."

She thought he meant it as a joke and wanted to laugh, but held back. "It's up to you. I'm willing to listen if you want to tell me."

"I always wanted to know what happened to my daughter, my first girl child."

"She was the one who left, right?" asked Olivia.

"Yeah, she left."

"Leon, how did she leave?"

He peered at Olivia and down at the table, again.

"I wish I knew how she made out. I wonder what she's doing now." He paused. "I told you someone told me that she was dead, but I don't guess I believe that."

"Why?"

"I don't know. Maybe I just want one of my children to turn out good."

"But you don't know what happened to her after she left?"

"No."

"You genuinely cared for your children."

"Don't get me wrong. As I said, I loved all my children, but for some reason, she was special to me. She would be about your age. She had spunk, you know? She was a little stubborn about doing what I asked, but she'd do something nice for me, you know? We had a special relationship. I would do anything for that little girl."

Olivia watched him, a million questions she could ask, but dared not. Leon must have guessed that she had questions. He continued talking.

"Not that I wanted her to leave. But I guess she wasn't happy with me." He paused.

"Why would she be unhappy?"

"She was adopted, or went to a home; one. I don't know."

Olivia was a little puzzled by the look on Leon's face. She questioned whether he was telling her the truth, but there was no point in challenging it.

"Do you know her adopted family or the home where she went?"

"She was about nine or ten maybe younger when she left."

"That's a long time ago. Any idea where she is now or where she went when she left?"

"No. But if she's still alive, she'd probably be married with a bunch of kids."

"Why are you thinking about her now?"

"I just, I wish, I just want her to forgive me. I loved her, but . . . ."

"Why would she need to forgive you? I don't understand."

"She always wanted to go to school."

"Did she attend school?"

"When she couldn't go, she asked me to teach her how to read."

"Did you?"

"I did the best I could. We had an old leather chair that I found, and we would sit in that chair and she would pretend to read to me. I couldn't teach her much. I never learnt to read myself."

Olivia thought about the memory she had of her own father sitting with her in a big leather chair while he taught her how to read. She understood Leon's need to hold on to that memory.

"I always wanted to go to school, learn to read. My daughter made me see the things that I wanted. I hope she went off and got those things for herself. But somehow, I doubt it. I guess you could say she didn't get a good start."

"I'm sure she hasn't forgotten you."

"What do they teach you at that church about heaven?"

"I can tell you what I believe heaven is like for me. The Bible talks about a land where there is nothing but love and peace. Heaven is a place where we will all be free."

"Free?"

"Yes. Free from harm, free from disease, free from any disability, free from the ugliness in this country now, like shootings, and war, diseases, heart attacks and other ailments."

"Free from parents making you do things you don't want to do," Leon added.

"In heaven, everything is love and beauty. The sky is the most beautiful shade of blue anyone has ever seen,"

"Yes, with big puffy clouds that float by," Leon said.

"And the grass is the most beautiful shade of green, and so comfortable that you'd want to walk on it, sit on it, lie down on it and never get cut by a blade." Olivia paused, then, continued. "The seas and waters are clear and pure and you can see the bottoms, and you can see yourself in any part of it. You can play in all the water, swim in it for miles and miles, and never get tired."

"People all get along, say nice things to each other," Leon said.

"And show how much they love each other by doing nice things for each other," Olivia said.

"Yes, that's good," Leon said.

"As they go about their heavenly work with the angels to help us all who are still on earth. In heaven, Leon, everything is beautiful; everything is perfect, everything is love."

He held his head down, voice cracking slightly, "Do you think someone like me can go to a place like that, to heaven?" Leon paused, eyes still facing down at the table. "No, never mind. Don't answer that."

"That's important to you, isn't it?"

"Naw. They said some bad things about me and I guess I have to pay for that. I'm willing to do that." He turned his head up.

"You do understand that I won't be here tomorrow. A priest will come and be with you all day or for as long as you want."

"You have to come and see me off. When I look through that glass, it would be nice to see you. No one else will be there for me."

"One thing you'll be happy about. You'll see Tony again."

"Thanks for saying that. That makes me happy."

The guards entered the room to take Leon away. She thought she saw him fighting back tears. When he turned to get up, she saw his birthmark again. She almost asked him about it, but restrained herself, instead.

"I'll see you tomorrow, okay? Look, I have a CD radio player and some CDs that Tony bought for me on my birthday one year. They're the things that mean anything to me. I want you to take them when I leave tomorrow, okay?"

She nodded. The fact that these two men had birthdays surprised her and Leon's sentimental feelings about his son's birthday gift astonished her even more. She saw the "humanness" in this man aside from what he did, and understood that she never got to see his other side. She wanted to ask more about his birthday, but the guards pulled him out of the room.

Fr. Wilson suggested that she find herself. She was beginning to see herself differently. Even though she thought of herself as someone who loved people, she now saw she hadn't understood people. She had opened her mind and her heart to this man—one of God's children—and saw someone different from the man she met on her first visit two weeks ago. Fr. Wilson asked her to open her heart and her mind and now she liked the new person she found in herself.

On her way down the hall, she thought how sad it was that Leon had no one who cared enough for him to attend his execution and the only other person who meant so much to him wasn't aware that tomorrow will be his last day.

CHAPTER 19

On Friday, Leon's last day, Olivia arrived at the prison, thirty minutes before midnight, and the requirement by the warden. Wesley took her to see Mr. Breen, the Warden. Mr. Breen explained his policy to Olivia and told her what she would see. She would not be allowed to talk to Leon. The warden seemed very strict about each man on death row spending as much time as he needed, even up to his last moment, with a priest on his last day. Olivia had no reason to interfere with the warden's policy. He explained the injection process that would end Leon's life and asked if she had questions. When she had none, Wesley walked her to the observation room.

Even though the warden explained to her that people who would witness the procedure would be present, still she was surprised to see so many people in the room. She sat next to an elderly woman who was bent over so far that her head seemed to rest in her lap. She had a cane next to her and her presence seemed out of place. Everyone else was obviously there for official reasons. A guard entered the room and handed Olivia a sealed letter with the words, "Open only after I'm gone" and "signed Sunny," scrawled across the front of the envelope. He also handed her a CD player and several CDs. Olivia glanced at each of the CDs to get an idea of Leon's taste in music. They were mostly country artists and she was not familiar with those artists.

There were so many things she wanted to know about Leon—his relationship with his daughter, what happened to his mother, and his strange family structure and why he wanted children. Maybe he would not have wanted to answer these questions. Now it's too late. Anything she wasn't able to find out about him would go with him when he closed his eyes for the last time.

She held the sealed letter in her lap. Sunny? Sunny? The sound of the name as she whispered it to herself wasn't recognizable to her. Did the guard give this to the right person? At that moment, the curtain that was drawn across the large glass window opened up and the guards brought Leon into the room, in chains. She questioned the need for chains, but anything to make this ordeal easier for him, even chains. The guards put him on the table, secured his legs and arms, and head, and removed the other chains from around his waist and hands.

Even though his movements were controlled, Leon strained and tried to look around at the guards on his left. He tried to turn to his right and then turned his head toward the viewing glass.

He let out a large smile to Olivia and he mouthed, "Thank you for coming."

The Warden asked Leon if he had final words.

"I'm so sorry. I meant no one any harm. I wish I could go to that place where everyone loves one another and everything is perfect. Thank you, Olivia Douglass."

He nodded to the Warden.

The Warden looked at his watch, held up his hand.

Then he lowered his hand and nodded first to the doctor, then to Wesley standing next to the doctor.

Wesley injected a needle through a tube that was connected to Leon's arm while the doctor took Leon's pulse and did something Olivia couldn't quite see to Leon's chest.

Leon batted his eyes several times.

Leon let out a loud sigh as he took his last breath.

Wesley stood watching him for several minutes as if he couldn't believe what had just happened. Then he turned toward the glass and nodded his head.

One of the guards drew the curtains.

The witnesses got up to leave.

The woman next to Olivia began to sob loudly, and Olivia turned to her and touched her arm. She continued to sob while nodding her head at Olivia. Then she quieted down and rose to leave.

Alone and in the half-darkness of the small viewing room, Olivia wasn't able to move. Somberness enveloped her, a drabness that momentarily paralyzed her. Even though Leon had taken the lives of many, she now felt his absence. A guard entered the execution room, drew back the curtains and Olivia noticed that there was nothing in the room that indicated Leon was ever there. The straps that kept him in place were no longer visible, and the bed was absent its covering. Leon never existed. That's what the death penalty is all about. The act of eliminating a person, or making the situation of the person's life so that he never existed.

She looked up when she saw Wesley enter the observation room. She turned to face the glass and toward the now empty table on the other side as if she thought that Leon would reappear. This was her first experience witnessing death. One minute, Leon lived and breathed, the next minute, his body devoid of life, limp, inert, overwhelmed her. It all went so fast, she wasn't able to grasp the moment. The swiftness, unexpectedness of the moment was too abrupt for her and images of the things she read about his life flooded her brain. The little girl cowering in the corner covering her eyes flashed through her mind. Wesley sat down beside her and held her hand for a moment. He must have realized what she was feeling.

She turned to Wesley. "It's all over, isn't it? Leon is gone."

He turned toward her.

She was puzzled when she saw tears in his eyes. She knew he had seen executions before, he'd told her that.

"Wesley?"

"I'm relieved."

"I don't understand."

"Olivia, this was my last week, too."

She was confused. "You never said anything."

"I wasn't fired, if that's what you're thinking."

"Why?"

"I was just here temporarily."

"What will you do?"

"Go back to practicing law. I know you're going to hate me for saying this, and it's the reason I haven't mentioned it before, but I had to see Leon executed. I know that sounds harsh and it was hard for me to tell you this at first. I thought you'd find out. I started to tell you several times, but then, I couldn't bring myself to talk about it."

"Find out what? What do you want to tell me?"

Wesley opened his mouth, "I," he began then shook his head.

"Whatever it is, you can tell me."

Wesley cast his eyes down at his hands folded in his lap. Then he looked directly at her. "Leon abducted my older sister. I promised my mother—the lady who sat next to you—that I would find Leon and see him executed." He waited. "Maybe my mother will be able to find peace now."

"Why haven't you told me this before now? Olivia asked. "You went with me to see Tony, you walked me to Leon every day I came."

"Yes."

"Only someone like you would have the courage to do something good like that."

She observed him and needed to find the right words to help him now. He needed to hear something comforting; she saw that.

"I can't begin to understand how difficult this must have been for you."

"I know," he turned, "I know. I know you're surprised and probably disappointed in me."

She took his hand.

"I'm not disappointed in you. I admire your strength." What she wouldn't give to put her arms around him right now and hold on to him tightly. She gripped his hand tighter and she just knew he understood.

"I know," he said so quietly that Olivia wasn't sure he said anything.

She had to stay with him for as long as he needed her. She held onto his hand, still tight, and he sat still as if he were summoning strength from deep inside him. He pulled his hand away when he heard a guard call out to him.

"I'll be right there," he said to the guard. Wesley got up to leave.

"Wesley, would you talk to me about your sister?"

"I need to." He turned and left the room.

* * *

Inside her car, she glanced at the letter that she now realized she'd carried with her since the guard brought it to her. She opened the envelope and pulled out the letter, but hesitated. She wouldn't have to read it. It was just a "thank you" note and she understood he was grateful. She had stayed with this man for the last two weeks of his life. She saw his pain— the pain of his life, and the pain and suffering he caused other people. It was nothing to be thanked for. Instead, she wanted to ball the letter up and toss it in the nearest trashcan. It was out of her sense of obligation and that she cared about Leon, that she unfolded the letter and read it.

Dear Olivia,

It always bothered me that my first daughter didn't want to stay with me. I know what I did was wrong and I tried to stop many times, honest I did. If you get the chance, maybe you could find her and tell her I'm sorry. I'm sorry she had to run away. She ran away before we moved. At that time we lived in a farmhouse off a back road near Smoke House road in Maryland. Maybe someone could help you find it.

I always thought she would return to that house and that she loved me as much as I loved her. Maybe she still lives in the area. I made up the story about her being adopted. I don't know what happened to her. You don't have to make this a promise to me or anything.

Just if you have the time could you go back to see if she is still there. You don't have to. You'll probably throw this nice letter away. Wesley helped me write it.

He's a good man, the kind a man you can trust.

Thank you for being with my son and with me these last two weeks. And thank you for telling me about Heaven and that I'll see Tony again. I doubt that I'll go to Heaven, but he will. I know he never wanted to do those things. I made him.

Yours truly,
Sunny

She placed the letter on the seat next to her. His letter made her both sad and empathetic for a man who broke the law and abducted little girls to create his own family.

Even after the Douglasses adopted her, a different path was open to her. She could have spent her life worrying about why her birth parents gave her away. She loved her adopted parents and that love grew over the years. She took advantage of everything they offered her. She did well in high school, went to college, and then entered the seminary. She had no hard feelings about her birth parents, and she had to admit that it was hard for her to miss something that she never had. Olivia put her car in gear and drove home. Tomorrow she would spend the day getting herself ready for her graduation on Sunday.

CHAPTER 20

Olivia woke from her restless sleep to the aromas of coffee and bacon. It had always been that way when she had something on her mind. She would toss and turn all night and just when it was time to wake up, she'd dose off, and fall into a sound sleep. Her mother used to say that it was the sleep fairy playing a trick on her. But this morning, she managed to sit up, though feeling as if she'd just been hit by a train. She reached out and then up for a long stretch. Getting the kinks out would help and the whiff of bacon, something she truly loved, was a strong encouragement for her to get out of the bed. When she brought her arms down, she noticed that she had held onto Leon's letter. When she had read the letter just before she fell into her restless sleep, she was again tempted to discard it, knowing she would never be able to locate Leon's daughter. During the night, thoughts about both Leon and Tony swam in and out of her dreams. She saw them fishing, walking through the woods together, laughing together. She saw Leon teaching Tony how to play baseball, him hitting a bear, then running and touching each base. She saw Leon digging behind the house, planting something. She saw them all night and into the early morning.

For the moment, she wanted her mind on one thing—the emanations of the coffee and bacon wafting from the kitchen. She rose up out of bed and allowed her nose to follow the aromas that took her downstairs to the welcomed delight of breakfast. When she entered the kitchen, she found Kara buttering whole-wheat toast, the kind Olivia would eat. Olivia saw the pleading look on Kara's face and realized that the breakfast was her way of making up, so she pulled out a cushioned chair and took a seat at the round wooden table. Olivia saw relief or happiness, sometimes it was hard to tell with her sister, sweep across Kara's face, the way a journalist would feel after meeting a deadline for what would be a Pulitzer worthy article.

"How long were you planning to sleep? Don't you have things to do today?"

"I do. I have a very busy day today and rehearsal tonight."

Kara poured Olivia a cup of coffee. Olivia took it, steam circling upward.

"Mmmmmmmm, just what I need."

Kara put a cup of coffee at her place and went back to the stove. She placed a plate of scrambled eggs, bacon and toast before Olivia and dished out the same for herself.

Olivia noticed that she seemed careful this morning, almost as if she wanted something.

Kara pulled out the chair, sat down, and pushed her plate away.

"What's the matter, Kara?" Olivia gave off a loud sigh as she asked her.

"I don't mean to disappoint you, Livvy. I hope you know that."

"You don't Kara." Olivia cast a questioning look toward Kara over her coffee cup.

The doorbell rang, and Olivia got up to answer the door. Her father stood on the landing.

"How are my girls this morning?" he said, his voice cheerful, and arms open.

"Dad, what are you doing here?" Olivia looked beyond him. "It's snowing again?"

"It's just getting started. I thought I was too early. I just came by to see if you needed me to do anything for you today."

"Come in. Kara and I are having breakfast."

They walked back to the kitchen. Olivia poured her father a cup of coffee and Kara got up and hugged her dad.

"Tomorrow is the big day," he said taking the coffee with Kara who was tucked under his other arm. "I just thought that there was something you wanted me to do for you."

"Dad, that's so nice. I'm going to pick up my cassock and surplice, I know they're ready. And try to do something with my hair. . ." She ran her hand through her hair, then gave it a final pat.

"After the ceremony tomorrow, your mother wants us all at the house.

She invited a few people from the church, too. I told her to keep it small. I know how you like things."

"I suspected she would do that."

"Who made the coffee?"

"I did. You like it?" Kara asked, peering up at him.

"Kara, it's good. Wow. I wish I could take this with me."

The doorbell rang again and her father put down the coffee and went to the door. Olivia followed him.

"Claude? Can I help you?" her father asked after he opened the door.

"Dr. Douglass, I'm here to see Olivia."

"Hello Claude. What're you doing here?" Olivia asked, stepping in front of her father.

"I hadn't heard from you and got worried. Can we talk in private?"

"Thanks, Dad."

Her father went into the living room.

"I got your message and after your—"

"I just wanted to give you this." He handed her a card and a small black box tied with a red ribbon.

When Olivia saw the small black box, she thought of one thing, and her eyes widened in surprise. "Claude, I—,"

"Open it."

"Claude—,"

"Open it."

Olivia untied the ribbon and opened the box. She saw that the box was a little larger than a ring box as she untied the ribbon and she relaxed a little. She opened the box and pulled out a silver cross on a silver chain bracelet. She cast her eyes up at Claude.

He smiled. "Just wanted you to have it. Thought maybe you could keep it in your pocket or something. I remember you told me you lost your last cross and so maybe you could use another one."

"Thank you, Claude." She stared at him for a while as if she'd never seen this man before.

"Have a nice graduation tomorrow." Claude turned to leave.

Olivia almost felt like calling him back, changing her mind about him. She closed the door and turned to her father and Kara now standing behind her, so close she almost bumped into them both.

"You all right?" her father asked.

"I'm fine." Olivia laughed. "Could you two stand any closer?" She felt an easy but quick tug on her hand and when she quickly glanced at her hand, she also felt a small piece of paper that her father had stuffed between her fingers and the box. Without thought, she gripped it tighter.

"You and Claude broke up?" Kara asked, looking from her father to Olivia. "Dad knows about you and Claude?"

"He figured it out."

"Some of us guys are not as clueless as some of you women think we are. After all these years, I learned to pay attention, that's all."

They laughed.

"Dad, you're anything but clueless," Kara said.

"I'll leave you two. You must have a million things to do today, Livvy." He looked at them both and Olivia thought he wanted to say something else, but he turned toward the door instead.

"Thanks, Dad."

Without warning, Kara did something that Olivia hadn't seen her do in a while. She gave her father a hug and said, "I love you, Dad. I love you."

Before she stepped back, he kissed Kara, wiped a tear from her eye, and whispered to her, "Me, too, Sweetheart, I love you, too." He stood in the hallway, not wanting to leave, as if he wanted to say something more, but thought better of it. Olivia knew what he wanted to say. She still hadn't told her mother. She knew it wasn't fair to ask him to continue to keep her secret, but she wasn't ready to say anything.

"Okay, then," her father said, eyes on Olivia. Then he opened the door and left.

Kara closed the door behind him. Olivia smiled at her sister. They went back to their breakfast and as they ate, Olivia talked Kara into spending the day with her and helping her get ready for her graduation.

After breakfast, they got dressed and went to pick up Olivia's surplice and cassock. Olivia wanted to stop by the salon in the mall and then the dress shop to buy Kara a new dress and shoes with the money her father had just slipped in her hand.

CHAPTER 21

When her parents arrived at the townhouse to pick her up, the minute Olivia opened her front door, her father took the garment bag that held her surplice out of her hand and carried it to a long black limo that sat in front of Olivia's townhouse. Olivia knew he'd find a way to honor her, but she never thought he would rent a limo to chauffeur her to the church.

He opened the back door bowing and extended his hand to help her in the car. Then he motioned for Kara to get in. He hung the garment bag on the holder over the door. He reached in the front seat, pulled out a white cone-like bag and handed her a bouquet of wild flowers. Olivia thought about putting up an argument, but her mother must have seen her face and that reminded her about the time that he had acted as a chauffeur when both she and Kara graduated from the University of London.

But, this was all for Olivia on one of those mornings in January where the sun lit up the earth in wide bright streaks. The temperature was much warmer than it had been all week, especially after the light snow the day before. The leftover snow was beginning to melt away. Olivia was thankful for that. They drove through the entrance of the seminary, and took the road to the left that led around the cemetery. Her mother and Kara had never been to the seminary and Olivia asked her father to give them a quick tour as they drove through. Olivia pointed out the dorm where she stayed, the library that was practically her home, the offices, and other buildings until they came to the church situated on a hill in the back. During the rehearsal the night before, Olivia learned that the fifty-two-people graduating that morning along with family and friends would make a tremendous crowd and she had suggested to Wesley and her parents that they get an early start to find a parking space and seats. When they pulled up to the church, Wesley was standing at the entrance dressed in a black cashmere topcoat looking more like a model than a captain of guards in a prison.

Her father pulled up in front to the entrance. He got out and went around to her side and opened the car door for her. She walked toward Wesley to greet him, and saw how happy he appeared with a smile that literally seemed to stretch from ear to ear.

"You ready?" he asked her.

"I'm ready," she said.

"Good."

"I know you have to go in, but would it be okay if we took a walk around? Wesley asked. "A self-directed tour until the graduation ceremony begins?"

"Sure. Some buildings may not be open and some parts of the dorm may be closed off to visitors, but you can walk or drive around the campus."

"I wonder if the bookstore is open. It's not very far; we could browse there while we wait."

She had a hard time trying to make herself turn away. His intense gaze, was so penetrating and paralyzing and made her feel vulnerable, almost like he knew what was in her heart. She saw how this day was just as important to him as it was to her.

In the prep room inside the church, the dean brought her a package that she thought Fr. Wilson left for her. She opened it and found a beautiful off-white satin Deacon's stole with panels of noble Coronation tapestry at the bottom. Carefully, she slipped the stole out of the box, angled it sash-style across her left hip and closed it with a woven cord. She couldn't imagine anything more beautiful. She thought about wearing it under her cassock but decided it would be too much. When she took it off, she noticed a cross, stitched with red thread, across the shoulder. She folded the stole up and placed it back in the box. It was just like Fr. Wilson to do something like that. Then she noticed the card signed by Wesley Johns and her heart stopped. She took the stole out of the box, unfolded it, and slipped it on under her cassock. She wasn't supposed to wear it in an official capacity until she was ordained. But since it was Wesley who had given it to her, why not? Who would know? And she had to admit that she did understand Wesley's message.

The graduates filed into the area reserved for slipping into the cassocks and surplices as well as lining up. Olivia wanted to take a step out of the picture to appreciate the moment, but the confusion, anxiety and the noise in the room, prevented her. Sidney, who roomed next door to her at the Residence Hall, rushed to her.

"Well, here we are. No more staying up late in the library."

"Ahh, taking away our fun," said Olivia, laughing.

"Yeah, no more nudging each other, trying to keep awake in class. I've spent these last two weeks almost entirely in my bed."

"Sidney, not you. You were the one, keeping me up."

"Look at us. We made it. I can't wait to start work," sang out Jeannie, while walking toward them. She hugged both girls as she talked, "I can't wait, I can't wait."

They pulled back.

"Have you found a place?" Olivia asked, watching Jeannie.

"My church will let me start there for now. What about you?" She turned from Sidney to Olivia.

"My Bishop found a place for me. A little church in rural Virginia. I know I'm going to love it," Sidney said.

"My church. I'm going to be at my church," Olivia said. She was a little uncomfortable, but she told the truth. She will be at her church. She will continue with the prayer group.

"All right everyone. This is it everyone. You need to line up," an advisor said in a loud voice.

At that moment the organ began, the noise in the room evanesced and everyone lined up to process into the church. Behind the dignitaries and speakers, the graduates—Masters level first—entered the church two by two and took the reserved pews in the front four rows on each side of the aisle. The dignitaries and speakers continued to the sacristy where chairs were added for them. The church service began with the opening prayers, and during the Collect, Olivia remembered that Fr. Wilson had submitted her name for an academic award. Since she was not going to be ordained, she thought that would eliminate her. It was just as well.

She took a last look around the church. For three years, she'd come into this church for services and prayer but never saw the beauty that she saw on this day. She loved the stone walls of the sanctuary, and its marble floor and wooden railing. She loved the smell of incense and the candles burning. She loved the smell of the wood oil that was used to clean the pews.

She remembered on her first night, she had arrived early and had come in alone before the service started, to pray alone. Then, after the service began she happened to look down on the floor as she pulled down the kneeler, and there was a penny just lying on the floor next to the screw that secured the kneeler. It wasn't the shiny kind or the rusted kind. It was a well-used dark brown penny face up and lying there almost as if it waited for her. She picked it up, held it in her hand and without thought, stuck it in the seam between the cushion and the wood of the kneeler. What's the likelihood that the penny would still be there now? She casually looked around her and saw that she was now sitting in the very same pew she sat in that first night, and in the very same place.

Surely, the penny must have fallen out by now. She slipped her fingers along the edge of the kneeler next to her leg feeling for the penny, her penny. She touched something and felt the roundness of the penny. She pulled it out where it had been hidden over the past three years. Turning it around with her fingers, she was amazed that no one had found it; no one knew she had hidden it there. She knew it was silly, but somehow, she thought the penny was there for her.

No one found it; no one was supposed to find it until she graduated. How many graduations had this penny witnessed? She placed it back on the floor next to the screw where she'd found it, ready for the next person who needed assurance, ready for the next graduation. During her years at the seminary, she remembered that she sometimes felt as if she was home, like the church was her place. Afterward, she discovered that it was just the "every-now-and-then-rest" from that haunting feeling.

Olivia turned toward the nave, where she sat, and at the row of stained glass windows that lined the aisles on each side of the church. During her second summer in the seminary, she enrolled in a seminar on the history of the windows and found that some of the windows were given as gifts. She remembered an evening when monks filled the choir pews and sang evensong for them. When the service ended, she remembered she wanted to stay and hear the monks sing forever. The voices of those men blending together in high notes chanting and singing solo, then groups, then all together, put her in such a calming, loving and euphoric state that when the service had ended, she had wished she had found a way to take it with her, put it on her phone, so that she could listen to it over again as many times as she wanted. Sadness washed through her as she realized, she would truly miss the place, her home for the past three years, the place that kept her safe and secure.

When the service ended, the graduation ceremony began first, with speeches from the advisors. The dean called the speakers, "Can we have each of the four academic advisors, come up now?"

The four priests left their seats and stood beside the dean.

"These men represent academic excellence, outreach, liturgy, and church history. They will tell you a little about what each graduate is called to do and how each one will carry out his or her," he paused and emphasized the word "her," "duty before their ordination." He nodded for the first priest to speak.

After the speeches and the choir sang several songs and psalms, the Dean rose and the four academic advisors stood on either side of him. They each presented several awards to the graduates before they called Olivia Douglass to receive the Harris Award for academic excellence. Olivia had written an essay on "Love and Forgiveness." She was surprised since she thought her name had been withdrawn.

After the awards, the graduates were ready to receive their degree. The dean gave them a signal, the candidates on the first row all rose, and walked across the chancel in front of the altar to receive their degree. When the Dean called Olivia's name, her eyes searched for her family and Wesley, all sitting together in the first unreserved pew. When it was her turn, she walked across the chancel, shook the dean's hand and accepted her degree. She turned toward her family and Wesley and smiled. When she sat down, she realized that one of the most important moments in her life had passed by too quickly, the same way Leon left this world. She wanted to capture her moment, savor it, hold on to it for much longer, so she could truly live it. But it was like all moments in time—fleeting. After they processed out and were back in the "dressing area" again, Olivia put her stole back in the box, and went to seek Wesley.

There he was, standing with her parents and Fr. Wilson. When she approached, Fr. Wilson shook her hand, and congratulated her. He looked at her as if he was proud and hoped she was too. Then he excused himself when he saw the dean. Wesley had a scowl on his face after he saw her carrying the box.

"Well, they're having a little reception here, but your mother has prepared something at home. Everybody ready?" Her father looked at Wesley as if he meant the invitation for him too.

Olivia took hold of Wesley's arm and held him back. He stopped and turned to her.

"Wesley, the stole. It's so beautiful. I've never seen anything so breath-taking. And it's not just the stole."

He kissed her on the forehead. "For a beautiful person."

"I want you to know that I wore it under my cassock."

He kissed her on the forehead again.

* * *

Olivia's mother had invited a few friends and church members to celebrate Olivia's graduation. Olivia was a little nervous. Her mother still did not know that she had chosen not to be ordained and Olivia hoped no one would ask her anything about being a priest.

She sat on the couch next to Wesley, both with a wedge of cake and a glass of white wine on the table in front of them. Without any warning, Wesley stood up in the middle of the living room, his glass in the air. "May I have your attention everyone?" He turned around in all directions and waited for everyone to come into the living room before proceeding. Olivia stood.

"I want us all to raise our glasses to Olivia Douglass. Look at where she is now. Today she graduated from the Virginia seminary. These past three years for her must have been grueling, and intense, yet a satisfying experience. A person who would want to do that must have patience, have a lot of love for people, not to mention a wealth of other good things that I can't even comprehend. Here's to Olivia Douglass who possesses those special qualities."

Olivia relaxed.

"Thanks be to God," her father said.

"May the Lord bless you and keep you," her mother said. She dashed over and kissed her daughter.

"May you always seek the truth," Elizabeth's friend and church member said.

The group let out a round of "here, here," clinked their glasses and took a sip of wine.

"What's next?' Mrs. Johnson, a church member asked.

"I'm still thinking about that," Olivia said.

"I hope you'll stay with us. I know I speak for many of the parishioners when I say we all love what you do."

Olivia looked surprised as if she had just realized that she was on the wrong bus going in the opposite direction from her intended destination.

"Just something to keep in mind," Mrs. Johnson continued.

Olivia's mother stood behind Mrs. Johnson and whispered something in her ear.

"It seems as though the women are being called to help. Can you excuse me?"

Mrs. Johnson and Olivia's mother made their way toward the dining room.

Wesley turned to Olivia, "I promised my mother that I would—"

"I understand," she said. She walked him to the door.

"I want to make it up to you. Let me take you to dinner. Would that be okay?"

"I'd love to have dinner with you."

"Can I pick you up at say, eight-oh-clock this evening?"

"I'll be ready."

He turned around, and she peered up at him. At first, she thought he wanted to ask her about a suggestion for dinner, but she couldn't tell that from the look on his face. But then, he turned to leave. Her eyes followed him across the street to his car and she watched him get in. When he started the car, he turned in her direction. Then, he pulled out the space and left.

"Don't worry," Kara said, coming up behind her. She leaned her chin on Olivia's shoulder. "I can say for certain that he wanted to kiss you."

Olivia, still facing toward the street, gave herself a huge smile.

CHAPTER 22

"Olivia, I hope you like this place," Wesley stood outside the restaurant, left hand on the brass plate ready to push in the door, and his right arm around her waist. A blue and white sign over the door read: HOG Restaurant. "I just want to warn you that it's quite different from the usual places."

"We will be able to eat normal food, won't we?" Olivia asked.

"As far as I know we will." Wesley laughed. "I just wanted you to expect something different."

"Now, I'm a little nervous. And starving."

"Trust me. I don't want to scare you away." He pushed the door open before she could read the words written in smaller letters under the HOG. He took her hand. They walked through the quiet half-empty restaurant to another door. Olivia was surprised that he had reserved a private room for them until he pushed that door open to the sounds of two guitars, a piano, two horns, drums, and a bass as the artists spread themselves out across a stage singing and dancing. She looked around at the crowded bar, the groups of people sitting at tables singing along and swaying and tapping to the fast tempo music. They found a table and almost as soon as they were seated, a waitress appeared.

"Would you two like something to drink?" She asked while wiping down the table.

"Two iced teas." He nodded at Olivia as he said it.

Olivia nodded back.

When the waitress left, Wesley turned to Olivia. "They don't serve wine and other hard drinks here. I told you this place was different."

This once quiet unassuming man had gradually morphed into someone else. Olivia liked this new person—this man who was alive and enjoyed life. He made her feel all giddy and happy inside; a happiness she welcomed.

The bandleader announced that *The Born Again Saints* would take a fifteen-minute break. The band members carefully arranged their instruments and left the stage one by one. Wesley pointed the leader out to her—the man with long dark scraggly hair and dressed in all black leather. He waved to Wesley as he left the stage.

Olivia found herself staring at Wesley admiring his strength and courage. By all accounts, he should be in a mental institution somewhere, but here he was all excited about *The Born Again Saints* band playing loud music. Olivia hadn't been paying attention to the kind of music the crowd was singing, when they came in, or the kind of music the band played. Wesley was a little old for rock music and she preferred religious music. It was of no concern to her at this moment. She just wanted the band to return from their break. Wesley made her happy and now she just wanted to sing along, loud, and with her lack of ability, off key.

"Everything okay?" he asked.

"Yes. Everything is just fine. This—"

"Can you excuse me a second?"

"Su—," she began, but he got up before she finished.

A woman came by to pass out a booklet of songs for the next session. Olivia took the booklet. She put it down on the table without looking at the songs. A woman in a group of men and women one table over yelled out, "Oh, I love this song. This is my favorite song. I love this song." Olivia picked up the booklet and saw that all the songs were praise songs, religious songs. She smiled as she looked around for Wesley. She nodded several times in approval. He would take her some place she liked. She saw Wesley in the corner behind her talking to the man dressed in all black leather, the band leader. The others wore jeans and T-shirts or all black leather with chains extending from their front pockets.

The waitress returned with two tall glasses of iced tea, sugar, lemon and spoons and placed them on the table. She rattled off a list of snacks that reminded Olivia that she was hungry. Olivia selected snacks for the two of them. In a few minutes, Wesley returned smiling.

"Come on," he said grabbing Olivia's hand and leading her toward the stage.

"Wait a minute. What's going on?"

He sat her down on the bench at the piano. "This is a Praise Bar, House of God, you know? HOG? Sometimes I play with the band. I asked if you could join us."

"But, Wesley, I don't know how to play anything. You mean on the piano? Oh no, I don't know how to play the piano."

"You don't have to. I'm going to give you something to play and all you have to do is play that throughout the song, okay?"

"Wesley—"

"You'll love it. I promise. And you'll do well. See this is all you have to do." He began playing a simple scale and asked Olivia to play the scale with him, an octave higher. After a few practices, she caught on, and he asked her to play it an octave lower.

"When do I play it? I don't know when to come in." She heard her own shaky sounding voice. She was nervous, but she had to calm down and play the notes he asked.

Still, he must have heard the anxiety in her voice. He smiled at her, gave a soft pat on the back of her hand, and said, "Watch me. When the drummer gives you three beats" he pretended to beat on drums," and I nod, you start right then. Practice with me nodding. I'll be standing right there." He pointed to a place on stage.

His effect was calming, soothing, and she was able to get a hold of herself. They practiced for a while with the nod. In a few minutes, the band members returned to the stage. Each one turned to Olivia, smiling, and she gave a nervous smile back. They each began tuning their instruments to the piano, the notes Wesley played. The bandleader introduced each of the members again, and Olivia might have heard her name as he introduced her, but she was so nervous and concentrated so heavily on the scale that she was to play that she couldn't take her eyes off the piano keys.

Wesley took a horn out of an open case, put something on it, and put it to his mouth. When this was all over, she would ask him about this, but for now, her mind was on coming in at the right time. The band began, "Lord of All Creation," and she watched Wesley intensely for his cue, the nod. When she saw him nod, she began the scale. After that song, Wesley joined her at the piano. While the bandleader spoke to the audience, Wesley told Olivia to continue with the scale. The second piece, "My Jesus, My Savior," began and when Wesley signaled, she began her scale again. On the higher octave treble keys, Wesley played counter to Olivia's scale while the band members played on. When her part had ended, Olivia tried to get up from the bench, but Wesley took her hand meaning for her to stay. As Wesley and the band played on, the audience danced, sang along, threw up their hands and joined in, feeling the urge to move. She sat beside him on the bench watching him, head nodding to the beat, eyes closed, as he ran his fingers up and down the keyboard, white keys, black keys, several keys together, both hands, with grace and ease. His touch was so perfect, so light, so intense. It was hard for her to believe that he had a hardened side, a side of him that worked in a prison. When the song ended, the audience screamed and yelled for more and sang out other songs they wanted to hear the band play.

"You did a beautiful job," he said sliding closer to her on the bench.

She kissed him on the cheek; she just couldn't help herself.

He smiled, turned to her. "Stay here."

The bandleader gave Wesley, who had the lead-in on this piece, the signal to begin, "All of You is More Than Enough," and recognizing the song, the audience members sang out loudly, and swayed back and forth, praising the Lord.

When the set ended, Wesley took Olivia by the hand and led her back to the table.

She picked up her tea and he took it away from her. "I promised you dinner. I hope it's not too late for you to eat."

She turned to him. "You were right. I loved it."

They held there a moment his eyes locked with hers. Without a word, he turned away and looked down at the table as if searching for something or was embarrassed about something. Then he stood. "Come on." He paid for the tea and snacks that the waitress brought, led her out of the Praise Bar and to the restaurant down the street on the corner.

When they were seated, "Well, well, well. Just when I thought I knew you."

He laughed.

"Wesley, a man of many talents," she began. "You play the horn and the piano, and where did you find that place?"

"I play the horn, guitar, piano, and violin. One of the ushers took me there one evening," he said. With a little more somberness in his voice, he continued, "I've been going off and on ever since; more on than off."

"How long have you been playing and singing? I thought I heard you singing, too?"

"I started with the piano first. Then I took up the violin and guitar when I discovered that girls like guys who play the guitar or horn."

"Your musical career centered around your romantic or potentially romantic life."

"Absolutely."

"You just threw the piano in there just in case?"

"You catch on fast." He paused. "I learned to play the piano because my parents wanted me to play duets with my sister."

"Your sister?"

"My sister was good on the piano." He cleared his throat. "I hope you don't mind, but I took the liberty of ordering a bottle of wine for us."

"That's fine. With the musical talent you have, why aren't you a professional?"

"I look at it as a good hobby. I'm not that good as a solo."

"You seem good to me." She pressed out the wrinkles in the white linen tablecloth and realigned her fork and knife. "This is a really nice restaurant."

"This is one of my favorite restaurants."

The waiter came and lit the candle on the table. The flickering of the candles cast a streak of light on Wesley and she noticed him staring at her. She was a little nervous and wondered whether her hair rested on her shoulders with bouncy curls and whether or not the navy-blue silk dress was feminine enough for Wesley. She tried to keep her smile, but he continued to stare. She let out a nervous giggle and straightened her shoulders.

"I'm sorry, Olivia. I don't mean to stare. I can't get over your decision."

She looked up at him, then cast her eyes downward.

He reached his hand across the table for her hand. She put her hand in his.

"Can you tell me why? I would like to know."

"Wesley, that's something that I don't know how to talk about. Can we leave it that way?"

"We can leave it that way for now. But I would like to know why you feel that way. You're a priest already. I'm surprised to know that you've decided against it."

"It's just difficult."

"When you're ready I want to know. If I can do anything that would change your mind, consider it done or said."

She smiled at him.

"What have you decided to do, instead?"

"I thought I might help my parents with the bookstore."

The waiter brought the wine and two glasses. After Wesley approved, the waiter poured wine in Olivia's glass. Wesley held up his glass to offer a toast. Olivia held up her glass.

"To Olivia Douglass; may she use her knowledge from the seminary to help guide members of the church through prayer and discernment."

They touched glasses.

"Thank you for inviting me to the graduation. That was the most beautiful service I have ever seen."

"I find them spiritual. For two years I went to graduations to watch those ahead of me move on." She paused. "The stole, Wesley, I've never seen a stole that beautiful."

"I just had to. After watching you these past two weeks, well, I just had to."

"Oh, I didn't do anything."

"But you did. I don't know how you could come back and talk to Leon like you did."

"Wesley, can I tell you something?"

"Sure."

"Please don't think badly of me." She hesitated a moment, watched his face. "But I was beginning to understand Leon. Seeing him was not only part of my responsibilities, but I also wanted to see him, to get to know him better."

"You changed him, Olivia. You changed that man. Maybe if someone with love and patience had gotten to him earlier in his life, he would have become a different person."

"I don't believe Leon was born hard-hearted. You were right, Wesley. He was afraid to die because of all the things he'd done over the years. He knew he was wrong. His environment made him that way. It was hard to get inside him, to break down that armor and get to know him. He shielded himself better than I've ever seen," she said.

"After so many years of building onto that shield, even he may not have known the real Leon." He paused. He spoke as if he was holding something in him. "Since working there, I've learned a thing or two. There are different kinds of killers. Some know the difference between right and wrong and feel they had no choice but to do whatever they did, and others just don't care. They get it in their mind that they are in the right." he said.

"Did you get to see him and talk to him much?"

"I had to know all the inmates. I read their records and I tried to learn their names, not just their assigned numbers. I tried to find out a little about them all, the information that they wanted to tell, that is. Sometimes they would let out a little more than they wanted to tell, mainly the lifers. Holding things in is the culture of the prison. You don't want people to get too personal with you. It leaves you vulnerable, and an inmate can take advantage of you."

"It's easy to see that the prison life is a different world."

"That it is. I had to learn it and learn it quickly. I was a guard and when I became captain, I couldn't make mistakes."

"You helped Leon write that letter to me. That was nice."

"It wasn't for him."

She smiled.

"I asked him how he wanted to spell the name, 'Sunny' and he said to spell it like the sun because you brought him more sunshine in those few days than he'd had in his whole dark life."

Olivia felt a pang in her heart. "He said that?"

"Yes, he did."

"Wesley, you didn't have to do it. You could have asked someone else, but you helped him. You did it."

Wesley gazed at her as if he hadn't realized what helping Leon meant for him.

"That house that he mentioned in his letter, is it still standing?

"Yes, it is. In fact, they both are and they're both empty. I guess after the public heard what happened in those houses it would be bad luck for anyone to live in them. The owner of one of them is tearing it down."

Olivia wanted to ask him how he knew this, but it was best to leave it alone for now.

"I can't imagine how hard it must have been for you, being at that prison every day."

"I thought I had put things behind me." He took a sip of wine. "My mother never got over my sister. She talked about Anne a lot over the years. She blamed herself." He paused.

Olivia waited for more. She wanted him to say more.

"My mother wouldn't let herself get away from what happened and I couldn't put what happened far enough behind me. But when you came . . . Watching you convinced me that I was stuck and I had to move on. I'll go back to my law firm full-time. My mother, well I hope that she can let it all rest now; make peace with it and forgive him."

"I don't think I've seen your mother at church."

"She refuses to come. My mother holds herself responsible for the way I've felt."

"Wesley, it's so easy to blame ourselves when things like that happen. You were not to blame and neither is your mother."

"I'm learning that."

"You gave up your law practice and took the job at the prison for your mother?"

"Pretty much. At first, I thought I'd be helping her put things to rest, but when I went to the prison, my feelings resurfaced."

"I read in one of my books about prayer, that you forgive, but you don't forget."

Olivia thought she'd said something to upset him when he looked at her with such seriousness and intensity.

"I have to know something."

"What's that?"

He arranged and rearranged his fork and spoon on the table in front of him. "Are you seeing Claude? I missed him at your graduation ceremony." He turned his head away and sat back in his chair.

She smiled. "No. No, I'm not." She could honestly say that Claude never made her feel the way she did now.

He looked up, and took both her hands in his. "Good," he said, "Good." He leaned across the table, Olivia leaned toward him, and he gave her a kiss on the lips.

This man always made her heart do things inside her. She would have sworn that for certain, she actually felt her heart flipping and twirling and swelling and she would have sworn that everyone in that restaurant saw her heart flipping around in her chest. She hadn't realized that Wesley believed that she and Claude were still seeing each other. However, she wasn't surprised that he held back; he was that kind of man which made him even more appealing.

CHAPTER 23

Olivia woke up with the notion that she would follow through with Leon's request. Nevertheless, she tried to talk herself out of it by telling herself that there was no purpose in searching for his daughter. Whatever Leon did or did not do was the past. Finding Leon's daughter and dredging up the past could also bring back unnecessary hurt and pain for his daughter. She wasn't sure she wanted to be responsible for that. Besides, it was not a request that could be fulfilled. It was one of those things that you asked to have done without expectation that it would be done. He said it in his letter. She also thought the request was his way of saying he did nothing to his daughter. During her visits with him, he never said he was sorry, at least not to her anyway, not that he had to say anything to her.

But as the morning wore on, the thought of the search satiated her mind and no matter how hard she tried to keep it away, she couldn't get it out of her brain. One thing that repeated itself in her thoughts was the question of his daughter—who was she now, how had she grown up and would she want to remember her past. Wesley was right. Leon had changed and she had seen a different Leon near his end. Olivia owed it to his daughter to let her know that deep down her father wasn't a bad person. She was obligated to tell his daughter who her father truly was. Maybe that would bring her some comfort. Olivia pulled the letter out of the trash where she had put it and read it again. Maybe, it wouldn't hurt to at least make an attempt to find his daughter. If that attempt led her to an end, without finding her, then she would leave it at that.

Even though she had talked herself into going, she wasn't anxious to go to the house alone. She thought about asking Wesley, but that wasn't a good idea. He was trying to put it all to rest. She would ask someone she trusted, her father.

She recalled that Leon lived two places that she knew about—the farmhouse, the one mentioned in the newspaper where they nabbed him, and the house he mentioned in his letter.

Now that she had decided to go, she decided to go to the house mentioned in the newspaper first, since it was in Virginia. Maybe she could get a good sense of how they lived, how he kept these children, if that was still possible. Olivia was sure that seeing the house would help her know him and help her talk to his daughter.

When she arrived at the bookstore, her mother and father were in the store as she had hoped. She knew her mother would try to talk her out of going and she hated to come between them, but she had to ask her father to help her; he was all she had. At this point, she needed someone to go with her, and asking Wesley wouldn't be right, after what she found out about his sister.

"Good morning," said her mother who must have looked up and seen Olivia enter when the bell rang. "You're up and about early. Aren't you going to take a few days off before you begin your training?"

Her voice sounded hesitant, as if her mother expected something to happen and she could put it off by talking about Olivia's rest.

"Training?"

"Yes, your six-month dia, well you know. I never could remember that word."

"Hi, sweetheart. Come to help?" her father asked, as he carried an armful of books.

Her mother turned to her father. "I thought she'd take a few days before she had to start her training as a priest. You need it after that ordeal with that man at the prison."

Olivia looked at her father for help. At this moment, she'd forgotten that she hadn't told her mother. She thought about the day when one of her father's friends asked him how it was living with a house full of women. His advice to his friend was to keep quiet because whatever you say or do will definitely be wrong. Olivia let out a slight smile as she recalled that incident, and now saw her father standing there in the center of the store, arms full of books, staring back at her, as if shocked, the way a person would who had just received news that he had a few days to live. She knew her father wouldn't have told her mother. She'd asked him not to and he hadn't. But as she watched her father, and saw the disappointment on his face, she had to say something now.

"Mom, the truth is, I haven't decided to continue. I don't know if I'll do the training."

She heard her father let out a long sigh, and she tried not to see his face.

"What? What do you mean? You aren't going to become a priest? Vinny, did you know about this?" she asked turning to her husband and quickly turning back to her daughter. "Livvy, why not?"

"I'm just not sure if being a priest is what I'm called to do. It's difficult and I want to be certain."

"Livvy —,"

"Mom, please, just give me more space. This is my life and going into the priesthood is important. I just need to consider it some more, okay?" She thought that would be enough to get her mother to stop the interrogation that was coming.

Chest sinking, her mother gave her an, "I don't believe what I'm hearing" look and slammed herself down in the nearest chair.

"Mom, please." Olivia bent down and kissed her mother on the cheek. She turned to her father.

"Dad, I need your help."

He sat the books down, walked over, and placed his hands on his wife's shoulders and began giving her a shoulder rub. "What is it?"

She pulled out Leon's letter and waited for him to read it. When he had finished reading it, he asked, "What do you want me to do?"

"Take me there." She looked for a response from her mother.

"Livvy what's going on?" her mother asked. Her voice filled with fear.

Vincent passed the letter to his wife.

After she read it, "Surely you don't plan to do this. You can't . . . Vinny, she can't . . .," she tried to suppress a scream and it came out a loud gurgle.

"Elizabeth, I have to. She wants to do this. In fact, she needs to go."

"No, Vinny, please." She turned to Olivia, "I knew something was wrong the minute you walked in the door. Livvy, you don't know what you're doing.

What do you hope to find?"

"Mom, I don't know. I don't understand why this is so upsetting to you. Leon asked me to go look for his daughter. I believe I should at least do something. If it's danger you're worried about, we'll be careful." She paused for a moment. "Dad, we should start with the house mentioned in the newspaper first." She showed him a copy of the news article she'd gotten from the library.

Her father skimmed it and passed it to his wife.

"Vinny, no, please don't take her. Livvy, what if people are there now? Someone may still be living in that house." She pointed to the news article still in her hand. "Or maybe the place is torn down?"

"Mom, you just questioned why I'm not going to be ordained. Wouldn't someone who had planned to become a priest want to do this for this man? If the place is torn down, then that's what I'll find." She gave an asking look at her father. Vincent bent down, kissed his wife, and grabbed his coat off the rack behind the counter. They left.

* * *

Olivia gave her father the directions to the house in Virginia that she had gotten off the internet. Her father drove them to the place where police found Leon and his wives and children. They turned off the main highway and took a state route that led to a cross road. Her father turned into the cross road and at the next road, route 691, made a left. They followed that to an unidentified road and turned right. About a half mile, they reached the house. The bulky weeds and thick grass had overtaken any road that was once carved out, or paved, to the point where there was no original road left. Her father followed what seemed like a newly made narrow trail for almost a mile as he drove around overgrown vines, bushes, and fallen trees until he came to what was left of the farmhouse.

Several long tree limbs grew onto the front part of the roof, and extended across to the end of the roof. Olivia and her father got out of the car and made their way to the front porch that was bolstered with cinder blocks on three sides. The tall weeds not only crawled onto the porch and hid the front door but they also covered the entire front side of the wood slatted farmhouse. On one side of the house, a chimney had crumbled and some of the bricks had fallen on the ground, some were hidden under the weeds and overgrowth. As Olivia carefully found and tested each of the three steps, using her toe before she stepped, she made her way to the front porch. After her father moved away some of the weeds, he found the door. A weatherworn sign warned of the dangers of entering. The door was already open and her father pushed it all the way in. They entered the house, he leading the way, and stood in the front room. Olivia looked around the room and saw the windows were almost gone, dirt and debris covered the floors. When she looked up, she saw the roof half gone, and tree limbs hanging down inside. She saw what seemed to be at one time a stove and a sink caving into the cabinets below it that once held it up. The room smelled of wet sneakers. A table with one leg rested against a wall and a chair seat protruded out. She heard a noise and turned to see Wesley Johns coming out of one of the other rooms.

"Wesley? Wesley?"

Wesley, wasn't himself. He mumbled to himself and ignored Olivia and her father when they tried to get his attention.

"Wesley?" her father asked. "Wesley, Wesley?"

Olivia turned to her father. "His sister lived here for a while."

Her father took a step toward Wesley, but stopped.

When she saw remnants of ropes and chains, Olivia turned in all directions to take in the entire room. She was in the same room, even in the same spot, where the children and his wives were tied up and chained. She remembered reading about it and Leon had tried to tell her that.

Wesley swiped his face with his hand, and turned toward her. "I'm sorry. I just had to." Tears streamed down his face. He swiped his face again and turned away, obviously not wanting her to see him.

"Wesley, you shouldn't be here." He was in great pain and she was lost as to what to do to console him. She recognized his need, but standing in this place, the midst of everything evil, the place where his sister was abused, and nothing soothing came to her mind.

After a few minutes, "Watch yourself," her father said.

Olivia looked down and saw that she was about to step on the uneven part of the dirt floor.

Her father walked into another room and Olivia and Wesley followed him. A bed frame with springs exposed, and eroded with rust was under the window that was now gone. A closet door hung open exposing a missing rod and three broken wire clothes hangers on the floor. She checked around for chains and ropes, but saw none and figured that she was standing in Leon's room. They followed her father to the third room where she saw more, dirty frayed ropes, broken and mangled chains and brown-red splotches all around the room. She imagined children screaming and crying, sick children, hungry children in need of their mothers begging Leon to set them free. She saw one child, with her outstretched hand, reaching for Tony begging him to help her get away. She heard babies crying for their mother's milk and at the same time, denied of their mother's love. She was sick to her stomach. This was the room where he had kept most of his children and wives and he may have disposed of some of them in this very room, even in the very spot where she stood.

At that moment, she hated both Leon and Tony for depriving these children of their right to live a long healthy life. The look on Wesley's face led her to believe that he thought the same thing. She had to get him out of this horrible place. She went back to the front room. Her father and Wesley followed. Wesley stood in the center of the room whispering to himself and turning in all directions. When he faced Olivia, he was crying harder, shoulders shuddering uncontrollably and long hard sobbing that made it hard for him to catch his breath.

"Come on Wesley, you shouldn't be here. You don't want to think of her being in some place like this. You want to hold onto her and remember all the good things about her and the good that you two did together," her father said.

Olivia moved closer to Wesley to take him by the arm to lead him out.

His face was contorted with hate and anger at this moment. "She was in this house, that room back there. She was here," Wesley said.

"Wesley, you don't know that," her father said.

"Wesley, my father is right. You shouldn't be here. This is too much for anybody."

Where they stood was beyond anything a human should experience or be exposed. No one could expect anything rational about this man's motive.

What had gone on in that house with the brown and faded red spots on the floor, the remnants of ropes, and chains made his motives obvious. How these children, including Wesley's sister, could have endured anything that terrifying, that horrendous was beyond reason. She wanted the house burned to the ground, and purify the grounds. Olivia wished there was something she could say to Leon's daughter that would bring her comfort. She had to keep in mind that she saw another side of Leon and she needed to remember that now.

"Wesley, let's go," her father said.

"I know; I know," he repeated nodding his head.

"Come on then, Wesley, walk out with us, okay?" her father said. "Walk out with us now."

She and Wesley took hands and with her father leading them, they left the house.

"Where is your car?" her father asked.

"Over there." He pointed toward a group of three trees that seemed to be growing together and attached to each other.

They had missed the car hidden by the trees and foliage.

Olivia walked Wesley to his car. After he got in, she stepped back, watched him back his car out and drive down the path.

She and her father followed him out to the main road. Wesley's driving back and forth to the house must have torn away the grass and weeds and formed the path. He must have gone back several days. How could he do that and then help the man who abducted his sister write a letter. She wondered whether Wesley ever told Leon that one of his wives was his (Wesley's) sister.

On the drive back, Olivia and her father were quiet for a while.

Her father was the first to speak. "Sweetheart, we ought to leave things like they are."

She heard a quiver in his voice. She turned to him. "You don't want me to go to the house in Maryland?"

"Well, you've seen this house. There's no need to go any further. I'm sure it'll be much like this one."

She was a little disappointed. He had taught her to follow things through to the end.

"You think that's best?"

"I do, I do. He must have moved around a lot. I guess people like that don't stay in one place too long. Eventually they'll do something that brings the law after them."

His fear permeated the atmosphere in the car. She had never experienced his fear like this before. She remembered the fury with which her mother spoke when she tried to stop her from going to the house. Her father and mother both knew something more than what little they told her. The house is empty. Leon is no longer. He could never ever do anything like this again.

Olivia glanced over at her father and almost asked him if this was all.

"Okay, Dad. If that's what you think is best."

* * *

Later, Olivia slipped in the side door of the church. Usually she had it all to herself, but on this evening, Wesley was praying at the altar. She stood in the aisle and watched him as he whispered something, made the sign of the cross and stood. When he turned around, Olivia stepped into the first pew. Wesley sat down beside her. She reached over, and took his hand.

Olivia sat waiting. He remained silent. She gave him a sideways glance, but his eyes were directed toward the altar. She felt the heat exuding from him and sensed that he was angry. He gripped her hand and held onto it. She gave him another glance. She moved as close to him as possible where her shoulder pressed against his and her thigh touched his. She heard him release a steady stream of air, a long sigh. Being a man always in control, he wouldn't want his anger to just spill out of him.

"Wesley, I'm so sorry."

He glanced at her, cleared his throat. "I need to thank you."

"Thank me for what?"

"For saving me."

She waited.

"As you have probably figured out, Leon was my primary focus."

She hadn't quite figured it out, but before he mentioned it to her in the viewing room after Leon's execution, she had guessed that there was more to his wanting to be a guard. He never seemed to be like all the other guards, particularly in his dress and the way he carried himself.

"Wesley, what happened with your sister?"

He cleared his throat again, and began.

"We were in elementary school; she was ten, and older by two years. Mom and dad always told us to walk home from school together. We were not allowed to leave each other. Ann, Ann was her name. Ann liked to go to the library after school, and I always went with her. We did our homework there. One afternoon, she said she wanted to skip the library. She got the idea to stop off at a little corner store where many of the kids coming home from school would stop for candy. She thought she would see this boy whom she liked, I don't remember his name. I didn't want to stop. I told her that we weren't allowed to do that and we needed to get home before mom got home. She insisted that we stop and even tempted me with some of the candy she had planned to buy. She'd been saving her money for candy, and even showed me her money. If she'd been saving her allowance for candy just because she wanted to run into a boy, then I thought that the boy must be important to her. So, one afternoon, instead of going to the library we went in the store. Once we got in, she made me wait for her outside. She said that even though the boy hadn't arrived yet, she wanted him to see her without her baby brother tagging along behind her. I was so afraid that if mom and dad ever found out we'd get in trouble. But, I went back outside, as she asked, and stood by the door. That way I could see her when she came out. In the few minutes I stood there waiting on her, only a few kids, mostly girls, went into the store on that day. After a while, when I thought she had taken long enough, though I couldn't guess how long I'd been waiting, I went in to get her. But she wasn't there. There were two other kids and the clerk. I asked the clerk and he said that she and a boy went out the side door. The store was on a corner and I never saw her leave out the side door since I was standing in the front. I asked him how long ago and the clerk said about twenty minutes ago. I went out the side door and ran down the street, but I couldn't find her. I waited a while longer hoping that she'd come back any minute, but she never did, so I raced home and told my parents."

"You feel responsible?"

"Yes, I am responsible," he whispered.

"Why?"

"I should have insisted that—"

"At age eight? None of that is your fault, Wesley, you have to know that."

"I should have —,"

"No, Wesley. You only see what you should have done later, after everything is done and as an adult. When it happened, you did what was right, and, remember you were eight. No one expects a boy to do a man's job."

"You deserve the credit. For two weeks, I watched how you treated Leon. This man kidnapped children. He took my sister. Yet, I thought I had put it all aside, but I hadn't gotten over it. Watching you come every day to pray with him, and be his friend, opened my eyes to people who do this kind of thing. It made me realize that once I had let my hatred for him take over my life." He paused for a moment and looked over at her as if trying to decide to tell her more.

"When I was a teenager, and then an adult, I was always angry and I didn't trust people."

"Wesley, then you've changed."

"You came in, said you would pray with that hardened criminal, and you fought him until he did. You dedicated yourself to that."

"But Wesley, my being there was different. I was there to pray with him."

"I know."

"What else? You need to talk about it. I want to hear it."

"The hatred I had for him, during those earlier years," he paused to gaze at her to see how she was taking everything, "turned everything I touched sour. I lost my girlfriend. At first, in my law practice, I wasn't a trustful person. Thankfully, over the years, I lost interest in Leon. I changed who I was as an attorney, made myself a little more likeable and almost became a new person. But my mother found it difficult to let my sister rest."

"Maybe you both can now. How did you find out about his capture?"

"My mother showed me the newspaper article where Leon had been apprehended. The police had finally found the man who walked away with my sister. I knew I couldn't let him out of my sight. I found out everything about him and what he did. My mother made me promise her that I would see it through to the end. She told me she had to witness his execution."

"You quit your practice to be near him?"

"I hired another lawyer in my firm and concentrated on Leon. I found out that the prison was short of guards and I applied, I was more than qualified. After I had been on the job a while, the captain retired, so I applied for his job. There was one other applicant and I just knew he would get it since he had been a guard much longer than I had. But the warden asked him to take another position as assistant warden in another prison and I got the job. I promised myself and my mother that I would stay there and make sure that Leon got what he deserved."

"Wesley, what were you planning?"

"After you came, I lost my reason to care about that anymore. I realized that I should have let Leon and his son go years before. Maybe I should have used what he did to my sister in a positive way in my life. I have to say that I feel free and relieved, like a huge burden has been lifted from me. I like that feeling. But, you have to know that your visits with Leon freed me."

"Why did you go back to the house?"

"I discovered that it's not easy to let things go." He looked at her. "I guess that's why it was easy for me to do what my mother asked."

"You've been there several times."

"Three. I've been there three times. This morning I was there to say good-bye to my sister. I won't go back. He's gone and I have to move on."

Silence for a long moment.

Olivia questioned, "What's the matter?"

"You're disgusted with me, aren't you? I shouldn't have told you all this. I haven't told anyone this."

"I'm not disgusted with you. I'm happy you picked me to confide in. Why would you believe I would be disgusted with you? You were carrying a heavy burden, and you've been carrying that since you were eight. I can't imagine what you have been going through, how you have felt responsible all these years, and managed your profession. You're very strong. You're much stronger than you think you are. Your sister would have been very proud of you."

They sat in silence and pressed together, his hand around hers.

Her three years in seminary has taught her that people carry so much hidden inside and a good priest makes the effort to bring the feelings or the hurt to the surface. Olivia had to admit that all this about Wesley took her by surprise judging him from his outer appearance. She never would have guessed that he was carrying a burden this heavy. He had felt responsible for his sister all these years. That must have been eating his heart away. Maybe now that Leon was gone he could put this pain in the past and move on, as he said. She was amazed at the fact that Wesley came to church which meant that he had already begun to heal.

She had spent almost two weeks with a man who wanted so badly to be loved that he caused so much pain and harm to those whom he asked to love him. She had grown to understand this man and she hated to admit it, she liked him. But now, she'd seen as much as she could bear. She had seen what he did and how he did it. She saw Wesley, a strong man weakened by Leon's actions. Her quandary now was whether she should go to the house Leon asked her to go to find his daughter, or leave things the way they were.

CHAPTER 24

Olivia rose early for the long drive to the house located in Maryland where Leon had asked her to go to find his daughter. Throughout the night, she had a dream about Leon and his daughter. She saw his daughter with a picnic basket and she and Leon sat outside at a picnic table under the trees eating fried chicken, Cole slaw and salad. The dream seemed so real to her until she woke up and found that she was just having a dream. When she fell asleep again, she dreamed that Leon and his daughter went in a store that resembled a commissary with cinderblock walls on all sides. His daughter pushed the cart and Leon smiled and laughed, showing everyone that he was proud of his daughter. He introduced her to the other men wearing gray uniforms. She woke up before the men in gray spoke.

Olivia had a sense of obligation, a sense of duty to Leon's daughter. Leon was gone. Still she had to prepare herself for what was to come. Maybe his daughter didn't want to be reminded of what she went through with her father. Maybe, there weren't all good things that happened to her. Maybe, she had found herself another life, a life where there was beauty and happiness.

Then, maybe she was just like Leon. In any case, Olivia wanted her to know the good she found in Leon. Even though she had seen what must have gone on in the house in Virginia, his daughter never lived there according to Leon, and Olivia thought that his daughter deserved to hear that he wasn't born a child abductor and that earlier in his life, he had good in his heart. Maybe in some way this would help her live a good or at least a better life. Olivia not only wanted his daughter to know that, but Olivia had to believe that herself.

Before she left, she needed to find out a few things on the internet. She was thankful that while she was in seminary she took a class one summer from a nearby community college that showed her how to set up a webpage, and which browsers were best for particular searches. She needed directions, a list of elementary schools in the area and their principals.

On the way out of the door, she tucked Fr. Wilson's letter and Leon's letter inside her purse along with a couple of protein bars and picked up several bottles of water.

She used her GPS to find the major four-lane roads, which took her to several back roads. She crossed over railroad tracks that ran alongside commercial buildings and drove down dirt roads, stirring up mud and dust until she arrived at the house. It was surrounded by huge trees and overgrown bushes. This time, she knew what to expect and she had put on her hiking boots. She pulled up as close to the vacant-looking house as she could, seeing that there was no driveway. She turned off the engine, checked around, and saw no one else there. The house appeared abandoned; and from the outside she couldn't tell whether it was livable.

A strange loneliness, the lull before a severe storm, first overtook her. The small one-story house seemed so out of place, out of tune with nature, hidden among the huge fir and oak trees and they spread out and over the house as if nature wanted it out of its picture.

Then, a fear so terrifying that it halted her, surged through her body. She remained paralyzed for what seemed like an eternity. After a few moments, she felt her seatbelt draw itself back and when she looked down, she saw her hand on the clasp. She had to say something to herself, urge herself to get out of the car, or drive away from there without coming back. She tried to get her lips to move. From far away, it seemed, she heard the car door open and looked down at her hand on the latch. She could see, and feel and think, but they didn't seem like her feelings and thoughts. She felt like she was at a movie watching someone else. Perspiration ran down her face and her clothes were wet up against her. She tried to keep herself in the present and took in deep breaths to gain control of herself. She sat in the car until she was relaxed enough to ruminate rationally. The other house had a different effect on her. Through her confusion, she tried to understand what would be inside that house that would cause this kind of fear in her. She slowly turned, lifted one leg at a time, and pulled herself out of the car. Her reasoning mind wanted to get back into the car, drive away, but something else, some kind of magnetic force, pulled her toward that house.

Once out the car, the fear began to slowly subside, and she was able to reason more clearly. Shoving one foot in front of the other, she compelled herself to move toward the front door. Along the way, she remembered the words her father said to her the day before, *There's no need to take this any further*. Again, the thought of turning back ran through her mind several times. But, her body would not allow her to turn back.

Fear returned when she was about half way and she began to shake. She knew the house was empty, she could see that, and besides Wesley told her that. Yet she felt a terrible fear so great that again she tried to turn back. But she still couldn't turn back. Instead, she continued the walk toward the house still forcing her steps. When she was almost there, she was surprised to see that the house was being restored. For some reason, that seemed to calm her a little. The outside wall seemed newer and some of the wood slats were painted. An almost empty paint can, with dried paint in the bottom, sat next to the recently painted wall. At the front door, she turned the knob that seemed to work, and slowly pushed the door in. She stood back as if she was afraid that someone would jump out from behind the door.

When she stepped inside, she saw that some of the floorboards in the front room were newer and had been placed alongside the others. Two of the four windows in the back of the room looked new, and were even painted a different shade of white. She walked to what was the fireplace with its decomposed wood and fallen bricks, the ashes and half-burned logs still there.

She thought she heard a noise, a baby crying and walked to one of three rooms in the back. She put her hand over her heart and felt a regular beat, gazed at her hands and found they were no longer shaking. She was more relaxed now; the fear was diminishing.

She stood in the center of the empty room and turned around in all directions, held there for a moment listening for the cry again. She heard nothing, and walked to a wall, ran her hand across something that seemed etched in the plaster, and discovered a bump in the wall. She waited to hear the baby cry again, but the crying stopped; and she realized that it was a bird or some other animal.

She left that room and went to the second one. Again, she stood in the center and checked around. In a corner, she noticed a small table with two drawers. She opened the top drawer. Inside there was an old dirty baseball with the red stitching unraveled. Olivia touched it realizing that she was standing in Tony's room. She remembered him telling her how badly he wanted to play baseball. He must have picked up a lost ball. She closed that drawer and opened the next. She found part of a page from a children's book. She took it out and ran her hand across the page. There was not enough of a picture or words for her to determine the story. She put it back, closed the drawer, and started out of the room.

Again, fear overtook her and she held onto the doorjamb to keep herself from falling. Her stomach churned, and churned, felt like someone had reached inside her, grabbed hold of her stomach, upended its contents. She grabbed hold of her stomach, an effort to try to keep from bringing up anything. After a moment when she felt better, she pulled herself away from the doorjamb and eased her way inside the room. There, she moved to the single bed with its half-eaten away mattress, still in place. She looked for chains and ropes, the things she saw in the other house. She thought that whoever was restoring the house had removed them all. She turned to leave, but before she did, she bent down to pull up a floorboard near the bed, but the floorboard was nailed solid in place. She didn't understand why she would do anything like that. It must have seemed lose and she just wanted to see but, otherwise she wouldn't know anything about the floorboard.

She went back out to the room with the fireplace and stood beside it. She touched the wooden mantle and the eaten away wood. In the alcove on that side, she saw two brown leather cushions that were from a chair or a couch. With her foot, she pulled back one of the cushions and saw that it was ripped up on the underneath side and most of the foam missing. She looked harder and saw that the cushion was not leather, but vinyl. For a fleeting second, the house seemed familiar to her and she thought she'd been in this house before. She rejected that idea thinking that she was familiar with this house because of her visits with Leon. He talked about himself and the house.

She looked all around the room and wondered whether Leon's daughter had bought the house. She would check the county records at the courthouse for whomever was making the changes. Leon said that his daughter wanted to go to school and Tony told her that he used to watch the children coming out of a school.

Before leaving the house, she went through it once again. There was no evidence of chains, ropes and no brown or faded red spots, proof she saw in the other house. Maybe more good happened here. Maybe the real owner removed it all.

Earlier, during her internet search, Olivia found the elementary school that Leon's daughter likely attended. It was the only one in the area. The site also gave facts about the school, when it was built, important people who once attended along with their teachers, and more importantly, a list of all the past principals with their tenure dates. Olivia found Mrs. Edna Dickey who was principal about the year, or months Leon's daughter attended. She also found an old phonebook, the White Pages, that she had been planning to throw away, but hadn't, and located Mrs. Dickey's address. Even though the phone book was considered "old school" she always found it easier than the internet where now a cost was involved. Using her GPS, she drove first to Scaggsville Elementary School and parked across the street.

A group of yellow school busses all packed with children, lined up in front of the school. One by one, the busses pulled out of the driveway and down to the two-lane road in front of the school. Olivia pulled into the driveway behind the last bus. The sounds of the children laughing, talking loudly, yelling out the window, and squealing were a stark difference to the quietude and grimness of the house she had just left. She understood why Tony wanted to go to school.

When all the busses left and the teachers turned to go back into the building, she could see the entrance to the school. The school seemed familiar to her. It looked like the one she attended shortly before she was adopted. She tried hard to remember her own past. This school couldn't be it. She and Leon's daughter couldn't have attended the same school. She had trouble recalling. Leon said that his daughter was there for a short period. Leon also said that they were about the same age. Maybe they met. She just couldn't remember.

Olivia pulled her car into an empty space and sat for a few minutes. Even though the school had a familiar feel, she couldn't have attended this school and if so, she wasn't there long enough to have met Leon's daughter. She recalled that soon after she went to live with her parents, they moved to England. As much as she wanted to know, she just could not recollect her birth parents, or any of the circumstances under which her parents adopted her. She started her car and drove to Edna Dickey's house, the woman who was principal during those months.

* * *

Olivia found Crazy Horse Drive and parked two houses down and across the tree-lined residential street. While she sat in her car trying to decide what to do, the front door opened and a woman came out of the house, walked down to the edge of the driveway, turned in the opposite direction, and walked down the street. She was dressed in jogging clothes and wore tennis shoes. When the woman reached the second driveway from her house, a woman also dressed in jogging clothes, came out of her house. At the end of her driveway, the two women greeted each other and took off. From the way these two women held their arms, and their quick, but sharp pace, they were on a power walk.

Later, the two women power-walked back. They slowed down at the lady's house and Olivia found the courage and her chance. She got out of her car and met who she thought was Edna Dickey at the edge of her driveway.

"Good morning ma'am, are you Edna Dickey?"

The woman stopped. "Who wants to know?"

"Mrs. Dickey, my name is Olivia Douglass. I'm sorry for approaching you this way, but you see, I just graduated from the seminary in Virginia. I wanted to be a priest, but I changed my mind and my rector gave me this assignment to go see the inmate who was being executed so that I could find myself and decide whether, or not to become a priest. I think he wants me to be a priest. Anyway, in talking to Leon, the inmate, he told me about his daughter and asked me to find her to tell her he was sorry and that led me here to you." She said as quickly as she could and in one big breath. Even though she was nervous, she hadn't intended to run Mrs. Dickey away.

"Wow, young lady. Take time to breathe. That's certainly a story. I don't quite understand how I'm involved. This sounds like a scam to me. What are you trying to do? Get me in my house so you can tie me up and take my few belongings? Get away from my house. I'm calling the police now." She ran up her driveway to her front door.

Olivia started behind her. "Mrs. Dickey, I'm not a scam artist or anything like that. Why don't you look at my ID from the seminary and I have a letter that my rector wrote to the warden of the prison giving me permission to see Leon Sunstrik Wilkerson."

Mrs. Dickey turned around.

"You can see my driver's license if you want to or you can call the police and ask the officer to stay with you while we talk. All I need to know is if you knew Leon's daughter and what happened to her," Olivia said.

Mrs. Dickey walked back down the driveway. "What did you say your name was?' She held out her hand for the papers.

"Olivia Douglass." She handed the papers to Edna.

"Why don't we go inside?"

Mrs. Dickey opened the front door and motioned for Olivia to enter.

"Have a seat," she said pointing to the couch in the living room.

Olivia stepped into the living room and immediately was in another world. She took a seat on the French antique couch with its ornate pink and yellow flower design. A French antique table was placed on either side of the couch, and in front of her, another French style antique table. She surveyed the room, first at the myriad of framed pictures displayed on the antique marble top end tables, then the mantel over the fireplace across from her, and on the marble top table in front of her. The tables were filled with pictures in all different types of frames, and showed groups of children, and classes of children. On one end of the carved inlay mantel, there were several pictures of Mrs. Dickey and a little girl. On the other end and on the marble top table were pictures of what must have been Mrs. Dickey's family. Olivia noticed more pictures of Mrs. Dickey and a little girl.

"Thank you for seeing me."

The retired principal didn't seem familiar to her and she watched Mrs. Dickey through her age lines, faded eyes and sagging skin trying to recognize her in any way. But, if Mrs. Dickey was her principal when she was at the elementary school, she had aged so that she was unrecognizable to Olivia.

"Mrs. Dickey, as I said, I had the opportunity to talk to Leon Wilkerson, a prisoner on death row. His last request, was that he wanted me to find his daughter, if I could. He has a message for her. He lived in a cabin in the woods near the school where you were principal. He also said that his daughter had attended elementary school for a short period. He didn't know the name of the school but your school is the only one in the area. I'm hoping you can help me."

Mrs. Dickey frowned in confusion, which made Olivia nervous, and she began to wring her hands. Mrs. Dickey smiled again, and looked over at the pictures of herself and the little girl.

"I remember that we had a little girl, a sweet little thing, all the teachers loved her. I want to say her name was Olivia, but I can't be sure, but that's because I didn't think she had a name. Either she made it up or one of the teachers named her, or maybe her father did say that was her name. I just don't remember. Anyway, she came to us out of nowhere it seemed. I remember that a man brought her, and said he was her father. We tried to get him to complete some papers on her, and bring in a birth certificate so we'd have some records, but as I remember, he said he had to get to work and he'd have her bring everything on the next day. He wanted to leave her with us that day."

"He never enrolled her?"

"Not really, not officially. As I remember it, he said he didn't have time to fill out the papers. He was late for his first day of work. We gave him the papers to take with him and we thought he would bring her back after he completed the papers, but he wanted to leave her with us that day as I just said. We let her stay that day. Things were different then. We were a small school with woods on three sides. The families were poor or working class. During that period, most of them were out of work. The officials from the school district let us care about our students the best way we could. We took care of our own. In that school, we were like a family. We had to be. After I saw that little girl, I told him that she could stay with us and that we needed to get her records from her other school system. He said they'd just moved from another state. One of the hardest things in the school system is to try and get records from another state, and now they have to try and get records from another country. That's even worse. Even with the use of computers, it's still very difficult. Sometimes the records come in a few weeks, a month, several months and in one case, a child who entered kindergarten went on to middle school before her records came."

"Can you tell me something about this girl?" Olivia asked.

"Well, let's see. At first, she was afraid. She wouldn't let anyone touch her. That little girl hadn't had a bath in a long while. Her clothes, well she needed new clothes. Her first day, we had to get her ready for school. Our utility closet had a shower and a washtub and Mrs. Hardesty, she was our female custodian at the time, and I had to get her in the shower and wash her hair before she could go in the classroom. That was truly a chore because she thought we were harming her in some way and fought us. She tried to keep us from taking off those clothes and yelled, 'Mine, mine, mine.' We got her as clean as we could," she chuckled, "she seemed to like the bubbles from the soap, as I remember. Then we searched around and found some clothes from the lost and found for her. I tried talking to her, but she seemed to understand very little of what I was saying. Mostly, she grunted or shook her head. Her father told us that she was eight-years old, so we had to put her in second grade, at least until we got her records. Mrs. Taylor, the second-grade teacher, said she couldn't read or write or do much, even talk. We suspected that she had never been to school. That was why he never got us her records."

"How did she get back and forth to school?"

"She walked. I'd get there very early and I'd see her coming out of the woods. She seemed to love school after she got started and figured out everything. And she was a quick learner. In the three months she was with us, she learned the alphabet, numbers, simple addition and some words. Her first week with us and we figured out that she had no food at home. She couldn't get on our free lunch program because we couldn't get hold of her father. So, every day the teachers pitched in and bought her breakfast and lunch. She came by the office every day after school and had a hearty snack before she left. I thought that would tide her over until the next morning. Every one pitched in and bought her clothes even the students and parents. Of course, we never told her where those clothes came from."

"Do you remember what happened to her?"

Mrs. Dickey glanced at Olivia, her face in a scowl as if she was not understanding why Olivia would ask her what happened to her. After a few seconds, Mrs. Dickey's appearance changed and Olivia could see that she was afraid to say anything more.

"Mrs. Dickey, do you remember what happened to her?" Olivia persisted.

"One afternoon, she came to my office and as best she could, said that she couldn't go home. She wouldn't say why. She lacked the words to tell us, but I thought her father left her. I called the police. When they arrived, she tried to tell them where she and her father lived, back up in those woods. When they went there to find him, no one was there. The police said that he had left some days before and the poor little girl was living there by herself. Her father said she was eight, and she couldn't have been more than eight years old. I really thought she was about late six to middle seven. I have some pictures of her that are very dear to me. I often wondered what happened to her." She turned to pick up a picture off the mantel and handed it to Olivia.

"Just before she left I asked her if I could take a picture of her. You know when she came early every morning, we talked, I did most of the talking, but I got used to her every morning and I knew I would miss her." She handed Olivia a framed picture of herself and the little girl. "This is soon after she arrived. I had to take this picture in case any questions came up." She handed her another picture from the table. "And this is just before she left." Then she handed her a third picture from the table. "And this one is with the family who took her in. I think they adopted her. Dr. and Mrs. Douglass."

Olivia looked at the pictures when Mrs. Dickey passed her the third picture. She sucked in her breath. "These are my parents. Is this the little girl they adopted?"

"Yes, that's you. The Douglasses had one daughter in the second grade or third grade at the time. You two became friends."

"But these are my parents. Are you saying . . . But this is me . . . I'm the daughter?"

Olivia held the picture up again. "See, I don't look anything like this little girl. Where'd you get this picture?"

"Another teacher took it. I wanted to remember us." She watched Olivia. "You are that little girl. I knew it the minute I went back down the driveway and stepped closer to you. You have those same warm eyes. I'll never forget those warm, caring eyes."

"I don't understand. The Douglasses adopted me. Could they have adopted another child, too?"

"Not that I know of."

At that moment, Olivia became someone high above looking down on herself or some poor creature. This creature took hold of one arm to feel that it was she. She saw the person stand up, sit down, stand up again, walk around the living room in a circle, heard this person scream out several times, "It can't be me. It just can't." She saw this person study the pictures that sat around on tables, walk around the room again, and finally sat down on the couch. She saw tears gushing out of this person and heard her yell again, "No, it's not me. It can't be me," and again, and again yell, "It can't be me."

She saw that the person had trouble forming her thoughts. "But what. . ., what, who, I can't, this."

She heard another voice. "It's okay, Olivia."

That evilness or curse that had been plaguing her all her life came to mind. She heard someone say, or was it herself saying. "See, I told you, you were an evil one." Then she heard laughter.

This is where that evil feeling had come from. She was Leon's daughter. Memories flooded her mind. She thought about a day when Leon had taken her and Tony and the three of them stood outside the school watching the children. She remembered how Leon took to one little girl and followed her movements as she ran around the playground and while the other children tried to tag her. She remembered how he watched that little girl one afternoon when that little girl's mother picked her up from school. She remembered one afternoon when the woods were icy and Leon made a fire for her and Tony. She remembered how Leon told the two of them fairy tales all afternoon and told them how sorry he was that they didn't have a better house as he stoked the fire trying to keep them warm. She remembered how Leon had taken her through the woods looking for wild flowers for her space in a room. She saw him picking some of the flowers and handing them to her. She saw him hug her and direct her to a patch of daisies. She remembered how he made her a doll out of old rags and how she slept with it every night. She called the doll "Doll" and cried when Tony ripped it. She remembered she was afraid to tell Leon about the doll, for fear that he would beat Tony. She saw him giving her something hot and soothing when she'd caught a bad cold. She felt his hands when he stroked her head and pulled the blankets up. She saw a little girl cowering in a corner, hands over her eyes. She remembered, and now she was no longer high above herself.

"I never should have come here. I was better off not knowing." Tears continued to gush down her face, a water main bursting.

Olivia's sobbing grew louder and she had trouble breathing from the intense sobbing.

"Listen to me. I know you're not going to remember everything I say to you now, but the little girl I knew and grew to love was a kind loving, smart little girl who I thought would grow up to be someone important, someone like the person you are now."

"How can I? Leon was my father. Do you know what that man did? What he told me he did when I visited him? It can't be true. I just have everything all mixed up, that's what it is. He can't be my father." How could she ever reconcile herself to the fact that she was Leon's daughter? The shock of the truth was so terrifying that it was debilitating.

"Leon, Leon was my father," she repeated. Stomach spasms overpowered her and she felt an eruption so great that caused her to heave violently.

"The bathroom is down there," she heard Mrs. Dickey say. She ran down the hall to the bathroom. After closing the door, she hovered over the sink, trying to calm herself, stop herself from heaving. After a while, she wiped her face and peered up into the mirror. Since she had held on to the picture, she put it up beside her face to see the resemblance. It seemed like the same girl. It had to be her. Did Leon ask her to look for his daughter because he knew she was his daughter? She tried to recall, to remember anything he might have said that would let her know he already knew. This was the reason why she couldn't remember her past. Her parents knew that was why they tried to stop her search for Leon's daughter. After a very long few minutes and she was composed as much as she could be under the circumstances, Olivia came out of the bathroom.

"I'm, so sorry. I didn't mean to upset you," said Mrs. Dickey when she saw Olivia returning.

"I know."

Mrs. Dickey gave her a wide smile and reached over to hug her.

When they pulled away, "Do you know anything about my mother?" Olivia asked.

"No. I thought she passed away."

"Do you know if she was someone he abducted?"

"Olivia, I'm sorry. I know you want answers, but I really don't know."

She stood watching Mrs. Dickey as if she could rewind the last few minutes and have her life take a different turn. "Thank you for your time."

"Don't go yet. Sit down. Let's talk more, like we used to. You're leaving because you're embarrassed. Don't be embarrassed, don't be ashamed, don't feel lost and don't give up. You have no reason to do any of that. I'm so happy to see you again."

"Thank you. I do remember you, now. You were always so kind to me. And I came to school early and stayed later because I wanted to be with you."

"I looked forward to seeing you every morning and every evening. And even though it was a short period, I missed you terribly when you left. But, in a sense, I was happy to see you go."

"I understand."

"Are you just finding this out about yourself?"

"Yes. I guess my parents felt it better to not say anything until I asked."

"Under the circumstances I understand that. Olivia, when you approached me outside, you said you were going to be a priest, but you changed your mind. Why? Why did you change your mind?"

Olivia halted herself at first, then Mrs. Dickey just found out about her so there was nothing to hide, anymore. "I couldn't be a priest. For as long as I can remember, I've had this feeling haunting me, like a curse, something evil, or something sinful. As I got older, I thought that I committed a terrible sin or did something horrible to someone. So, you see, I couldn't be a priest if I'd harmed anyone."

"But now you see that you couldn't do anything like that."

"I still don't know."

"Olivia, who were you before this day, this moment?"

"I was many things— a high school student, college graduate, and I just graduated from the seminary in Virginia. I like helping people and I wanted to, but now . . ."

"You had a life with a loving family who helped you accomplish all those things."

"My family. I have a mother, father, and sister all whom I love dearly and who love me. My parents helped me through seminary. They are the parents

I know and I don't know what I'd do without them."

"Don't you see Olivia, who you just described to me is the person you are. The Douglasses wanted to take you. They wanted to give you the chance you deserved. You have to use that chance and do something important. Be the priest that you want to be."

"I don't know how I can forgive him. How could I ever forgive him for such gruesome acts?"

"I can't answer that, but I know who can. Maybe you're being called to the priesthood so you can forgive him and for you to understand that you don't have to be like him. You came here out of kindness. You came here to help someone else. You know we all have choices and you have already made your choice. You've selected something different. I'm sure you'll find a way to forgive this man. In fact, it seems to me that you've forgiven him already. And you needed to tell that to his daughter. Then tell it to her."

Olivia reached for the doorknob, but Mrs. Dickey opened the front door for her. She handed Olivia a card. "You know I always thought you'd do well. You were such a lovely girl and as I said, so sweet and kind. Everyone loved you. I am so excited to see you now. I missed you so much after you left and always wondered what happened to you. Now, I see. This doesn't happen often to teachers and principals. Olivia, I am so happy to see what a good person you've turned out to be. Please keep in touch with me."

Olivia heard joy and happiness in her voice,

"Thank you, Mrs. Dickey." Olivia turned to leave.

"Olivia, you know all I know about your past. Dr. and Mrs. Douglass may not know much more than that, either. Your future will be your doing. You have to know that. I'll always be here and if you find it in your heart, and I know you will, please invite me to your ordination."

Olivia tried to smile, nodded, and turned to go to her car.

Chapter 25

As Olivia drove back, she was filled with a mixture of confusion, hurt and anger. In her quest to find Leon's daughter, she found herself. On one hand, she needed to know everything about who she was before her adoption. On the other hand, she refused to believe that she'd committed the most heinous acts possible, that she'd helped Leon with those little girls, the way Tony helped. She couldn't continue living if she found out she was responsible for the death of those girls. She was relieved to know that those feelings she'd had came from her life before she was adopted; her life with Leon.

On the drive back, Olivia couldn't get who she truly was out of her mind. She drove in a fog and several times car horns blew at her as she had crossed into the next lane. Several times, her car weaved in her lane and drivers sped around her. She was consumed with the thought that she was the daughter of a child abductor and killer and that whatever made him that person would also make her the same kind of person. She was afraid of herself, that she was born the way he was and given the chance, she would do what was innate.

She could hardly see the road in front of her, she cried so hard. She wiped her eyes every few seconds as she continued driving aimlessly on I 95. She would never go back to that place. Perhaps if she kept away, she wouldn't be like Leon.

When she saw the sign, she realized that she had driven to the bookstore, the place where her family was, the place where she was safe and loved. She needed to know what more they knew about her, about her biological mother. She needed them to help her see whether or not she was involved in helping Leon and Tony abduct those girls. She needed to know that where she came from, those first six or seven years of her life, would not matter to them.

She pushed opened the door, and the bell tinkled as she entered. The store was empty, and she switched the "Open" sign to "Closed" and turned the lock on the door.

"Hi," said her mother, caution in her voice as she came out from the back room. "What's wrong? Oh, sweetheart, you're upset. What's wrong?" Her mother moved toward her.

At that moment, her father came out of the back room. "Hi, sweetheart."

"Why wouldn't you tell me? Why did I have to find out from someone else?" This time she meant to be accusing. She held her body stiff.

"No, no, no, no, no," repeated her mother while shaking her head, hands on her face.

"Who am I? Tell me, please. I need to know who I am." Tears formed in her eyes that begged, pleaded for answers.

"Sweetheart, you are our daughter," said her mother. "You've always been and you always will be our daughter, Olivia Emily Douglass." She stepped closer to Olivia.

Olivia took a step back. "Am I Leon's daughter?" She could no longer control her tears and they ran down her cheeks like a hard rain beating against a window. Her body sank in the way a person would when giving up, all is lost.

Her mother, tears now running down her face, grabbed her daughter, held on to her as tightly as she could. "No. sweetheart, no, no."

Her father separated his wife and daughter.

"Sit down, Sweetheart." He pointed to the chairs at the table, then pulled one out for Olivia. He turned to his wife, pulled out a chair. She sat down.

He drew in a deep breath. "We only knew that your mother had died and your father left one day while you were in school. The police thought that your father had left several days before, but we weren't sure about that. You were too young. When we found out that you had no place else to go, we wanted to take you with us. We arranged for an adoption. Our attorney, someone we found, said that given your circumstances it wouldn't be a problem. When the judge found out that we were moving to England, he moved things along as fast as he could."

"The man who left, was his name Leon?"

"Honey what does all this matter?" her mother said.

"I just have to know."

"What are you saying that we're not your parents anymore? Are you leaving us?" her mother asked, looking at Olivia, eyes still filled with tears.

"Why can't you just tell me the truth; just say it?"

"We think it could be, but we're not sure. We knew he had a funny sounding name, but no one knew his entire name. The principal said you called him Sunny or something like that," her father said.

"Mom, why were you so against my going to the house?"

"I just have a very bad feeling about all of this and though it's just a feeling I couldn't see any good coming from it. Honey, you have to know that we don't want to lose you."

"Why? Why did you and mom pick me? Of all the children at that school, why did you pick me?"

"We wanted to adopt you. We couldn't just leave you there. We loved you right away. And because of Kara; you saved her life."

"I did? How?"

"The principal wouldn't give us the whole story. She told us that you went to her office to talk to her. There was no way to confirm it, but we thought that you told her that your father had gone off and left you. She had to call the police and child welfare. Afterward, she called us. We weren't told more than that. For your protection, I guess. Your mother and I didn't need to know more than that, especially since child welfare told us that they would have to take you with them. We wanted to adopt you and that was that."

"I remember, now." Olivia stopped crying, and looked away as if seeing the past. "I remember he wanted me to bring Kara home with me. I liked Kara and I didn't want to do that. I knew what he would do to her. He told me if I didn't bring her home that day, he wouldn't let me go back to school, and I knew I wouldn't see Kara anymore. I wouldn't have a friend. I went to the principal's office. I had to tell her and she called the police. If I'm his daughter, I'm tainted, evil. I'm a killer, too." The times she tried to see if she could kill her cat, Purdy, flashed through her mind.

"No, Sweetheart. You've never hurt anyone," her mother said. "From the very second you became ours, you were a sweet, thoughtful and kind person. Don't you remember how you always had to know if your mother or I had milk and when the carton was empty, you'd give up yours? You learned to cook and you and Kara made dinner for us almost every Sunday; always something new and different on the menu. We've always been family and you've been a part of it. Please, sweetheart, don't let any of this change that. You are who you are, a sweet loving, kind little girl, who has now turned into this kind sensitive woman, the person you are now. You weren't born like Leon. Ugliness is not inside you or else you wouldn't want to be a priest." her father said.

"Do you still love me?" Her voice was weak and tiny as if she was afraid of the answer.

"Livvy, we thought that you'd be resentful at first, especially since we had to move to England as soon as we adopted you, but you weren't. You were always so grateful. We loved you from the first moment we saw you. You needed our help and we loved you back. None of that has changed," said her mother. She took Olivia's hands in hers.

"Don't do that." Her father wiped away her tears. "Don't do that. You have nothing to cry about. You have brought us so much joy and happiness. You've been so giving and encouraging to Kara. Clearly, God sent you to us and we hold you special. We're very proud of you."

He kissed her forehead.

"There's no way you could believe you're tainted," he continued.

"Your father is right, sweetheart. You have to know that."

"Do you think, I . . . do you . . . do you think I helped Leon with Wesley's sister?"

Her parents looked at each other as if they'd never thought about that. "I seriously doubt that, Livvy." Her mother took Olivia's hands in hers, again. "We had no way of knowing that Leon had taken Wesley's sister. That must have happened after we were in England. You said you would find out more about him, did you?"

"Yes, he was found in Virginia and charged with murder in Virginia."

"Then you couldn't have helped him. He lived in Maryland when we adopted you. When the police went back to his house after you talked with the principal, Leon and his son were gone. There was no mention of other children in the house at the time. They must have left then and gone to Virginia. Maybe they figured out that you called the police." her mother said.

"You also know how to put your foot down when someone tries to make you do something you don't want to do. I doubt that he could have made you do that," her father said. He wiped away her tears again, and then continued, "You refused to take Kara to that house; instead, you called the police. Even then you knew right from wrong."

"How old was I then?"

"We took you to a pediatrician after we got to England and she said you were an early seven," her mother said.

Remembering a conversation she had with Leon, she asked, "When is my birthday?"

"We don't exactly know. The pediatrician gave us an estimate about when you would turn eight. We used that month."

"My age is close to correct?"

"We believe so," her mother said.

"But that doesn't change anything. I . . ." She frowned, twisted in her chair.

Her father picked up the cookie bowl now empty, handed it to Olivia.

"You're upset with us. You assumed that we held information from you. You're very angry and I don't blame you. I'd be extremely upset, too. Take this bowl and throw it at me. Get even with me." He handed her the bowl.

"Dad, no."

"Vinny, this is crazy?" yelled her mother. "Stop, Vinny, are you out of your mind?"

Ignoring his wife, he continued, "Here, take the bowl." He tried to force her to take it, shoved it in her hand. "Take it. Throw it at me. If you aim right, you could kill me. I deserve it. Hurt me, Olivia, I did you wrong. Get even with me. You have to."

"No, I can't do that. What's wrong with you? Why are you asking me to hurt you?" Olivia tried to stand up, get away.

He grabbed her arm. "Livvy, throw this bowl at me," he yelled.

"No, I can't do that. I can't. Stop it." She pulled and jerked until she freed her arm.

"Well, now. That proves it."

"Proves what? What are you talking about?" Olivia asked, hiding her hands under her arms.

"Sit down." He pointed to her chair. "You can't do that; you couldn't hurt anybody. I knew you wouldn't throw this bowl at me; you have too much good inside you. Why would you even accept the fact that you could help anyone do harm to someone else?"

"Honey, we've been trying to tell you that you couldn't hurt anyone. You're not like that man," her mother said.

"You're both just saying that. I'm evil in my heart."

"Livvy, please stop it," her mother cried out. "I can't stand it any longer, please stop it. Just because you were, you, you lived there, doesn't mean that you had to do the things that he did."

"I know I'm evil, a sinful person. I've felt this evilness, this curse hanging over me for a several years, ever since I was a little girl. I even tried to kill Purdy. Why do you think I can't be a priest?"

Olivia snatched her hand away from her mother. "Olivia, we got Purdy shortly after we all moved to England and he died two years ago. Purdy was old, sweetheart."

"No. Don't touch me. Why would you anyway? I'm evil. I knew all along that something was wrong with me . . ." She got up, ran out the door, and made her way down the street to her car.

She looked back and saw her mother running after her. Olivia opened the car door and was inside the car before her mother got to her. She turned the engine over just as her mother reached her and tapped on the window.

"Livvy, honey, come back inside. Please."

"Watch out." Olivia pulled her car out of the space.

Her mother stepped back out of the way. "Where are you going?"

Olivia drove to the church, and pulled up to the side door. She used to have the idea that no one knew the door was open, and that it was her special way of entering the church to pray whenever she needed to, but her thoughts were all confused at this point. She entered the dimly lit sanctuary and walked down the aisle to about midway. Suddenly she turned around, walked out of the church to her car, and drove home.

CHAPTER 26

The next morning, Olivia rose early, went to the closet, and pulled out a large suitcase. Searching through her drawers, she packed the suitcase with sweatpants, sweatshirts, wool socks and anything else she would need. She had to get away and mull things through. She was confused, angry, and without hope. She needed to ground herself, put things in perspective, find order out of this chaos. Downstairs, she grabbed her grill and searched through the cabinets for cheese and crackers, peanut butter and crackers, canned foods, coffee, and things good for camping. She threw her clothes and the food in a suitcase that she struggled to close, she'd packed so hurriedly. Getting it into her trunk posed an even bigger challenge, but she managed to lift it up enough to roll it into the trunk of her car. Just before taking off, she remembered Kara's bourbon and wine, or rather what was left in the bottles. Seeing the bottles, reminded her that she needed paper plates or cups, so she went back and got what she had in the cabinet and brought out plastic store bags for the wine and bourbon. She placed them both upright on the front passenger seat.

She drove to a camping goods store and bought flashlights, a heater, a tent and anything else the man talked her into buying. She got in her car and aimlessly drove around. She hadn't planned a trip and she had never felt as lost as she did at this moment. She had to come to grips with what she had just found out about herself, figure out who she was, and how to shape her future. At this moment, she was out of place in this new foreign world. She needed to sort things out and find a position for herself. Even though Mrs. Dickey and her parents were certain about her, she had to be the one to be certain about herself.

Before she realized it, she was at the turn off to the road that led to Leon's house, the house where he had kept his daughter who ran away, where he had kept her. She had told herself that she would never return after her last visit, but maybe this was the place to put things in perspective and put them to rest one way or another. She pulled up to the house. When she knew she was alone, she got out of the car and walked toward the door. She stepped just inside the house and stood in the doorway, almost afraid to go all the way in. Then she walked through the house making certain that she was the only one there. The house was empty. Without presence of mind, she turned around, walked back to the car, opened the trunk, took out the suitcase, and somehow managed to get it into the house. She let the case drop in the middle of what was left of the floor and went to get the other things and the camping equipment the man in the store insisted that she needed.

After bringing in everything, she searched through the bag for the wine and bourbon and found the scotch that she thought was bourbon. She pulled out a paper cup that had gotten smashed, straightened it out a little, and filled it with wine.

Olivia sat down on the floor in the main room, lit some candles that she sat around the room, and sipped the wine. She tried to consider who she would have been as Leon's daughter, what she saw herself doing. After she'd had several sips of wine, she set the paper cup down. She remembered living in the house when she was younger. Like it or not, she was Leon's daughter, but how does that matter to her now? She tried to pretend she was that little girl from years ago and Leon, her father, wanted her to read to him. The memories that came to her were the memories that she had with her father, the man who adopted her. He taught her to read. She loved those many nights they sat together reading story after story. He never seemed to mind telling her the same words over, and over or answering the same questions. Just when she thought he was tired and out of patience, the next day he would bring home a new book for her to learn.

Dr. Vincent Douglass. He was the one who also got her interested in religion, and interested in school. He taught her how to ride a bike, how to count the stars at night, and he taught her how to drive a car. He was the father who stayed up late waiting for her to come home from her dates. He was the one who took her to a movie when she was sad. Dr. Vincent Douglass was her father and it was clear to her that she was more like him. She had experiences with the things he exposed her–the experiences that she wanted. And she recalled how hungry she was, starved for the good things a good life would bring.

She got up and moved toward the window. She closed her eyes still trying to remember. She saw herself looking out of the window when she was maybe six, or seven. There was a full moon that couldn't push its way through the tall trees, but gave off a sprinkling of light. Olivia couldn't see who was standing outside behind a tree nearest the house. Leon? She felt herself being afraid, but not because the person would harm her. She was afraid that this man, her father, would harm the person hiding behind the tree. Olivia wanted this person, child, it was a child, to leave, run away before this man took it away and Olivia wouldn't see it again. Olivia saw herself trying to open the window, yelling to the child to go away, saying to it to get away fast. But now, as Olivia stood near this same window reflecting back about this day, she thought the child was familiar to her. A girl, it was a girl and Olivia had locked eyes with her. Olivia wanted to save the girl, to keep her from harm. This was the opposite of what Leon would have done. Again, she saw that she was not like Leon.

Before she knew it, she had finished the wine in her cup and poured what was left in the bottle, into her cup. She noticed that the cup was barely half-full. Kara had gotten into her wine and drank most of it.

She had a desire to know more about her mother and if her mother was in that house with Leon and Tony. Did Leon love her mother like he said he loved his daughter? Was she also Tony's mother? Olivia recalled that Tony was quite a bit older than she and since Leon liked early teenage girls, her mother would have to have been at least older than Tony. Olivia regretted the fact that her biological mother missed out on so many things, things that her adopted mother taught her.

Olivia remembered the many afternoons and evenings her mother would hold her and comfort her when she came home from school crying because the other children teased her. She remembered the days her mother went with her to soccer practice and helped her try out for cheerleading. Her mother cheered with her to help her remember the words to the cheers. She recalled how her mother helped her find a dress for her confirmation and high school prom. She remembered the many talks they had when her mother picked her up from school. She recalled the many times she and Kara went shopping with her mother and the funny arguments they had.

Olivia began to feel badly for the child she was then, the little girl who lived in that house. She felt bad for Tony and for all Leon's children who had lived this way. Tony had no other choices, no one else loved him. She was, for the first six or seven years of her life, a part of this life, whatever went on in this house. She had to find a way to forgive herself and Leon for anything that she did from that life that was evil. She thought about the comment Leon made to her during one of her visits to the prison. He said he could only treat his children the way he was taught. Leon wasn't born evil or born a killer. He learned that from his mother.

She had graduated from high school, college, and gone on to seminary school. She realized that she had found a way to replace the bad things from her early life, with the good things in her life from the Douglasses. Did she have to recognize that she was Leon's daughter even after her life with the Douglasses for the past twenty-three years?

She got down on her knees, folded her hands in prayer.

The thought that came to her in prayer, "sending the Douglasses to me" stuck in her mind and she recalled the time when she was in the woods and out loud asked for help. It was late at night and she woke up. She couldn't sleep, and sat up in her twin bed. She was worried about two girls who had lived there for a while, but first, one, then the other, were no longer there. It was cold and the wind blew in through the cracks in the wood planks. She got out of bed, took her two unwashed, discolored pink blankets, wrapped them securely around her, opened the front door and went out into the night. She had no idea where she was going and after a while, she was lost. She sat down on a log that had fallen, and said aloud that she was afraid. She asked aloud where the other two girls had gone; one got sick a few days before, the other took sick before that. She missed them, and wanted to play with them. She kept asking Sunny, her father, where he had taken them. Earlier that day, when she went to look for them, Sunny made her stay on the front porch. He told her not to play in the yard. She sat on the porch pretending to read a page from a book that she found in the woods and saying over and over that if the girls left because she wouldn't let them play with her jar of crickets, then she was sorry. She would let them play with it if they came back. She was sorry she was mean to them and wouldn't let them play with her crickets.

She sat on that log, talked out-loud to the night and the dark woods. She wanted a nice family and she wanted to go to school, a school like the one Tony, the boy who also lived there told her about. Tony told her about birthdays, and cakes, and people singing "Happy Birthday." She wanted that, too. She wanted a home where she could go places even go to the city that Tony told her about. She wanted those things for herself and she asked aloud for those things. She needed to speak to whomever was in charge of people and their lives and she asked that person to hear her and help her. She had seen girls come to the house screaming and crying and over time, got sick, so Sunny told her, and had to leave. She was always afraid that one day she would get sick and would have to leave. After a long period sitting on the log, she grew tired and when her heart and eyes were empty of tears, she slid down on the ground, rested her head on the log, drew her blankets around her, and drifted off to sleep.

The next morning, Tony found her just a few feet away from the house. She was so cold and he warmed her by putting his coat around her. He yelled for Sunny who smiled when he found her and carried her back to the farmhouse. Sunny fixed a fire and sat her on the floor in front of it to warm her. Now, she remembered that night in the darkness of the woods when she asked the night to help her. She saw his scar and asked him if she could touch it and he let her. She traced it with her fingers, "You, Hurt you?"

"No, my baby. I had it my whole life. It don't hurt me."

"You, not hurt?"

"Call me Sunny. No more 'You' call me Sunny."

That was why she didn't recognize his name. She never knew his first name was Leon or the last name Wilkerson for that matter. What did he name her? Was she always Olivia? Should she rename herself Olivia Wilkerson? If she did, that would mean she was part of Leon's family. She was now a Douglass.

She now understood that she was selected, saved from a life of horror and from the dangers of the kind of life that her father lived abducting girls. She could see how He showed her the way to the Douglasses. She now had no doubt about who she was. She was a Douglass. She was sorry about her mother, sorry about Tony, and sorry about Leon and all his children, but she was a Douglass.

Later that night, she sat up in her sleeping bag. With the wine in her and the swirling around of all her unanswered questions, her stomach wrenched, and twisted and knotted and she heaved. She coughed and heaved up Leon and his obsessions as well as the choices Tony made. She coughed and heaved up that house that she used to live in, that evil feeling that she'd had all her years, and all that happened in that house. She heaved up any responsibility that she thought she had. Olivia let go of all the questions that could continue to crowd her mind. She had hoped that she could find answers, but she understood that she had to go on. She could have gone her whole life without finding out about her father or meeting him, but they were brought together. She was supposed to meet him. She was supposed to see who he was and what she was so that she could make the choice to be free, so that she could choose life, so that she could choose blessings over curses. She recalled her reading in church, the one that she read about Life death, blessings and curses and choosing life. She was sent to that prison as part of God's plan. God wanted to help her rid herself of that evil feeling that haunted her. She knew what she was to do with her life, now. She knew who she was now and who she had always been.

CHAPTER 27

The next morning, she felt more like eating, and just as she began to open a can of peaches, she heard a car outside. By the time she got herself up off the floor to see who it was, the front door slammed against the inside wall and a man appeared in the doorway. Olivia froze, and remembered that homeless people, squatters searched for abandoned places to stay. She tried to find something to defend herself.

"Who the hell are you?" the man asked.

"Olivia. Who are you?"

"Eddie Beasley, the owner. What are you doing here?"

"The owner? I didn't know anyone owned this place."

"Well what did you think? That the government just built this place for anyone who wanted to squat for free?"

"No. That's not what I mean." She hesitated for a moment, then decided to say it. "I used to live here, but I'm . . . .. I mean, I used to live here a long time ago."

"It must have been. No one's lived here for many years, far as I know. I asked what you were doing here on my land. Do I have to call the police?"

"No. I'm sorry. I just came because like I said, I used to live here. Did you know the family that lived here last?"

"I took this house over from my father after he died four years ago."

"Was the house occupied then?"

"Look lady, I don't know why all these questions. You just need to pack up and get out of here. How many people are with you, anyway?"

"No one. No one is with me." She cast her eyes down at the floor, realizing that she had made herself a little too vulnerable.

"Look lady. I don't allow squatters. My father was the easy one, but not me."

"Could you tell me a little about the house before I leave?'

He let out a loud sigh. "I don't know much."

"Do you remember anything your father might have told you? I just want to know if you knew the man who lived in this house about twenty years ago."

"That was many years ago. I was about twenty-five then. I used to help him every now and again. There was a man living here about that long ago." He looked off into the distance. "Yeah, I remember something and if I remember correctly, the man had a family."

"A wife and children? You saw them?"

"As I remember it, they stayed pretty much to themselves, but it seems to me he had a boy and a girl. The boy looked to be about fifteen, seventeen and the little girl looked to be about four or five."

"What about a wife? Did you notice a wife?"

"A wife, a wife. You know, I remember someone in town said that he did have a wife, but he wouldn't let her out of the house."

"Did you ever get to see her?"

"No, I don't think so. Lady, I can't stand here and answer questions. You just get your things together and get the hell out of my house."

"Thank you for the information. I needed to know because I believe he was my father and I believe the woman that he held here was my mother. I came here to, well I don't know why I came here. But I'll leave now." She turned to begin picking up her things.

"All right, all I know is what the town gossip was. He had a teenage girl here in this house. Maybe she was your mother. I don't know. I never saw her. I did see a teenage boy and a little girl from time to time. When he came to the store for supplies, he was usually alone, I heard. About twenty or so years ago, my father came to the house to collect the rent and the house was empty. He skipped out owing almost six months back rent. The house was a mess. We tried to fix it up, but no one wanted to live in it. One day a group of hunters asked to rent it during hunting season and I've been letting hunters stay here since then. I'm trying to fix it up so I can rent it."

His eyes gave off a questioning look, "Something else?" she asked.

"It's possible you're that little girl?" He looked her up and down as if trying to determine her age. "You're about what her age would be now. You are that girl."

"I could be. I thought maybe the house would tell me something. I was adopted about twenty-two years ago."

He shifted from one leg to the other and held his eyes down. After a moment, he looked up at her. "Okay, I tell you what. I plan to come back through here at the end of the week. If you're not gone by then, I'll have to charge you rent."

"Thank you."

He turned to leave, then turned toward her. "I'm sorry. I hope you figure it all out. But I don't understand why you need to." He closed the door and left.

In a few minutes, she heard the car drive away. She stood facing the door. It was beyond her understanding, also. After all, she knew all she needed to know.

CHAPTER 28

After she'd finished her peaches, Olivia heard a car outside the cabin again. She'd promised Eddie Beasley that she'd be gone before he returned, but he wasn't due to return until the end of the week. She was nervous and looked around the house for something to defend herself in case she needed to. She had been a little too forthcoming with Mr. Beasley and maybe he wanted to take advantage of that. After she'd found a flashlight, she went to the window, stood next to it, and peered out. A man dressed like a hunter with an insulated coat that puffed out and gave him an appearance of a balloon, and a red plaid hat pulled down over his eyes, almost covering his face, got out of the car. He opened the back door of the car and pulled out a duffel bag. He closed the car door, threw the bag over his shoulder, and headed toward the house. It seemed to Olivia like he was planning to stay in the house. As the man moved closer, she recognized him. Just as he stepped on what was once, the stoop, Olivia opened the door.

"Wesley, why did you come here?"

"You are here." He stepped around her and went inside.

"What are you doing here? Please, go home. I'm okay, just go home."

Wesley dropped the duffel bag on the floor where he stood. His face softened. "I couldn't find you. Your father said he thought you'd be here."

"Why were you looking for me?" She wasn't ready to talk to Wesley. She tried to straighten her clothes, patted her hair once or twice, and swiped her face with the back of her hand.

"With the snow day and yesterday made the second prayer class we missed. We watched the video, but the discussion after was a lousy one. It lacked substance. We missed you; we needed you there. Besides, your parents and I were going crazy because we couldn't find you," he said softly. He took his hat off and began unbuttoning his coat.

"I've only been gone one day. How did my father know I was here? He had no right to tell you I might be here." She had trouble facing him and went to make instant coffee, but she had never made coffee on the grill. She poured water in a cup, and dumped in a spoonful of coffee. She sipped it and tried hard not to make a face. She couldn't decide whether she wanted him to go or stay. She was such a mess. She couldn't allow him to see her so distraught. She wanted him to see her as someone strong, at least better together than she was now.

"He said you'd be here. Your parents had to get back to England. Remember? I told them to go on and that I would find you. But they wanted me to bring you back before they left." He watched her as she continued to try to make coffee. "They have to see you before they go back to England." He took off his coat and dropped it on the floor. "I went to your house, twice, and no one was there. I went to the bookstore and Kara said that you hadn't been to the store at all. I came out here. And here you are."

"You don't have to worry about me. Tell them I'm okay and not to worry. Wesley, thank you for coming, but I need to be alone. I have things I need to contemplate. When I'm ready I'll return, but not before then." She walked to the door believing he would follow, but when she turned around, she saw he hadn't moved.

"You want to talk about it?"

She took a sip of her cold, bitter, instant coffee, and looked away.

"Olivia?"

"Wesley, I'm not . . . I . . . can't you just go? I need more time." She felt him closing in on her and looked away from him, again.

"What's wrong? Why can't you look at me?" He stepped toward her.

She immediately stepped back, slurped another long sip of the nasty coffee. She wanted to toss it out, but she couldn't. She needed something to come between them now.

"You know what? I hope you're out here making your mind up about becoming a priest." He moved closer to her, reached for her hand, the one with the cup of coffee. He took the cup out of her hand and placed it on the floor.

She wrinkled her face, trying to hold back tears.

"Tell me. What is it? Please tell me. Let me help you with it."

"Help me? No one can help me. No one." She tried to take her hand back, but he tightened his grip.

"Try me. Sweetheart, I just can't leave here while you're angry and hurting."

"I'm here because my real father, my real father was Leon Sunstrik Wilkerson. How's that for news?" She looked him directly in the eye, knowing he would find an excuse to leave.

"Okay, now what?"

"Don't you understand? I may have met your sister."

"Yes, I understand. But, you didn't meet my sister."

"How do you know? Wait a minute. How long have you known?"

"I had no idea until your parents told me."

"Did Leon know?"

"I doubt it. He couldn't get over you going to see his son. I doubt that he saw much beyond that. Nobody had been that kind to him. How did you find out?"

"This is the house he wrote about in his letter. I recognized the school Leon talked about. It was the same school I attended before we moved to England."

"Okay."

"I went to see the principle and before I realized it she was talking about me." Tears formed.

"Olivia, why did you really come here?" He looked around the room and pointed to her things. "You brought camping equipment with you."

She watched him, as if she was seeing something fresh, new, untarnished. "I came because I wanted to find out who I am and what I should do about it. I've been living a lie all these years. What if I'm not the person everyone says I am? What if I'm someone else?"

"You thought that being here, in this house would tell you that?"

After a long pause. "Yes."

"Okay then, who are you?"

"Wesley, please—"

"No. You came here for answers, now what did you find?"

"What that man did—"

"No, Olivia who are you?"

"I was given a chance that the others weren't given. I had a chance to get away. I'm the person who took advantage of that chance. Maybe I'm the one to turn everything around. Maybe I'm supposed to try and ease all his wrong doing."

"You can't worry about him, Olivia. You can't change anything he did or said. That was his job. All you can do is live your life. Be who you are, who you are in your heart."

"I understand that the Douglasses gave me a way out."

"So, everything is okay then?"

"Wesley, I thought you would hate me. I thought you'd want your sister to be the one to get away, not me. Wouldn't you believe I aided him? I was the one to lure your sister just like I was supposed to lure Kara."

Wesley held her in his arms. "You think that I would be upset with you and believe that you and Leon abducted my sister. You think that I would believe that you helped him and held her captive. But that was such a long time ago."

"Yes, and you would not forgive me for it. I couldn't forgive myself."

"Don't do that to yourself. Olivia, I don't hate you. Even if you did, which I know very well can't be true, you were a child then, a very young child and probably afraid of what he would do to you. How could I believe you were responsible? Isn't that what you told me? Remember? I do."

"I know, but this is hard news Wesley, hard to accept and hard to endure."

"Sweetheart, you knew what that man had done, but you came to that prison every day, subjecting yourself to his abuse, and you talked to him and had a good relationship with him. You believed that even he should be able to pray; even that man should be able to have someone to walk him through his last days on earth.

"That was before I learned who I was." She tried to pull away from him, but he wouldn't let her. He held her tighter in his arms, stroked her hair.

"Your heart hasn't changed. You're just angry now. It'll pass soon and you'll forgive yourself."

She pulled herself away from him and stepped back. "Stop trying to be nice to me. I don't need your sympathy." She tried to walk past him to the door.

He blocked her path. "No, I won't stop trying to be nice to you. I've been trying to get you to notice me since I stepped into that church three years ago. I won't stop trying to be nice to you."

"How could you have such good thoughts about me? Couldn't you see something was wrong with me?"

"No, I did not and still don't see that. Olivia, I fell in love with you the first moment I saw you. You're the reason I come every Sunday, for a chance to see you."

She looked at him, a half smile on her face. "Really?"

"There's nothing you could ever say or do that'll make me change my mind about you." He kissed her lips gently, kissed her lips gently, then put his arms around her, holding her tight. He pulled back slightly, "Who you are made it important for me to tell you about me."

She pulled back slightly. "Wesley, I was gone by then?"

"Yes. That's the thing that's bothering you, isn't it?"

"I don't want you to see me as the one who—"

"Stop. Stop it, Sweetheart, just stop it, okay?"

He tried to kiss her. At first, she wanted to pull away, she still thought of herself as defiled and more importantly, she hadn't had a full bath recently, not to mention the coffee, now making her mouth feel like she'd swallowed a big ball of cotton. But she couldn't help herself. Slowly, she gave in to him. She needed to let herself go. She was so exhausted so drained by her inner fight to be clean, guiltless and pure of heart. She needed him. Her body began to give in, to sink into him until she just gave in to his kiss. She tightened her arms around him, her safety net. After a moment, she was calm, and could no longer feel the anger that curled inside her. Instead, love filled up every part of her body.

Soon, too soon, he gradually loosened his hold. No words were spoken, their hearts communicated.

After a moment, he said, "I can't believe you stayed here by yourself. Weren't you afraid?" He kissed her on the forehead.

She pointed to a large bag of water that she'd gotten from the camping store. "Wesley, I wasn't expecting you to come here. I want to clean up a bit."

He smiled at her. "Get cleaned up. We're leaving here."

She smiled back at him. Never to return. She would never let this part of her life interfere with her again.

Chapter 29

When Olivia entered the bookstore, Kara was busy adding the new collections to the shelves.

"Livvy, where have you been? We . . . mom and dad were worried about you."

"I'm fine. I'm fine. Kara . . ."

Her parents came out from the back.

She stretched out her arms as far as she could, for Kara and her parents. She closed her eyes and gave them the tightest hug. When she opened her eyes, she saw Kara watching her and she pulled back.

"Kara, I feel like you've been wanting to say something to me since forever. Won't you please tell me what it is? I'm ready to listen, now."

Kara just stared at her, no expression on her face. Finally, "Maybe." She walked toward the backroom.

"Then why not talk to me." Olivia said to Kara's back. "Why not tell me? I want you to say it, speak the words."

"I don't have anything to say and even if I did, you don't want to hear it." She stopped walking, and stood still with her back to them.

Her father went to the door, flipped the "Open" sign to "Closed," and turned the lock on the door.

"Sit down everyone, please." He pointed to the four chairs at the nearest table.

Kara, her mother, and Olivia sat down at the table. He sat down.

"We have to talk about everything. We have to say it all. You're my girls and I know we've been keeping secrets from each other. I want to see my girls happy."

"What do you want us to do?" her mother asked.

"There is anger in this family and I want us to talk about it. Can we do that? Can we do that Kara?"

"Yes."

"Livvy, can we start with you?"

She looked at her mother and father. "I understand why you both kept things from me and I'm very grateful to you for giving me the chance and the opportunities you provided for me."

Olivia's mother held her hands. "We felt you deserved a chance and we had to do it the best way we knew how."

"Elizabeth, is there anything else you want to say?" her father asked.

She reached over to Kara. "I just want my Kara to get rid of her anger and to show her parents more respect. Sweetheart, can you please talk to us? When you were little, you used to ask me if I loved Olivia more than you—"

"And you would say no, that you loved us both the same."

"That's right. Then what is it?"

Kara opened her mouth to speak, then closed her lips. She looked at each one of them, around the room, and, "You, none of you would like what I have to say. You'll say what I did was despicable."

"None of us feels that way about you, Kara," her father said.

"I remembered something. One night, I happened to look out of the window of the house where Leon lived, the house in Maryland. I saw someone hiding behind a big tree and staring into the house. Kara, was that you?"

Tears swelled in her eyes, but Kara held strong. "No."

"It was you, wasn't it?" Olivia asked.

Olivia took Kara's hand. "Kara, I was so afraid for you that night."

"I followed you. I don't know why I did it; I just did. You asked me to go home with you. When I asked Mom and Dad, they told me I couldn't go. Not that I wanted to go to your home with you, I was just curious. All the kids talked about how weird you were and how afraid they were of you. But I thought you were so nice and kind and I wanted to show you that I wasn't afraid of you. So, one afternoon, I followed you home. I hid and waited until it was almost dark and then I peeped into your house." Tears seeped out and Kara tried to cover her face with both hands. "I couldn't believe what I saw. Kids chained to the furniture. Kids, who looked like they hadn't had enough to eat, were crying and hurting. Then a man came outside. I thought he would find me and then I'd become one of those kids in the house. I was terrified. He looked right passed me and when he went back inside, I ran as fast as I could to my house."

"It was you I saw hiding behind the tree. Kara, I was so afraid that he would get you. In my head, I begged you to get away, run, run home as fast as you could," Olivia said.

"When I got home, I wanted to tell. But I couldn't. I knew, and I couldn't tell anyone," Kara said.

"Kara, Sweetheart, what did you know?" her father asked.

"I knew, I knew, no I saw children chained up and I did nothing. I saw what was happening and I did absolutely nothing. Don't you understand what that makes me?"

Olivia reached over and hugged her sister. "All that made you was a scared little girl. Kara, it wasn't necessary for you to do anything. The next day I told the principal."

"I know, but I should have told someone. I wanted to help, but I didn't know what to do. I thought no one would believe me and then I'd get you in trouble. As we got older, I wanted to talk to you about the children in chains, but when I tried to bring it up, you never remembered anything. Once, I asked you about a story about a man who held children in chains and you said you thought it was not a story but a movie. So, I thought maybe it was some kind of a game for you. Over the years, I couldn't get those children out of my mind. Each time I thought about them crying and hurt, I still thought I should have told someone. I kept quiet. I thought you were afraid and for some reason you wanted to keep it a secret. So, I kept quiet about it, too."

"Kara, you kept all this to yourself?" her mother asked.

"No, Kara, no. You did do something. When I saw you, I knew I had to tell someone. If you hadn't peeped into my window that night, I doubt that I would have said anything. You can say that you saved me. I must have had a feeling deep inside that I'd be next."

Her father got up, went to Kara, stood her up and put his arms around her. He held onto her so closely that Kara seemed hidden in his arms. Olivia and her mother joined in and her mother rested her head on Kara's.

Chapter 30

The next afternoon, Olivia opened the door to her townhouse and saw Kara sitting on the couch, two suitcases in the center of the room.

"I need you to know that I have to leave with mom and dad. I called my boss to ask for a lead to anything else. He broke down and gave me the name of a newspaper editor. I called and, he said he'd try me for three months."

"That's nice Kara. I'm so happy for you." She hugged her sister. "Before you know it, you'll be one of the country's stop reporters again. And I'll brag on my sister."

"Livvy, the first day you came into our class you asked me if you could stand behind me in line. You made me feel as if there was something special about me. I've always remembered that."

"I remember that. You smiled at me when I had to introduce myself to the class. You were the only one who smiled at me." Olivia paused for a moment, "Kara, is Olivia my real name?"

"I don't know. Right after we met, you told me that you'd always loved the name, Olivia. I always thought it suited you."

"How are we now, Kara?"

"I don't want to be angry or fight with you anymore. The book of essays that you wanted me to read again, made me see that."

"Do you have to go back to England? You could stay here with me."

"I just have a hard time here. I want to talk to a priest away from here so I can sort it all out get my reputation back and maybe work out things with my husband. He never really wanted a divorce. I was the one who wanted it."

"I understand. Maybe you could write another book of essays, about what happened and how you brought yourself back."

Kara smiled at Olivia. "Maybe I will."

The doorbell rang and Kara rose to answer it. Her father gave Kara a kiss and then stepped inside to get her bags. "You ready? Your mom and Wesley are waiting in the car."

"Hi Dad," Olivia said.

"Hello, Sweetheart," He looked from one to the other.

"We're okay, Dad," Olivia said.

"Yes, we're okay," Kara said.

"You know girls we could all go to counseling together, group sessions; start with forgiveness. What do you say?"

"Dad, I just need some time. Now that everything is out in the open, I just need to think about everything and make some decisions about my life. Who knows, I have a three-month trial in England, maybe then, I'll decide to come back here. Or, Dad, maybe I'll decide I'll come back when you retire, and help you and mom run that bookstore."

"Okay, Kara. I'll leave that to you. I want what's best for you, I know you know that. Well, let's get to the airport. And Livvy, no matter what, we'll all be back in July for your ordination."

"You'd better be. When I glance out into that congregation, I want to see my family smiling back at me."

"That's a promise," said Kara.

Olivia finally learned how she saved Kara from Leon. She was not involved in helping Leon with any of the girls he claimed were his wives. She had to believe that. Maybe Leon did love her as he said he did. Maybe things were good for her in that house. It could be that Leon loved her because she wasn't evil. Somehow, knowing that her biological father loved her brought her a little peace. At least that was one worry she no longer had to carry.

CHAPTER 31

Later that afternoon after seeing Kara and her parents off to England, Olivia got dressed for dinner with Wesley. He'd called and asked her to be ready earlier than planned which made her happy.

He picked her up and they drove to a small modern-looking office building just behind the new courthouse in Rockville. He made a right turn and pulled into the parking lot in front of the building. Olivia noticed several cars in the lot and the name, "Law Office," in big black letters on one of the glass doors that marked the entrance to the building. He held open the first set of glass doors and when he pushed in the second set and she stepped inside, suddenly the office came to life. Olivia raised her eyebrows in surprise.

A woman walking with two men stopped and talked to each other before they separated and went into different directions. Two men shook hands, walked across the room and entered an office on the other side. A woman seated at a big round desk which seemed to be the stopping point, talked on the phone as she juggled papers and gave out directions to each of the two people who stood over her. She hung up, and placed the papers back in the folder just as Olivia and Wesley reached the desk. The woman looked up and smiled when she saw Wesley and Olivia standing in front of the desk. Wesley bent over the desk and spoke quietly to the woman. She handed Wesley papers clipped together and nodded. Olivia turned and gazed around the outer office and at the three people in the waiting room, and a woman flipping through a magazine.

Olivia wanted to ask Wesley where they were, but figured she already knew. His arm around her waist, he directed her to the left and down the hall. She smiled at him and he smiled back, but she was determined not to ask him where they were. She trusted him and she just wanted to relax in that trust. But she was curious as to why he wouldn't tell her. At the end of the hall, he opened the double doors with his name and the title, "Corporate Law," on the plaque. Once inside the lushly carpeted office, he offered her one of the white leather armchairs opposite a desk that seemed to be made out of glass all around including the legs. She looked under the table for drawers in the desk. There were none. Two computers side by side were on the right side of the desk, but did not obstruct the view from the glass wall that spanned across the entire side. Olivia saw everything going on in the Rockville Town Center and for miles beyond, it seemed. She would not survive in this office. Most of her day would be spent watching the people in the town center coming and going.

The aroma of coffee brought her attention back to where she was and she turned around to check for Wesley. He stood at the bar and to the right where he was tending to the coffee. He poured two cups, brought them to her on a tray that he placed on the small table between the two leather chairs.

"Well?" He asked while handing her a cup of coffee.

"I don't know. Is this---?"

"My office, yes." He sat in the other white leather chair.

"Just out of curiosity, why wouldn't you tell me we were coming here?"

"I thought I'd show you. I want you to see the other me."

"It certainly is modern, and different, very different from your other office," she said while looking around. Then she put the cup on the table, and turned to him. "I don't judge, but I'm impressed. This is a different side of you. But after the Praise Bar, let's just say that I'm liking the surprises."

He leaned over and kissed her.

"You trust me. You neglected to ask me where we were going. I know you wanted to."

"No, I didn't. I really didn't." She giggled through her tease, pleased that he knew her so well.

Just as he leaned over to kiss her again, the phone rang. He kissed her on the cheek and went to his desk to answer the phone.

"Yes, Sammi. . . Okay. Can you transfer the call, please?" Still holding the phone, he looked over at Olivia. "I'm not officially back yet. I thought this problem was being handled. I have to take this call. Do you mind?"

"Of course not."

He nodded. "Yeah, Walt. Okay. . . I have to call you back first thing in the morning. I'll have more for you then. . . Okay . . . Tomorrow morning." He hung up and dialed another number. "Hamp? I just talked to Walt. I need you here in my office with everything first thing tomorrow morning." He hung up.

"I'm so sorry about that," he said as he walked back to his chair. "We're having a problem with an account. Even though I want to be with you, I had to take the call. Are you ready? I want to get out of here before anything else pops up."

"Let's go then."

"First, I want to take you on a tour of the office before we go."

Olivia was fascinated even more with Wesley. Even though he lived in a high-powered world where corporations fought to make more money, and used his law firm to do it, he managed to hold on to his faith, so tightly that he joined a prayer group and played the piano and horn in a praise bar.

After the tour, he took her to his favorite country French restaurant off River Road in Potomac. The maître de escorted them to their table as soon as they arrived. After they were seated, Wesley seemed a little nervous for some reason. Somehow, his fork managed to get caught in his sleeve and when he went to hand the waiter his menu, the fork flew out of the sleeve and fell just before hitting the man at the table next to them.

"Oh, sir, I'm so sorry," said the waiter to the other patrons as he picked up the fork.

"It's not necessary for you to apologize. It was my fault," Wesley said leaning over to the man and waiter.

He checked his sleeve for other sharp objects and then put his hands in his lap. Olivia reached for the butter to spread it on the bread that the waiter had just placed on their table.

"Oh, it's frozen," she said when she couldn't cut the butter.

Wesley moved the butter dish closer to him and tried to cut a piece of butter for her with his butter knife. "It's softening up," he said. With a final stroke, the butter and butter dish slipped out of control and flew to the center of the table. The waiter was nearby and saw what happened.

"I'll bring another one," he said.

"Thank you. I don't know what's wrong with me," Wesley said, head down, embarrassed.

She couldn't understand why he was so nervous. She started a conversation about his law practice. That would help relax him. He told her that he'd been in practice for the past fifteen years. He was with a firm until about seven years ago when he went out on his own.

"Why corporate law?"

"When I was in law school, I wanted to be a defense attorney, but I found it hard to defend people who were guilty. I changed to corporate law. Besides, my father who was a lawyer turned me off to being a defense attorney."

"Is he one?"

"Was. He was a defense attorney. He passed away five years ago."

Once she saw that he was beginning to be a little more comfortable, she asked more questions about music and the instruments he played. He promised to teach her how to play the piano. She was so wrapped up in his life that she forgot all about the time until the waiter brought the dessert menus for them.

"What would you like? We have to get a dessert." He said it like she had to have a dessert and that she had no choice in the matter.

"Can we sh—," she began. "Can you excuse me for a minute?" They asked at the same moment. Then he suddenly got up out of his seat and hurried toward the men's room.

"Sure," She said to an empty chair. She noticed that he was beginning to perspire. Had he eaten something that wasn't agreeable with him? She rubbed her stomach for a second searching for discomfort, but she was fine. She worried about Wesley. In a few minutes, he returned.

"Are you okay? We can go if you need to."

He starred at her pensively, as if trying to make a decision. He reached into his coat pocket and pulled out a small black velvet box.

Elbows on the table he held the velvet box up in front of her.

Her eyes grew larger as she watched him.

He opened the box, tilted it toward her.

She gazed into the box at something flickering and saw a diamond ring. The white gold ring had emeralds on either side of the two-karat diamond.

"Olivia, if you'll have me, I promise you a long and prosperous life with me. I want to raise a healthy family with you, help in our community and I want us to enjoy each other for the rest of our lives. Olivia, would you marry me?"

"Is this what was wrong? You were nervous?"

"Yes."

"Then I'd better say yes. Yes, Wesley, I will marry you."

He eased the ring out of the box and slipped it on her finger.

"Whew," he began, "am I glad this part is over."

"I can't believe you were so nervous."

"Are you kidding? First, I thought you'd say we haven't known each other that long. Then, I thought that dinner was a bad idea and that I should have been a lot more creative. And then I was worried that we weren't getting to the dessert part soon enough, and . . ."

She took hold of his hand, and he stopped talking.

"Wesley, I want to say something to you I've wanted to say for a long time."

"I hope it's the same thing I want to say to you, again."

"Wesley, I love you."

"Now that's what I want to hear. Sweetheart, I love you with all my heart and soul."

* * *

In the car on the drive home, Olivia held her hand up in front of her, admiring her engagement ring, turning her hand in all directions. "This ring makes my hand look nice, doesn't it?" she laughed.

Wesley turned to her. "I thought by the time you'd get it your fingers would be a different size."

"How long have you had this ring? Did you already have it?"

"I bought it about two years ago when I knew I wanted to marry you."

"Two years ago?"

"I almost bought it the moment I saw you, but I thought it was best to get to know you first. But then, I doubt that you even knew me."

"Wesley, the truth is, I was aware of you."

"You were?"

"Yes, I couldn't do much about it. But I did try to find out about you."

"When was that?"

"I had to leave a message with your usher team. I went to the secretary to get Ned's phone number when I saw your name on her list of ushers. I asked if you were new to the church. She said that you and your wife had been coming for a while."

"So, that's why you kept your distance, I mean aside from Claude. Olivia, I never had a wife and I never brought another woman to the church."

"Wesley, if I had known you weren't married, I would have been just a wee more aggressive."

"You? Oh, that's funny. Set a date, set a date, now, this very moment. I want to marry you before anything happens."

"August."

"August? Are you sure?"

"Yes, it will be after the ordination. Let's get married in mid-August. We will have the ceremony in the church for about 50 people and the reception immediately after in the church. How's that?"

"That's what I want."

"Can we honeymoon in Aruba?"

"I'll take you to wherever you want to go."

Olivia couldn't believe this was happening to her. After everything she knew and found out about herself, she was handed this wonderful gift. She would spend the rest of her life with Wesley.

CHAPTER 32

Standing in the back hall with everyone serving and getting ready, Olivia was surprised that she was nervous. She had just peeped out into the nave and had seen that the church was filled with people. She'd thought that her ordination would only bring a few people. After all, it was a Saturday afternoon, when everyone had their "Saturday things" to do. Since she had elected to work with children who were waiting to be adopted—her final project for her ordination—continued with her prayer group, had taken on a Sunday class that Fr. Wilson asked her to teach, and of course, finding evenings to see Wesley, she had little time to get to know the members of the church. She realized the irony in that thought.

Peeping out again, she saw her mom and dad—dad turning around looking for her—always making sure about her. They had flown back from England, as they had promised just to attend her ordination. As her mother said, "We have no choice." The summer term at the university was in session. Her father must have found a substitute so that he could watch his daughter officially become an Episcopal priest. She panned the congregation, and seated midway and on the end of the pew was Mrs. Edna Dickey. The pew was filled with other women about Mrs. Dickey's age. She not only kept her word, but she must have brought some of the other teachers who were at the school when Olivia was there.

The organ began and the violins joined in at the opening hymn, *Love Divine, All Loves Excelling*. Wesley sat in the front row pew next to her parents and Kara. The acolytes started down the aisle followed by the choir, the churchwarden, the Lay Eucharist Ministers, Olivia, the assistant rector, the rector, and finally, the Bishop. This time when she walked down the aisle she would not be behind the acolyte carrying the Gospel Book, she would walk down behind the Lay Eucharist Ministers.

When the procession ended, Fr. Wilson asked the congregation to sit, so that everyone could see. The church Warden stood before the Bishop with Olivia and presented Olivia to the Bishop. Olivia laid face down on the floor, arms out above her head in front of the Bishop. After the Bishop said a few prayers, and rites, Olivia sat in an office chair in the sanctuary.

Afterward, the congregation was asked to hear the Word. They sat to hear the readings from the Old and New Testament. She saw Wesley who was watching her intently. She thanked God that He sent Wesley to her and prayed that God would always be in the center of their lives. She saw Edna Dickey and the other ladies smiling back at her.

After Olivia gave her very first sermon, the Induction began. She rose to stand before the Bishop. Her mother, father, Kara, Wesley and other members from the congregation came forward to present her with the tools of her work. She accepted the Bible from her father, to proclaim the Word. The Bishop presented a vessel of water to baptize in obedience of the Lord; a stole from Kara to represent herself as a pastor and priest; the Book of Common Prayer from a member of the congregation; olive oil as a healer and reconciler from a member of her prayer group. The Warden presented her with the keys to the church to allow the doors to be opened to all people. Fr. Wilson gave her the Canons to share in the councils of the diocese. Wesley gave her the bread and wine. The Bishop helped Olivia put on an Alb, chasuble and stole, full vestments for a priest. Fr. Wilson presented Reverend Olivia Douglass to the parishioners and everyone clapped to receive her.

When the service had ended and they stood to recess out of the church, Olivia looked around the church and at the congregation. The next time she entered that church, or any church, she would enter it as a priest. She recessed down the aisle with her head high and smiling at Wesley first, and then, Mrs. Dickey. A few pews up on her left, she saw Claude. He seemed sorry, sad, a depressed appearance about him. For a moment, she was sorry for him. Sorry because he couldn't see that he would have to change. At the same time, she was relieved and exhilarated that she saw she needed to change her feelings about herself. Maybe her leaving him will open his eyes and he, too, will see. She continued down the aisle and to her right, she saw

Mrs. Cox smiling at her. She smiled at everyone she passed as she walked out of the nave.

Later, after the reception and after everyone had gone home, Olivia had gone back into the church and sat in the first pew. She was happy she'd followed her heart. The church was her calling, her home; the place where she belonged. Wesley found her there and when she saw him, she slid down a bit. He sat beside her, his right shoulder against her left, right leg against her left and took her hand.

"I knew you'd be here."

"Just reflecting."

"About the past months?"

"Isn't it all so very amazing? We were supposed to meet. You know that, don't you?"

"You're right." He paused. "Olivia Emily Douglass," Wesley said.

"Wesley Franklin Johns," Olivia said.

They sat there next to each other—holding hands, her head on his shoulder—for a while longer.

"Let's go. I have a wedding to plan next."

They rose up out of the pew, still holding hands. Then he let go and slipped his arm around her waist and together they walked down the aisle to the outside door, the door where she had been slipping in to pray in the evening, the door that she thought was left open for her, the door that was now their door.

View other Black Rose Writing titles at www.blackrosewriting.com/books and use promo code **PRINT** to receive a **20% discount** when purchasing.

CPSIA information can be obtained
at www.ICGtesting.com
Printed in the USA
LVHW09s1942280918
591750LV00001B/8/P